UNDER the RADAR

Judith Clark

UNDER the RADAR

DCB

The publisher gratefully acknowledges the support of the Canada Council for the Arts and the Ontario Arts Council for its publishing program. We acknowledge the financial support of the Government of Canada through the Canada Book Fund (CBF) for our publishing activities, and the Government of Ontario through Ontario Creates, an agency of the Ontario Ministry of Culture, and the Ontario Book Publishing Tax Credit Program.

This is a work of fiction. Any resemblance to actual events or persons, living or dead, is purely coincidental.

Library and Archives Canada Cataloguing in Publication

Title: Under the radar / Judith Clark.
Names: Clark, Judith, 1962– author.
Identifiers: Canadiana (print) 2019023072X | Canadiana (ebook) 20200170546 | ISBN 9781770865662 (softcover) | ISBN 9781770865679 (HTML)
Classification: LCC PS8605.L362265 U53 2020 | DDC JC813/.6—dc23

Cover image and design: Angel Guerra / Archetype
Interior text design: Tannice Goddard, tannicegdesigns.ca

Printed and bound in Canada.

Manufactured by Friesens in Altona, Manitoba in February 2020.

DCB
AN IMPRINT OF CORMORANT BOOKS INC.
260 SPADINA AVENUE, SUITE 502, TORONTO, ON M5T 2E4
www.dcbyoungreaders.com
www.cormorantbooks.com

For HK

Somewhere Under the Rainbow

ON SUNDAY AFTERNOON, I did bicep curls in our walkout basement while I waited for my friends to show up. I wondered if they'd heard about what happened at the party. My stomach fluttered.

My little brother Tor sat on an old beanbag chair in the corner playing a game on a tablet. The last thing I wanted was for him to listen in. "Myk and Jason are coming over," I said, hoping he'd take the hint.

"So?" He didn't look up from his game. Every time my twin sister Elin and I thought he'd hit peak pain-in-the-ass, he exceeded our expectations. If I gave him the smallest sign that I wanted him to get lost, he'd make a point of sticking around. I let it drop. He'd get bored and take off eventually.

Bang bang. Myk's usual *I'm here* courtesy knock. He threw open the heavy back door and entered, gym bag hanging over one shoulder. "Hey." He tossed it onto the battered couch near the door and propped himself against the wall to take off his shoes, pausing long enough to brush his curly, dirty-blond hair back from his face. If he let it grow too long, he looked like a poodle.

Jason followed Myk inside. "Hi." He toed off his shoes, put them on the heavy rubber boot tray, and stowed his stuff under the row of sturdy coat hooks. Then he crossed to the wrestling mat and started stretches.

Myk dropped onto the couch. "Dude. You didn't text." They had heard.

"Mum has my phone." Locked in Dad's desk all weekend. Dinner table infraction. It was just one text. I didn't know she could see me from the kitchen.

"Sucks. So — tell."

I racked my dumbbells and draped my hand towel around my neck, stalling for time.

Myk leaned forward. "I heard Cari Van Pelt started grinding on your crotch —"

"Whoa. Whoa. Whoa. She sat on my lap."

"She's grinding. No way she isn't."

Jason looked over my shoulder, and I didn't have to follow his gaze to know Tor's eyes were huge. I just hoped he could keep his mouth shut.

"So she's grinding on your crotch and lays a lip lock on you and you make her stop?"

"She was wasted."

"And your point is?"

"Dick move." I pulled my sweatshirt off and tossed it aside, revealing the old T-shirt underneath.

"Are you kidding? If Cari Van Pelt wants to kiss me, I'm not stopping her."

I jumped to my feet. "I can spot somebody. Who's first?"

Myk held up a hand. "Dude. Deets."

I wasn't going to get out of this, so I sighed and dropped back down on the mat. "Brody was trashed, and he was doing his usual wrestlers-are-pussies-football-players-rule schtick." And Ryder was goading him on, the way he always did. Ryder loved starting fights — as long as it was someone else getting punched. "And then Cari came over."

Laughter and squeals and camera flashes put me on alert. Cari Van Pelt headed toward me, weaving and staggering across the big back yard, accompanied by her giggling entourage. Before I could escape, she straddled my lap, clamped her mouth to mine, and pried at my lips with her tongue. I stood, attempting to disentangle myself from her without dumping her on the ground, but she draped an arm around my neck and hung off me. "Why don't you want to kiss me?"

"So that's when things started with Brody? You made Cari stop and he called you a f—" Myk cut the word off with a glance toward the stairs. If Mum was close enough to hear him from upstairs, he'd be in deep shit.

"No," I said, wondering who'd told him about the "f" word. "Brody told Cari he'd kiss her, and then he grabbed her and started macking all over her."

Cari shoved Brody hard and he staggered back, his sense of balance long gone. Some of the guys standing around laughed. He flushed in anger and lurched toward Cari. I got between them. "Leave her alone."

"I told him to stop, and he took a swing at me."

I'd parried his wild hook easily, snapping a straight right into his solar plexus. Fastest way to end a fight. He went down, gasping like a fish on land. A second later he was spewing all over the grass.

"Dude, seriously, you need to kick Brody's ass. He's always calling you —" Myk glanced at the stairs again. "You know."

This kind of conversation was exactly what I was trying to avoid. I didn't want to lie. I didn't want to deny who I was. But I wasn't ready for this. What could I say? *He says that about anybody he doesn't like.* That felt a lot like lying, even though it wasn't an outright denial.

Jason rolled to his feet. "Maybe he should be telling everyone that Gunnar's a good guy who doesn't take advantage of people who are shit-faced. And Gunnar did kick Brody's ass."

"One punch," said Myk. "One punch is not an ass-kicking."

"If I kick Brody's ass, Mum will kick mine." That was so obviously true it stopped the discussion. I didn't dare look at Tor. He had major dirt on me now, and the more casual I could play it, the less blackmail power he would think he had. I didn't *really* think he'd screw me over on purpose, but Tor does his worst damage by accident.

Jason took off his sweatshirt, retrieved hand wraps from his gym bag, and perched on the end of the couch. "I'm starting with the heavy bag." He hooked a loop over his left thumb, hand splayed, and began wrapping.

My shoulders relaxed. I'd tensed up without realizing it. I jerked my head at Myk. "Come on, let's go."

Myk sighed, heaved himself to his feet, and hopped on one leg to pull off his track pants. Underneath he wore Valgard Vikings wrestling shorts, like me and Jason.

Official wrestling practice wouldn't start until mid-October, but the team would be doing conditioning in Phys Ed. Myk, Jase and I had wrestled and sparred and worked out together all summer. Lifting and boxing built the kind of stamina you needed for wrestling season. When I started at Valgard High, coaches tried to convince me to play football or rugby or even basketball, but my big brother Gary and his best friend Sam were wrestlers. And Mr. MacKennon, the wrestling coach, was the only coach who didn't give me shit about my hair in Phys Ed: he just said if I wanted to be on the team, I'd have to wear a hair slicker.

I liked wrestling because you're on a team, but your battles are your own. Coach Mac talked about the mental game, and some guys believed that meant psyching out the competition. I thought it meant not letting your head make you lose. That's the real battle — the one with yourself.

Myk didn't try to talk during his reps, and he didn't expect conversation while I did mine, which was a relief. Finally, we all stopped for a break, poured glasses of water from the pitcher in the beer fridge, and collapsed onto the floor. Tor's chair was empty. Just as well. He already knew way more about last night than I wanted him to.

"I thought Cari had a boyfriend," said Myk. "So why was she climbing all over you?"

I groaned. "Can we not talk about this?"

"He's irresistible." Jason winked and stage-whispered, "It's the hair."

I flipped him off, and he laughed.

My hair is honey blond with highlights from the sun — heavy, thick and straight, down to my shoulder blades. Last night I had ponytailed a fistful at my crown, with a couple of braids on each side and the hair in back left loose. Kind of like Orlando Bloom playing Legolas, except I've got way more hair and mine is real. Girls really go for my hair, which is ironic when you think about it.

"I can't believe Brody swung at you," said Myk. "He must have been wasted."

He'd had more than a few, but he wasn't blackout drunk. More like envious — and mean with it. People like Brody don't bully others because they feel strong. The louder the talk and the bigger the swagger, the smaller they feel inside. And with his buddy Ryder right there egging him on, once he started, he couldn't back down.

It felt good sitting here with my best friends. For a second I had a crazy impulse to just tell them. *Guys. I'm gay.*

But wrestling was the only thing I was looking forward to this year, and I couldn't risk it being awkward. I just couldn't. There's enough potential humiliation built in already. Like your body making embarrassing noises. Or smells. The worst is a hard-on in a match. Any guy can get one. Dick malfunctions are no picnic in practice, but in a match that people are recording, that total strangers can see, that your parents might spot … There's a *just let me sink through the floor* moment sooner or later for everyone.

Right now, I'm just another guy on the team. No one thinks twice about all the sweaty groping on the mat, but the second I'm out, all that could change.

Being out would be a relief for about one minute, and then everything would go to hell. I would just keep my secret for now.

A Not-Boring Sunday Night

I WAS PUTTING the soup tureen on the dining room table for Sunday dinner when Dad and Gary came in from the fields and took their seats. They'd scrubbed off as much dirt as they could, but their hair was matted from being mashed under hats all day. Dad had a farmer's tan that stopped at the neck of his work shirt and a lined face from living life in the sun, but the crinkles around his hazel eyes were as much from smiling as from squinting. We have the same eyes.

My big brother Gary lived in the apartment, which was really the granny flat at the back of our house that my grandma Tryggvason lived in before she passed. He still ate with us, but he didn't have kitchen duty anymore because he's a partner in our family's farm now and works full time with Dad. This time of year they didn't get to take many Sundays off.

I concentrated on eating while Gary and Dad and Elin talked about the wheat harvest and whether rain was going to delay hay cutting. They actually found this stuff interesting.

I have zero farmer genes in my makeup. Elin and I were going into Grade 12 this year and I had no idea what I was going to do after graduation, but I knew it wouldn't be farming. I hadn't exactly broken that to Mum and Dad yet, but I had a feeling they already knew.

I probably wouldn't be going Elin's route, either. All her classes were advanced placement. And me? No one could believe we're twins. Elin said it wasn't that I'm unintelligent, just uninterested. I didn't know about the first part, but the second part was true.

"Gunnar," said Dad. I came to attention. "Derek Milam called a while ago. Parker fell out of a hayloft yesterday. They'll need some help for a while and wondered if you'd be interested in working there until school starts up again next month."

"Is Parker okay?" Elin asked.

"I think so," said Dad. "He's a little banged up, but nothing serious."

"It's a terrible time of year for something like that to happen," said Mum. She pursed her lips, thinking, and I knew I'd be delivering pie and casserole before long.

"Sure," I said. "I can call after we're done."

Derek Milam and Parker Shannon farmed four quarter sections that bordered the western edge of my family's property. Derek moved to Alberta in the seventies to protest the American draft and the war in Vietnam. Parker joined him later after serving a tour, according to local gossip. They had to be around seventy, but they both looked a lot younger. Even more interesting to me — they weren't just business partners.

"How was the party last night?" Mum asked. "You were home earlier than we expected." I froze. So did Gary and Elin.

Mum hadn't been suspicious about the party, but when the three people who had been there all went stiff, she got that way fast. I didn't miss the glance at me. *She's thinking about June, that day when I kind of let things get out of control.*

Elin shrugged. "It was boring."

I could read what was going through Tor's brain by the expressions that flitted across his face. *Why would she say it was boring? It didn't sound boring when Myk and Jason were talking about it. There was a fight. And kissing.*

Silence. Mum waited for more, but I gulped water so I wouldn't have to talk. I was draining the glass when Tor asked, "Would you have kissed Cari if she wasn't drunk?"

Everyone went dead silent and stared at Tor. Except for me. I inhaled the last swallow of water and started to cough.

Elin rescued me. "May we be excused?" At Mum's nod, Elin grabbed Tor. "Come on. We've got cleanup duty." He scowled but stacked plates.

I risked a glance at Mum, and she and Dad were having one of those conversations where they don't talk. They must have decided a frontal assault wasn't the way to go, because there were no more questions.

AN HOUR LATER, as I jogged down the basement stairs, I heard the rhythmic thwack of boxing gloves on the heavy bag. I knew it was Sam, and I stopped on the last step to watch.

He was six feet even — two inches shorter than me. He was ripped, but not in a bulked-up way. All skin over muscle under his too-tight wet T, lean and lithe. He burned off fat like Dad's big farm truck burns gas.

I could tell he knew I was there, but his feet didn't stop moving and his focus never wavered. He breathed in through his nose and out through his mouth as he threw punch after punch. Finally he slammed a last round of blows, stepped back, and bent over with his gloves on his thighs. He grinned at me. I hoped he hadn't noticed me checking out his abs.

"Gunny."

"Samwise. Movie night?"

"Yeah."

Sam and Gary have been best friends since kindergarten. Mum calls him her fourth son. I'd had a crush on Sam since grade school, when I decided I wanted us to be boyfriends. Back then, I thought being someone's boyfriend meant he'd like me best.

Then puberty hit. I got taller. My voice got deeper. I couldn't even think about skipping a shower after a workout, not if I wanted anyone to sit by me. I was hungry all the time, and I ate constantly, but I didn't get fat. Instead, I built muscle. And I started figuring out what a boyfriend would be good for besides liking me best.

"Water?" I said.

"Yeah, sure."

I pulled a pitcher of cold water from the beer fridge while Sam toweled off sweat and plopped down on a weight bench. Then I handed over a tall glass and sank onto the rubber floor mat beside him.

"Thanks."

His throat moved as he chugged. I made sure I wasn't staring at him when he drained the last drops.

Gary ran down the other basement stairs from his apartment. "Want a beer?" he asked.

"Yeah, gonna clean up." Sam headed off to the basement shower we all used after workouts.

"Hey, Gunnar, want to watch a movie with us?" Gary took two Grasshoppers from the beer fridge.

"No, he doesn't," Elin said from behind us, crossing to the bench by the back door. "He's going with me to water the babies." We'd planted replacement trees in each shelterbelt on the farm, and they needed plenty of water.

I sat next to Elin where she was lacing her work boots and retrieved mine from underneath the long wooden seat. Like me, she wore faded jeans and a long-sleeved button-up work shirt over an old T. Twins, all right.

"We can't do all the shelterbelts tonight," I said. We still had a couple of hours of light, but that wasn't nearly enough time.

"We can do the close ones. I'll do the others tomorrow."

"What's the rush?"

"I want to talk to you."

At the equipment shed we rolled out the water cart, and I steered it to the nearest catchment pond. Elin removed the intake cap from the barrel while I primed the hand pump. Fast, smooth, coordinated: we'd done this so many times we didn't need to talk about it.

"Mum thinks Cari was hitting on you and you were too much of a gentleman to take advantage of her condition," Elin said. "Which is true. She just doesn't know that you hit Brody." Elin's eyes narrowed. "And Tor is going to keep his mouth shut." Was that even possible?

Mum and Dad were working on Tor's filters, because much of the time he didn't seem to have any. Sometimes he didn't understand that he'd just said something you really can't say, and he only figured it out when Mum exclaimed, "Torvald Reynir Tryggvason!" and followed it with "People will think you were raised by wolves!" I got as far away as possible any time Mum said that because — collateral damage.

I said, "Thanks for running interference. Did anybody post anything?" *Please no.*

Elin frowned at me. "You need to get your own accounts."

I shrugged. "Too much trouble." We'd had this argument a million times. I hated social media. All of it. No exceptions.

I finished filling the barrel and removed the hose as Elin popped the intake cap back on. We pushed the cart toward the closest shelterbelt and worked our way up the long row of trees, stopping beside each sapling while Elin gave the soil at its base a good soaking.

Elin still hadn't answered my question. "Did anybody post anything or not?"

"I heard Jessica posted some pictures of Cari throwing up. I haven't seen any of you."

A breeze rustled the leaves of the mature trees, and a pair of quacking ducks flew overhead. Elin gave me several sideways looks. I knew the signs: she was working up to some kind of touchy-feely conversation.

"Can I ask why you don't want to tell anyone yet? That thing with Cari last night wouldn't have happened if people knew." My sister figured me out a long time ago.

"I'm just not ready." We moved to the next row. "I don't want to fight my way through Grade 12."

Elin drained the rest of the water onto the last baby tree, and we parked the cart in the equipment shed. Then she pulled me toward the double glider swing in the back yard, shaded by a cranberry red canopy. The glider was far enough from the house that we could speak without being overheard, though Mum had the windows open for fresh air.

Elin sat across from me on the facing seat, and I pushed off, keeping the swing moving with nudges from my foot.

"There's zero tolerance on fighting at school," said Elin. "Brody and his goon squad won't pick fights if it means getting cut from the football team."

"You really want to be the sister of the fag all year?"

"Don't make me part of this decision." Elin nudged my thigh with one foot and when I moved, she rested both feet on the seat beside me, ankles crossed.

"They call them shitkickers for a reason," I said, rubbing at the bits of mud and worse she'd left on my jeans.

Elin gave me a snarky smile and stretched, arms reaching up and back toward the prairie sky streaked in blue and pink as the sun inched down at summer's slow pace and painted the clouds like a watercolor wash. She propped one elbow on an armrest and the other on the back of the glider's wide bench seat.

I folded my arms and waited.

"Have you kissed a guy?" she asked.

"Not yet, but it's on my to-do list."

Elin laughed. "Wouldn't that be more likely to happen if you were out of the closet? Even Valgard High has some out kids."

I shifted, uncomfortable with the conversational direction. "The only out kids aren't really my type."

Elin frowned. "And what is your type?"

No way was I giving my sister a rundown on my taste in guys. I let the glider slow before pushing off again.

"Give me an example of someone who isn't your type."

I pushed my hair back from my forehead with both hands. "I don't know."

"Gunnarrrr." Elin's tone told me she wouldn't let this go until I gave her some kind of answer.

"Look, can you see me hanging with Collier Barnes?"

Collier Barnes was in the fashion and design track of the Career and Technologies Studies program. He had nothing in common with some wrestler who took Building Construction and Trades Math. "He doesn't even know people like me exist."

Elin crossed her arms. "Judgy."

I shrugged.

"Okay, what about Elliot Chesney?"

Elliot Chesney? Elliot played bass guitar in his dad's country-rock band, which ought to be the uncool kiss of death, but somehow it worked for him. He always looked like he was starring in a music video, with rocker wind-machine hair and a slouchy walk so cowboy you expected to hear spurs jingling. He and Collier had been best friends forever. They hung out with the artsy/fashion/theater types.

Why was Elin asking me about Elliot Chesney? Wait. No way. "Elliot is gay?"

Elin face-palmed. "How do you not know this?"

Maybe because who might be gay at our school was not a conversation I was ever going to start. Unless a guy was wearing something like a rainbow flag "I'm queer and I vote" shirt, how was I supposed to know for sure? No gaydar here, if that's even a real thing. Which probably had a lot to do with why I was seventeen and had never kissed a guy. Well, that and living in a small town in rural Alberta.

Elin thunked her boot heel against my thigh. "They're both nice guys. You should get to know them."

That wasn't exactly my decision. "You know how many times Collier has said hi to me in the hall? Zero. Same for Elliot."

"You could say hi first."

Right. And then what? If they didn't drop dead from the shock, they'd just say hi back and that would be it. Sure, they were cool enough guys. They were friends with Elin, and she didn't put up with assholery. But I didn't have anything in common with them except the gay thing. Everybody's got friendship firewalls. I couldn't get through theirs and — honestly — maybe they wouldn't get through mine. One thing in common doesn't make a friendship.

I didn't know how to explain all that. So I shrugged.

Seconds ticked by. Finally Elin said, "Your choice. But what will you say if someone asks if you're gay?"

"I'm not going to deny it, but I'm not going around announcing it either." And I intended to make damn sure I stayed under the radar so nobody would ask. Stick it out in the closet for one more year and then ... I hadn't thought that far ahead.

Elin rested her head against the back of the glider seat. "Is there someone you like?"

My face got hot. "Yeah, but he's straight, so it doesn't matter. What about you?" I was eager to redirect the conversation, given my sister's talent for discovering secrets.

Elin gave me a look that told me she knew exactly what I was doing. "There's someone I like. But if we did go out, it would probably be too complicated."

And if I wouldn't tell her who I liked, she wasn't going to tell me.

We glided in silence. I closed my eyes and breathed in the scent of cut grass and the stain I'd applied to the cedar glider frame last weekend. One of the horses in the barnyard snorted and stamped a hoof. Magpies squawked in a battle for something tasty, and a phoebe called nearby.

"Gunnar, you're not going to stay on the farm, are you?"

I opened my eyes and shook my head.

Elin's going to study accounting and business at university and then come home and be the farm's accountant and business manager. She'll be a partner like Gary.

But how can she know for sure that's what she wants?

"Don't you think you might want to do something different once you've spent four years away?" I said.

"No."

"What if you want to marry some guy who doesn't want to live on a farm two hours from the nearest big city?"

Elin shrugged. "Can't build your life around what might happen." She looked past me and sighed.

Running footsteps on grass. Tor slid to a stop. "Why didn't you get me when you went to go water? I wanted to go."

"I thought you'd only want to go if we took the ATVs. We didn't," said Elin.

"I don't care about the stupid ATVs."

"You can go with me tomorrow."

"Is Gunnar going?"

"I'm working at Derek and Parker's."

Tor's face fell. "Mum says come in if you want pie and ice cream. And Dad says check the locks. Please." He bolted toward the house.

Elin and I checked the locks on the equipment bays and storage units. Everything was secure. As we walked toward the house, the wind picked up and rustled through the nearby fields of ripening wheat: under the darkening sky, the movement looked like rippling water and sounded like a hundred people all going SSSHHH SSSHHH SSSHHH at the same time. The breeze carried scents to us: the spicy nose-tickling smell of Mum's tomato plants, fresh-baked apple pie.

A great horned owl called: *hoo-h'hoo-hoo-hoo*; maybe it was one of the pair I'd stumbled across in early spring, raising owlets in a tree near the remains of an old soddy. The parents had squawked and snapped their beaks at me until I backed away.

I really loved our farm. I just didn't love the farming part.

Make Hay While the Sun Shines

I SLAMMED THE truck door and walked to the barn where Derek stood waving me over. "Gunnar, you have no idea how happy we are to see you." Parker joined him in the wide-open doorway, and the injuries from his fall were easy to see: one arm was in a sling, and I suspected that the green and purple bruises on his face had plenty of matching ones elsewhere.

Derek was a stocky, scrappy-looking guy who'd given up the battle with his thinning hair and now shaved it close to his scalp. He looked like a take-no-prisoners bouncer, but when he smiled, the warmth in his brown eyes totally killed the big, scary dude vibe.

Parker had silver-gray hair that set off his green eyes. He was so good-looking I had to force myself not to stare. Looking at Parker as if he were a six-foot slab of Mum's triple-layer dark chocolate cake with inch-thick fudge frosting would pretty much out me.

I nodded at them both. "Hi."

"I told your dad I'd pay you whatever he does and feed you, and we can use as many hours as you can give us. That all right with you?" Derek said.

"Sure. I can put in full days until school starts."

"Good." Derek gave me a once-over to make sure I'd dressed for the job. I wore my work boots, jeans, and a long-sleeved T, heavy work gloves tucked under one arm. I'd clubbed and secured my hair with several of the elastic hair bands that Elin finally bought me after she got tired of me stealing hers. Long hair and machinery don't mix, except in a bad way.

We rode in a battered pickup to their hay fields, bouncing along dirt ruts, and stopped under the shade of a shelterbelt. We spent the morning baling the cut, raked, and dried hay; Parker drove the tractor with the baler and hay wagon even with his left arm in the sling, while Derek and I corralled the rectangular bales as they emerged from the baler and wrestled them into neat stacks starting at the rear of the wagon. When we'd worked our way to the front, Parker drove to the hay barn,. we unloaded, and then repeated it all. Every so often, we took a break to swig cold sweet water from the orange Coleman cooler in the back of their pickup. It was dirty, sweaty, hard labor and I loved it. Doing real work beats lifting weights any day for building muscle.

Something occurred to me, and on our next break I asked. "Wouldn't it be easier to do round bales?" They wouldn't need extra help if they did.

"This is what we call our boutique hay," said Derek. He tilted his head toward the bales we'd just unloaded. "That's a blend of timothy grass and birdsfoot trefoil. We have some regular customers who'll take as much of it as we can grow, and they want the smaller bales." That made sense to me: at home we baled rectangular bales that we could stack in our old barn's hayloft for our horses, but big alfalfa rounds to sell.

When we stopped for lunch, Derek carried a red chest cooler to the truck tailgate, while Parker took paper towels and plates from a canvas bag. We rested on the grass in the shade of the shelterbelt and cleaned our hands as best as we could. With no engine noise,

I could hear bird song and crows cawing nearby. Tree leaves rustled in the prairie breeze. A peaceful late-summer day.

Parker popped the lids off the plastic containers that had stayed chilled in the cooler all morning, and we helped ourselves. "Grab whatever you want to drink, Gunnar."

"You doing all right, Park?" Derek asked.

"I'm fine." Parker smiled at me. "Gunnar's doing a hell of a job."

I turned red and was glad I'd just taken a huge bite so I had an excuse not to talk.

"Hey, babe," said Derek, and pulled a piece of straw from Parker's hair. It was an affectionate gesture, exactly like what I'd seen Mum do for Dad. They smiled at each other the way Mum and Dad did too.

Derek glanced at me. I swigged water, as if I wasn't paying attention. I wanted him to do what he'd normally do. Usually I saw them in public places, with other people around, where they were always careful. I wanted to see how partners — men who were lovers — would be together when they could just be themselves.

Aidan

WHEN I GOT home, I put my boots on the tray by the basement back door and headed toward the laundry, removing my shirt as I went. I threw it in the hamper reserved for really dirty clothes, grabbed a clean pair of sweatpants from the top drawer of a battered chest, and finished stripping in the bathroom.

In the shower, I savored the hot water on my tired muscles. I smoothed several squirts of something on my hair that was supposed to free me from static before I dried off and pulled on the sweats, which hung low on my hips. Dangerous since I was going commando. I shoved my feet into sandals, hung the wet towels over the laundry sink to dry, and took a clean T from the dresser. It was last year's and too small. Had it shrunk, or had I grown that much?

I worked the shirt over my arms as I rounded the short wall that hid the laundry and bath from our workout space. I finger-combed damp hair out of my face — and froze. A page from GQ had come to life in our basement. He — a guy my age I'd never seen before — was looking at framed photos that Mum had taken at our wrestling meets, but now he turned in my direction. He stood, hip slung, hands in pockets, and checked me out.

I returned the favor, starting with his seal-brown hair, parted on the left side over thick but tidy brows that angled across clear indigo eyes. He wore sage green pants made of a soft fabric that hugged him, a dark blue checked, cotton shirt with thin white lines and a golden-brown suede bomber jacket that hit at his waist, leaving a hand's breadth of shirt hanging below it. On the most fashionable day of my life, it wouldn't have occurred to me to wear those three items at the same time, and yet it worked. More than worked. He oozed style. I wished I knew how to dress like that. If I tried, I'd just look stupid. I'd figured out a long time ago, fashion was a language I didn't speak.

"Uh. Hi," I said, when I finally got my voice to work.

Mr. GQ's eyebrows rose. Before, his face had been ordinary — a nose, cheekbones, a chin, attractive though nothing special — but when he lifted his brows his face got all smart and sharp and old-fashioned handsome, like in a black-and-white movie.

What am I doing? I can't look at a total stranger like I want to eat him up with a spoon. Not in my own basement. I'm totally outing myself.

Elin pounded down the stairs. "Sorry, Aidan. That took longer than I thought. Oh, Gunnar, good, you've met."

"Not yet," I said, subtly adjusting my stance so it said: *Athlete, not flirty fan boy. Poised guy, not drooling-over-you loser.* Aidan's face shifted in response: he'd just gone shields up like the Starship *Enterprise*.

"Aidan, this is my brother Gunnar. Gunnar, this is Aidan. His dad is Mr. Standish." Our insurance agent.

"Good to meet you," I said, stepping forward just as Aidan did the same. We shook, a single strong-gripped pump, and stepped back, not as far back as we had been, but still at a hetero male social distance. I'd thought he was checking me out the way a guy who likes guys would, but anyone might stare at someone wearing pants about to fall off, trying to get into a too-small T with wet hair in his face.

"Aidan's going to Valgard High this year with us," said Elin. "He's in Grade 12 too. He just moved here from Toronto. His mum's spending a year in Africa with Doctors Without Borders."

How long had he and Elin been talking? Knowing my sister, she probably already knew his life story, his future career plans, the last movie he'd seen and liked, and the party he'd vote for in the next Federal election.

"Cool," I said. Time to make polite conversation. He'd been looking at the wrestling photos. "Do you wrestle?"

His expression said *Are you kidding me?* Great. Way to sound like a dumb wrestler.

"Aidan's taking two of Mum's classes," said Elin. "He made his shirt."

"Nice," I said. "I could never do something like that."

Aidan raised his gaze and held mine. His expression said *No, really?* Then I realized where he had been looking — the gap between the too-tight T and dangerously low sweats. Had the pants slipped further than I realized? My eyes flicked down and back to his, and he reddened.

"Elin," Mum called. "Mr. Standish is ready to go."

"Okay, coming up." Elin and Aidan climbed the stairs, his socks (the same shade as his jacket with thin bands of lime green and orange) muffling the thump of his feet as he climbed. I followed, enjoying the view.

Mr. Standish shook Dad's hand, then Gary's. "Thanks again, Trygg. Gary, nice to be working with you too now."

"If you want to ask anything about school, give me a shout," said Elin, giving me a *Why are you making me do all the work?* look. I couldn't get my mouth to open. I couldn't think of a single thing to say.

"Thanks," said Aidan. He glanced at me, his expression unreadable, as he put on his shoes at the door. "Nice to meet you."

"Yeah, likewise." I gave the automatic response that didn't require conscious thought, which was good, because there wasn't any happening in the Gunnar-sphere just then.

When Aidan and his father had gone, Elin dragged me into the kitchen and shouty-whispered, "Would it have killed you to actually have a conversation?"

"He didn't seem too interested." *Yeah, no wonder.*

Elin's eyes narrowed. "He was friendly and chatty, and I get to the basement and he's like a different person. What happened?"

I shrugged. "Maybe he doesn't like wrestlers." *Maybe he doesn't like socially awkward weirdos.*

"Why wouldn't he like wrestlers?"

"Maybe he had a bad wrestler experience. I don't know. Do I look like a mind reader?" I couldn't possibly explain what happened in the basement to my sister. My head would explode if I even tried.

Hands on hips, Elin scrutinized me. "But he's cute, right? And he has to be gay. Don't you think?"

"How would I know?" Yeah, I thought he probably was gay, and he was hot, but there was no point in me getting interested. He'd be part of the artsy/fashion/theater crowd the first week of school. I'd bet my next paycheck from Parker and Derek on it. And since none of them seemed to know wrestlers existed, I'd be lucky to get a nod if our eyes met as we passed in the hall.

Tall Tall Charlene's

SATURDAY MORNING, SAM, Gary, and I went to Medicine Hat. At Prairie Farm Supply, Sam backed the truck to a loading dock and the staff stowed Sam's dad's order. He shoved the paperwork into the glove compartment.

"Ready for TTC?"

"Yeah." This was always my favorite part of a trip to the Hat.

Tall Tall Charlene's Coffeehouse was a hangout that attracted what Elin called "an eclectic mix." While Sam and Gary ordered drinks, I claimed a table, taking a seat that gave me a view of four guys dressed like a Ralph Lauren ad. The dark blond facing me wore a body-hugging peach shirt with a royal blue silk tie, sleeves rolled up to his elbows displaying tanned and toned forearms. His hair was short on the sides and long on top, gelled and slicked back in a smooth swoop from a side part.

Blondie caught me staring. I jerked my eyes away, sure I'd just turned bright red.

Gary set down our drinks. "Sam's talking to a couple of girls he knows in the back room. I'm gonna hit the washroom."

"Okay." Thank goodness he hadn't noticed my glowing face.

I sipped my latte and cut my eyes over to sneak another look.

Blondie and two of his friends had their heads together conversing, watching me. *Shit.* I would *not* look again. I checked out the funky store décor instead — until I had that feeling you get when someone is standing next to you.

"Hi."

I looked up to see Blondie. "Hi," I said, my mouth instantly dry. I sipped my latte to moisten it.

"I wondered if we could take this chair. If you're not using it." He nodded at the fourth chair at our table.

"Sure."

"Thanks." He smiled and stood there for a beat. "You must get this a lot, but your hair is totally amazing." The way he was looking at me — this was new. Anything you could read into that look would get you into a fight at Valgard High. He could look at me this way all he wanted.

"Thanks." Some part of me was marveling that I wasn't blushing or stuttering.

"Do you go to Medicine Hat College?"

"No. I'm in Grade 12 this year."

Blondie's brows rose in surprise. "You look older." Then he glanced over my shoulder.

"Here comes your friend." He didn't give the word any special emphasis, like *special friend* or *friend who's really your boyfriend*. Just a simple statement, but a question at the same time — a question only a gay guy would hear. All of a sudden, I wanted him to know the truth. I wasn't out to anyone besides my sister, but at least this guy, this total stranger, would know something about me nobody else could.

"If he's blond, he's my brother. If he's a redhead, yeah, he's just a friend."

I could see him making the connections. Me, making it clear I wasn't "with" Sam. Me, making it clear that a guy being more than a friend wasn't out of the question.

Blondie lifted the chair by its back. "We're here on weekends a lot. Maybe we'll see you around." He turned and walked away, my eyes on him all the way, and knowing without looking that his friends were watching me watch him and would tell him. A guy had flirted with me. A cute guy. Holy shit.

Sam sat down and watched me as he sipped his coffee. "Everything cool?"

"They needed another chair," I said. When the little muscles around his lips relaxed, something tight in my chest unwound. He hadn't seen gay guys flirting: he'd been thinking about what happened in June.

A second later, Gary sat.

"So, you excited for Grade 12?" said Sam. He grinned at my expression. I'm never excited about school. Only wrestling.

"There's a new guy in your class, right?" Gary prompted.

"Yeah. Aidan Standish. He looks like he should have a zillion followers online." I described Aidan's outfit.

"Maybe you should ask him for some fashion advice," said Sam.

I snorted. "I'd look stupid in his clothes."

"Why do you think you couldn't pull that off?" said Sam. "You rock your hair. You could rock whatever clothes you wanted."

I wished I could believe him. "You have to have the right attitude to wear clothes like that."

Sam and Gary laughed. How hard would they laugh at me if I admitted how much I really wished I could dress as cool as Aidan did and not look like an idiot? Except when I thought *dressing cool and not looking like an idiot*, what I meant was knowing how to look right for places I might want to go someday. On the farm I needed work clothes, school clothes, one suit for special events. Ordinary clothes. But I wasn't going to stay on the farm.

Once we went to a funeral for the son of one of Dad's high school classmates. His pallbearers were his oil sands co-worker friends, and they all wore new white T-shirts and dark blue jeans. Dad explained later that the family didn't want them to be uncomfortable. Most of them didn't own a suit. They would have felt strange wearing one. I wondered if they didn't feel strange anyway, because everyone else was dressed up. Not being judgy, just — I don't want to go through life feeling like I'm in jeans at a funeral.

Time to change the subject. "When do you leave for Calgary?" I asked Sam.

"Two weeks from today. My program starts the week after that." Sam had his future mapped. He'd always wanted to be a paramedic. "You thought any more about what you're doing after graduation?"

"No. I mean, I've thought. I just haven't figured anything out."

"Sure you don't want to be a paramedic?"

This was an old topic of conversation. "I'd be a lousy paramedic. And I'd have to cut my hair."

"Unless you're planning on a career as a Hell's Angel, you're probably going to have to do that anyway. There aren't too many jobs besides biker and rock star where you can grow your hair halfway down your back."

"Farmer," said Gary, with a quick smile to let me know he was teasing.

Sam laughed. "Don't stress. You'll figure it out."

To my relief, Gary asked Sam about the girls in the back room.

I slouched and watched Blondie and his friends as they gathered up their things and walked out. He glanced back, caught me looking, and grinned. I couldn't stop a smile in return.

Thrown to the Fashion Wolves

THE LAST WEEK before school, I was back at Derek and Parker's Monday through Wednesday. On Thursday, Mum was making me go shopping for school clothes: she had scolded me when she found out I'd gone all summer without buying any.

"I have clothes, Mum."

"You need to go through and set aside everything that's too worn. I think you'll be surprised how little is left."

Elin smiled smugly at me from behind Mum, and I scowled. Mum thought my frown was directed at her. Her hands went to her hips and her eyes sparked like an arc welder as she looked up at me. In my head, Mum towered over me, but in reality I was taller than her.

"Elin is going shopping on Thursday. You can go with her."

Elin's mouth fell open. "But Mum —"

"No discussion. You're taking the minivan, and I agreed to pay for gas, and I might as well take care of two for the price of one." Mum's stance told us she wasn't giving an inch. "Gunnar, I want to see piles of worn-out clothes and a shopping list no later than Tuesday evening."

As Mum walked away, Elin said, "What if I buy my own gas?" but not loud enough for Mum to hear.

We stared at each other, wearing identical *pissed* expressions.

MUM KNOCKED ON my bedroom door early Thursday morning, and didn't stop until I got out of bed and said I was getting ready. As I came down the stairs twenty minutes later, the doorbell rang, so I detoured into the living room and answered it.

Aidan stood on the front porch. I was so surprised to see him that I didn't say anything at first, and his lips tightened. Two vertical lines appeared between his brows.

"Can I come in?"

I stepped back. "Yeah, sorry. Come in."

Elin appeared — pale, in sweats and slippers, with a box of tissues under one arm. "Hey, Aidan." Then she sneezed three times, turned her back to us, and blew her nose. A two-tissue blow. So glad I wasn't eating right then. "Sorry," she said.

"How are you feeling?" said Aidan.

"Same as when I texted. Like crap. I hate summer colds." Elin turned to me. "You guys can still go." She smiled at Aidan. "Gunnar can use all the fashion advice he can get."

What the hell?

Aidan had to be horrified about shopping with me. Too late for him to get out of it without being rude.

"Sure," he said, but his expression was wary.

Aidan wore a long-sleeved crew neck T, white with thin, black, horizontal stripes, sleeves pushed to his elbows. On top was a short-sleeved red silky shirt splashed with black and white shapes. Over his shoulder, he carried a caramel-brown suede bag, and on his left wrist he wore a leather thong strung with five beads the colors of a rainbow.

His outfit looked like something you'd see on one of the men's fashion sites Elin loved, like *British Vogue* or the *Mr. Porter* online store — the ones that always made me feel clueless when she showed me clothes she thought I'd look good in. Aidan's look appeared effortless. Awesome. Chic. And if I wore that outfit, people would be posting my picture online: #FashionEpicFails. Or maybe #Farmboy-ShouldaStayedHome.

We stopped by the kitchen long enough for me to eat a couple of muffins and swig down a glass of milk. When I went to brush my teeth, Elin followed me to the foot of the stairs. "Be nice," she said in low voice.

"I am."

Elin took a step back.

"What?" I asked.

"I don't want to be hit when the lightning strikes."

My sister thought she was way funnier than she actually was.

Ten minutes later, I drove Mum's van past fields of wheat and canola and barley in total disbelief that I was going shopping with Aidan.

Silence dragged on.

Think of something to say. "Um …" My brain blanked.

Aidan glanced at me before returning his attention to the road.

"Is that a purse?"

Aidan shot me a look somewhere between disbelieving and offended. "It's a messenger bag. I have to have my asthma inhalers with me at all times, and it's easier to carry them this way."

Oh great. I'd insulted him. I had a feeling that was going to be a regular thing with us. "I didn't mean I didn't like it."

He glanced at me again, one eyebrow shooting up.

"I do like it." Not exactly true, but more polite. "I like your clothes too." That was true. "What are you shopping for?"

I got another one of those Looks, but he sighed and relaxed back into his seat.

"I need to find ideas for my portfolio."

"What kind of portfolio?"

"I'm applying to fashion programs. I've got examples of my pattern making and couture sewing and design, but I have to pull them together somehow so it stands out. What I need for my portfolio is a fashion story — like a theme or a narrative."

A narrative? "And you think you're going to find that in Calgary?"

Aidan gave me a sharp smile that didn't look amused. "Fashion stories are everywhere if you know how to look." Obviously I didn't.

Another two minutes went by in silence.

"What kinds of clothes are you shopping for?" asked Aidan.

I shrugged, keeping both hands on the steering wheel. "Just clothes." Without taking my eyes off the road, I pulled my shopping list from my front pocket and handed it over.

Aidan took it without comment and scanned it. I could feel him looking at me. He handed back the list, and I shoved it in my pocket. It couldn't be more boring. Socks, underwear, jeans, shirts. Same as ever.

I was afraid of what people would say if I showed up in something besides my usual stuff. I probably wouldn't do it right. I'd be that loser guy who tries too hard. I'd be that guy wearing jeans to a funeral.

Shop till Your Head Explodes

OUR FIRST STOP was a consignment store. The racks of clothes in my size were a big sea of colors and textures that didn't say anything to me. Fashion was a language I couldn't speak.

Then Aidan was in my face holding a pair of white jeans. "These are Ralph Lauren and would have cost at least $200 originally."

Was I a white pants kind of guy?

"They're versatile. But you'd have to try them on because they're cut narrow, and you're ... athletic." He pinked.

A couple of minutes later, I stepped from the dressing room. "They're kind of low, aren't they?" And form-fitting. Good thing I'd spent so much time on my six-pack.

"Hold up your shirt so I can see." Aidan stepped closer. "May I?" He circled me, tugging at the waist and seams along my hips, his fingers warm against my skin. Then he stepped back. "The fit is good. They're supposed to sit below the natural waist and emphasize your hips. There's a bit of stretch, just enough to give them a nice silhouette. Try sitting in them. Move a little."

I sat. Stood up. Bent to touch the floor. Stood again.

"Try these with the jeans." Aidan handed over a light golden-brown leather belt and a short-sleeved shirt in midnight blue with a pattern of tiny chevrons.

I stepped outside the fitting room and looked in a three-way mirror. The shirt was soft cotton and fit my body closely, but without feeling like I could tear it by flexing. It had slim-sewn cuffs that hit at that sweet spot where the biceps meets the deltoid. My muscles popped, and the color made my skin look tawny. The belt wrapped low around my hips. These clothes looked awesome. Seriously hot. Was this really me?

Aidan twirled a finger. "Turn."

I faced him.

"Do you have shoes near that belt color?" said Aidan.

"No."

"You'll need the right shoes."

Aidan held out another garment. "Try this on. Don't tuck it in."

In a minute, I was back wearing a V-neck lightweight purple sweater. The hem hit right at the belt so it covered me, but if I lifted my arms high, I'd show flashes of skin. The sweater flowed over me, silky soft. I fingered the fabric, liking the way it felt.

"Dark lavender looks really good on you," said Aidan. He crossed his arms. "That's a cotton cashmere blend. People with muscles can rock the hell out of it. If you've got a belly roll, it's unforgiving. That's probably why it ended up here for a fraction of what it would cost new."

Somehow I left with bags full of clothes, there and at each of the next three stores we visited.

"Are you ready for lunch?" I asked as we stowed our purchases from the last consignment store.

"Sure. Where do you want to go?"

"How about Rooster's Grill?" I said.

Aidan's expression suggested I'd said 'The Dead Rat.' "I'm vegetarian."

Oh. I thought for a second. "Mum and Elin like Beans and Grains and Greens. It's vegetarian."

"Sounds perfect."

AIDAN LOVED THE menu. "I thought I'd be the only non-meat-eater in Alberta."

Way to buy into the stereotypes.

Our waiter, *Benjamin* according to his name tag, returned to take our orders. He exchanged a look with Aidan that was an information dump lacking only his phone number. Even I, with no gaydar, got it. Aidan caught me watching. I snapped my gaze to the menu.

"Can I get you anything to start? Drinks? Or are you ready to order now?"

"I think we're ready," said Aidan after a quick glance my way to confirm.

We placed our orders, and Benjamin's hand brushed Aidan's as he took his menu.

Time to make more conversation. "I guess it sucked for you to get dragged out here for your last year."

Aidan shrugged. "I had options. I wanted to come. I was looking forward to working with your mum."

"Mum?"

Aidan looked at me like *are you kidding?* "My favorite teacher in Toronto graduated high school here and studied at the Ontario Couture Institute, which is really hard to get into. One of the admissions committee members said she had the best portfolio they'd ever seen from a high school student. That was thanks to your mum, because she's a great mentor. And she's good. She probably could have been a big-name designer."

Every year, Mum designed a few wedding gowns and formal dresses for ritzy events and proms. When she worked on those commissions, she put on her favorite tunes and sang along and glowed. It had never occurred to me to wonder if Mum had any regrets about landing on a farm in rural Alberta.

Benjamin arrived with our meals, but the restaurant had filled by that time, so he was too busy to linger, which was good, because all those flirty looks he and Aidan were trading earlier were making me want things I couldn't have, not until after graduation.

For a few minutes we concentrated on eating. Finally Aidan sat back and dabbed at his mouth with a paper napkin. "That was a great find you made at that last store."

Cargo-style trousers in a light military green. They were awesome.

"What will you wear with them?"

And just like that, I panicked. All those clothes I'd bought. What was I thinking? What if I looked like a big idiot dork?

"I don't know," I finally said.

Benjamin swooped in and removed our plates. "Anything else?"

We shook our heads.

"I'll be back with your bill." Benjamin gave Aidan an intimate smile. "Love your bracelet."

Aidan returned it. "Thanks."

My heart felt as if it were being squeezed in a giant fist. *I want that. I want a real life now.* Aidan was still smiling when he turned to me. His expression blanked. "Is something wrong?"

I grasped for words that wouldn't give away how much that look they'd shared had thrown me.

"I'm not going to stop wearing jeans and Henley shirts."

Aidan studied my face. "You shouldn't. But it's good to have some variety in your wardrobe."

Still flustered, I blurted out what I was really thinking. "Maybe I'm not the kind of person who wears the stuff I bought today."

Aidan frowned. "You lost me. What do you mean you aren't that kind of person? What kind of person are you talking about?"

I looked at my feet, through a window, anywhere but at Aidan. "Just — a person who can pull them off." A person who always knows the right clothes to wear wherever he is. A person who knows how to make clothes say what he wants them to say.

"You can pull those clothes off, Gunnar." We both realized what he'd said, and he flushed. "You just have to be confident."

"Right." I pushed my hair back, sliding lower in my seat. Why hadn't I just gone to Discount Dudes the way I usually did?

"Be as you wish to seem."

I stared at Aidan.

"For people to see you as the kind of person who belongs in those clothes, you have to be that person."

"You mean fake it till you make it."

"Don't think of it as faking. You aren't faking. First day of class, you wear your white jeans and the blue short-sleeved shirt and be that person. Fashion isn't about trying to be the center of attention. You're not a little kid running around screaming 'look at me.' You just do you, and it's like you're having a conversation with the world."

Sure, Aidan was having a conversation with the world; he spoke the language.

Benjamin arrived with the bill. "I've got it," Aidan said. "You're driving." He put down cash that included a generous tip.

As we walked to the door, Benjamin ran after us waving a folded piece of paper between two fingers. "Don't forget your copy."

Aidan accepted the slip. "Thanks." In the van, he unfolded the paper and laughed, then shoved it into his messenger bag. At my questioning look he said, "His phone number."

"Does that happen a lot?" Then I wanted to kick myself for being nosy.

"Not really, no." Aidan gave me a curious look.

Are you going to use it? Something clenched in my chest again. After graduation I could wear rainbow bracelets. Hell, guys had flirted with me in Medicine Hat. Just a few more months. Okay, another whole school year. But after that I could start my real life.

At the mall, I got a pair of shoes to match my new (formerly consigned) belt. Seventeen stores (I counted), two rounds of lattes, and more of my hard-earned dollars later, we drove back to Valgard. We listened to music all the way. Aidan didn't seem to be in a talking mood. Once we arrived at the farm, I helped him carry his bags to his car.

"So. Thanks for the shopping help." Now would be the time for me to say *Hey, actually I'm gay too. We have something in common.* Maybe he could tell me everything I didn't know, answer all the questions I had.

I took a breath. The words gathered at the back of my throat, wanting to get out. Wanting to be said.

Tell him.

No.

Having one thing in common doesn't make a friendship. We're too different. Stick to the plan. Fly under the radar until graduation.

Sweet Tea

THE LAST FRIDAY before the start of school, I shook the loose dirt and chaff from my pants, left my boots at the door, and followed Parker and Derek into their kitchen. Derek padded off to get my pay.

Parker's bruises were mostly gone now, but he still had to wear the sling, so he opened the fridge door with his good hand. "You drink sweet tea, Gunnar?" God, he was hot, even filthy and wearing smelly socks.

"I guess," I said. "What is it?"

"Something we make where I grew up. We've got pop too."

"I'll try the tea."

By the time Derek reappeared, I was drinking a glass of iced sweet tea at the kitchen table and eating a cookie from a plate that Parker set in front of me. Derek handed me an envelope that I folded and slid into my back pocket.

"Thanks," I said. "This is good tea. It's better than the canned stuff."

Derek snorted. "Don't get him started. Four decades here and he still complains about not being able to get decent iced tea in Canada."

"Where'd you grow up, Parker?"

"Tennessee."

"You don't sound like it," I said. "Maybe a little twangy sometimes."

Parker quirked his lips. "I've been hanging around Mr. Yankee there for a long time."

"And a good thing too," Derek said. "When he first got here, we'd go somewhere for dinner and Park drawled so slow I'd already be eating dessert by the time the waiter got his order."

I grinned, but kept my eyes on the cookie plate. Why was I so shy around them?

"We were wondering if you might be able to put in a few hours after school starts," said Derek. "Would you have any interest in that?"

"What would you want me to do?"

"My broken collarbone has been a bit of a wake-up call," said Parker.

"We're getting older," said Derek. "We don't have kids or family to take over. Before we make any decisions, we've got to do some chores we've been putting off a long time. There's a storage building and equipment shed full of stuff neither of us has looked at in years, and we have to go through all of it. We could use some help."

"Okay," I said. "But I couldn't start until after wrestling season, and that doesn't end until mid-spring."

"We'll wait," said Parker. "We'd rather have you later than some-body else sooner."

I drained my tea. "I should be getting home," I said. The two men stood when I did.

"Thanks for all your help," Derek said. "We would have been in a lot of trouble without it." He and Parker stood on the porch as I slipped on my boots. Parker had his arm around Derek's waist, and I didn't think he even noticed. Would I ever be able to do that? Would I ever have a boyfriend?

"See you," I said, and they waved as I drove away. I glanced in the rearview mirror and caught them in a kiss.

Like a Date but Not Really

SATURDAY, MUM AND Dad drove to the Hat for a date-night dinner and movie. They would stay there tonight so they could do some shopping tomorrow morning. Tor was sleeping over at a friend's house. Elin and Gary had gone to an event in Killam where they were going to see research plots and learn about "advanced barley agronomy research and lentil agronomy" courtesy of the Alberta Ministry of Agriculture and Rural Development. They wouldn't get home until late. At our house, someone was always around, so the emptiness felt strange, but in a good way.

I texted Sam.

Gunnar: *You packed? Dinner here? Ride first?*

Sam: *Packed. Sounds good. When?*

Gunnar: *3. Meet at corral.*

Sam was leaving for Calgary in the morning. This was my last chance to see him for a while. Of all our friends, he was by far the most horse crazy: he wouldn't think it was odd if I asked him to go riding even though Gary wasn't around.

I PREPPED FOR dinner, the ordinary kitchen routines calming my nerves. Afterward, I went to the horse pasture and caught up Deck, a blood bay quarter horse gelding, and Mackie, a red roan quarter horse mare. They were saddled and bridled, and I was double-checking Mackie's girth when both horses pricked their ears and swiveled their heads. A second later, boots crunched on the gravel drive leading to the corral.

"Gunny."

Sam sauntered toward me, his usual grin in place.

"Samwise." I couldn't stop my loopy smile.

I mounted Deck, while Sam swung onto Mackie, and we followed the dirt tracks that paralleled the fields on one side and the shelter-belts on the other. We rode side by side, the horses fresh and eager. They tossed their heads and snorted, impatient at being held to a walk.

"Want to run?" I said.

"Yeah."

We galloped until the horses had burned off some energy, reined back to a trot, then slowed to a walk to give them a breather. A snow-shoe hare shot away through stubble at our approach, its fur still mostly summer brown, but with patches of winter white already visible.

"So who do you see for wrestling team captain?" asked Sam.

I reddened. "I don't know."

"I think it'll be you and Jase as co-captains. You want it, don't you?"

"Sure, I guess." I wanted to be team captain or co-captain more than anything.

"Being a senior wrestler is awesome. You're going to love it." Sam's expression sobered. "I've been hearing some stuff. Brody is still pretty pissed about that party." Sam was at the party where Brody took a swing at me.

"You think he'll do anything?"

"I don't know. He probably doesn't want to fight you, because he knows how that turned out last time. Just watch your back. If he can find some way to get at you, he will."

"Thanks for the heads up," I said, but I didn't see how Brody could get at me short of physically attacking me.

Back at the barn, we looked after the horses and then cleaned ourselves up at the house. A little while later, Sam perched on a stool at the bar, chin propped on hands, watching me cook. "Should I be worried?"

"Have I ever poisoned you before?"

"I don't think you ever cooked for me before by yourself." He was right. Usually he was with me and Elin and Gary in the kitchen, often with hungry friends lined up along the bar, trading jokes and stories and insults.

"Here." I set out Mum's salsa and chips. "Mum made the salsa so you're safe. Beer?"

"Yeah."

I pulled two Grasshoppers from the fridge and handed one to him. "Can I do something?"

"Sure. Fill a couple of glasses with ice and water." *When I have my own place and a boyfriend or even a husband, will we hang out in our kitchen, chatting while we make dinner? If I had a partner, I'd touch him every chance I got. I'd brush my hips against his even when there was room to move past unobstructed. I'd skim my arm along his shoulder reaching past him for a dish. Our bodies would slow dance as we worked, the way a cat twines about your legs when it wants attention.*

Sam and I moved around each other, but the distance between us was unyielding, as if by crossing it, we'd hit some kind of invisible electric fence that would send us ricocheting off the cupboards.

"THIS IS GOOD," said Sam, over salad and spaghetti and meatballs and homemade whole wheat rolls. "Better than I'll be eating next week." He had an aunt in Calgary whose basement apartment he was renting. "You know, any time you want to visit, you've got a place to stay. If you want to check out schools or look for a job or just hang out. Or cook. Especially if you want to cook." He grinned.

Would I still be invited if he knew about me?

We'd just pushed our plates back when the doorbell rang. I opened the front door and froze, surprised.

"Hi," said Aidan, a cardboard box in his arms. He wore a beat-up denim jacket open over black jeans and a camo T. Extremely hot. "Your mum told me to leave this stuff on the porch because she wouldn't be home, but I saw lights so I thought maybe Elin was back. I shouldn't have bothered you. Sorry."

"No. I mean, Elin's not back. But you didn't ..." Why did I feel so awkward around Aidan? "Bother me."

Aidan's lips thinned, but then he wiped his expression. "Can I set this inside? Then I'll get out of your way."

"Come in." I closed the front door behind him.

Aidan set the box on a side table. "I didn't know you had company."

Sam stood in the doorway.

"This is Sam Glasgow," I said. "Sam, this is Aidan Standish."

"Hi," said Sam and Aidan nodded a greeting. "We were about to eat dessert," I said. "Come have some."

Aidan's eyes moved from my face to Sam's and back. "I don't want to be in the way."

"You're not. Come on."

Aidan shucked off his black high-tops, and I followed him and Sam back to the kitchen.

They chatted as I set a French press on the table, following it with dessert plates and forks, the cream pitcher, sugar bowl, and a plate of oatmeal raisin cookies.

I poured the coffee and passed around the cookies. Aidan asked Sam about his program. How many times had I sat across from Sam over the years? He probably thought he knew me, but he was missing a big piece of the picture. Sometimes I wondered how much I knew him or anyone else. If I could keep this enormous secret, what were the chances that other people were hiding parts of themselves too?

"You and Gunny went shopping?" *Crap*. What had I missed?

Aidan smiled at Sam. "I went shopping, and Gunnar came along kicking and screaming."

"Oh wait — you're the one."

Aidan looked surprised. I shot Sam a *Dude, shut up* look, and he turned pink.

"Gunnar said he met someone who had style. Fashion sense. You know what I mean."

"Really?" Aidan smiled, enjoying my discomfort, then removed his jacket and draped it over the back of his chair. He wore the leather thong bracelet with rainbow beads that I'd seen before.

Sam stood abruptly. "Gunny, can I help clean up? I need to call it a night."

"I've got it."

"Nice to meet you," said Sam, but his easy friendliness was gone.

"You too," said Aidan. Maybe he felt the sudden chill, because he didn't come along when I accompanied Sam to the door.

Sam pulled on his boots and I followed him onto the porch. "Thanks again for the ride and dinner."

I had to swallow before I could get words out. "Yeah, no worries."

Sam glanced at the screen door and then back at me, his eyes unreadable.

"Tell Gary I'll be in touch."

"I will."

"Okay, see you around. Good luck with wrestling." Sam climbed into his truck and I lifted a hand in response to his wave. He was the straightest straight guy in Valgard. I knew that. I shouldn't have let myself crush on him, but when hearts are involved, knowing you shouldn't do something is easy. Actually not doing it is the part people screw up.

I returned to the kitchen as Sam's truck growled up the drive. "He seems nice," said Aidan, his hands submerged in soapy water.

"Yeah," I said. "You didn't have to do those, but thanks. I can finish." Aidan stilled. I offered him a dish towel, and he dried his hands.

"I'm sorry if I overstayed my welcome."

My head was shaking without me even thinking about it. "No."

"I thought …" Aidan folded the hand towel and positioned it on the counter. "I just thought maybe I did." He ducked his head. "Okay, well … good." He slid his jacket on. "Thanks again for the dessert. Tell Elin I'll text tomorrow."

I followed him to the door, quiet as he slipped on his shoes.

He paused on the porch. "See you at school, I guess."

"Okay."

After he left, I closed the front door and then leaned against it. *What just happened?*

Incarceration, Day One

MONDAY MORNING, I dressed in the white jeans and blue shirt, plus a bracelet Elin bought me for last year's birthday: a strand of tiny, round, black glass beads and a strand of small, square, onyx beads that joined and then separated into two distinct strands again, with one tiger's eye accent bead. I'd never worn it to school before.

I trudged to class and sat through the usual boring speeches — class goals and objectives, teacher expectations. I wanted to burst out the door and not stop running. School was grinding day-in-day-out tedium — like incarceration with bag lunches.

Phys Ed was just before lunch. Everyone got the standard first-day pep talk from Coach Chenoweth, the head coach. Then Coach MacKennon waved the wrestlers to an empty section of bleachers and used the rest of the time to talk about training and scheduled practices.

"Make sure your participation forms are submitted no later than next week. Schedule's online and also posted on my office door. Questions?"

No one raised a hand, so Coach directed us to the men's dressing room for locker assignments. I'd brought my lock so I could stow my gym clothes.

A while later in the cafeteria, Myk and Jason plunked trays down at our table where I was unpacking my lunch. Wrestlers had their own tables, like all the other sports. Nothing official: we just always sat in the same spot. We didn't mind non-wrestler friends either. No guy wrestler had ever brought a boyfriend. I could have been a ground-breaker — if I wasn't flying under the radar, and if I had a boyfriend.

"So what's up with …?" Myk waved a hand in my direction.

"What?"

"You never wear anything but jeans."

"These are jeans. They're just white."

"You look good," said Jason.

I scanned the room. Where was Aidan?

"Who is she?" asked Myk.

"What?"

"Whoever you're dressing up for."

I blushed. "Don't be stupid."

Myk laughed. "I knew it."

There. Elin chatted with Aidan and Collier in line. Aidan glanced my way, our eyes met, and we exchanged nods, me trying to look normal and not self-conscious.

Aidan was drawing looks. He wore a pair of tapered trousers in a light khaki color, covered in a big print I couldn't make out from this distance. Over it he wore a white short-sleeved polo shirt that he'd buttoned all the way up. His messenger bag hung at his side and his left arm sported a wrap bracelet and two silver bangles. And his brown leather shoes were classy, like something out of a really old movie.

"Who's that guy with Elin and Collier?" asked Jason.

"Aidan Standish," I said. "He moved here from Toronto."

Myk snorted. "Ya think?"

How long had it taken Aidan to style his hair into its current graceful messiness that seemed to say *rolled out of bed and ran a brush through it?* Except if he had, it wouldn't have looked so good.

"When did he move?" Jason asked.

"I don't know. He and Elin have been hanging out and sewing."

Myk laughed. "Don't worry, Jase. No competition."

Jason's face was red, his mouth tight. "Shut up, Myk."

What? Jason and Elin? Was Jason the complicated love interest she'd mentioned before school started?

"I don't think he's competition for any guy, except maybe Collier." Myk grinned. "If you know what I mean."

How was I going to stand this all year?

Elin saw us, smiled, and waved. Myk, Jase, and I did a hand raise and guy-in-public smiles.

My gaze drifted to the football table. Brody sat at the end, across from Ryder. He stabbed at his food, frowned, and tossed his fork into the middle of his plate. His face was pasty, and even from a distance, I could see violet circles under his eyes.

Jason leaned in.

"You know Brody's dad is running for provincial office?"

"Yeah." Pastor Gilmore preached in a small evangelical church in Valgard, and I'd seen his campaign placards around town.

"The media found something he posted a few years back that said that gay people would roast in eternal hellfire." I flushed and looked away, hoping Jason hadn't noticed. He grabbed his phone and accessed a web page.

"Here. It's over the top. He's trying to make it seem like he's sorry for the poor, doomed gays, but he comes across like he couldn't be happier. You get the feeling he'd like to have front row seats."

We weren't the only ones bent over a phone, looking from the screen to Brody and back again. Brody spotted the phone in my hand and glared.

"Dad was pissed," said Jason. "He was going off all through breakfast about how anyone with his mind nailed shut could possibly hope to represent people not exactly like him." I could see Mr. Archuleta saying that. For an accountant, he could be fiery.

The five-minute warning buzzer rang, and Myk, Jason, and I joined the rush to class. Students pushed alongside each other like salmon slamming up a fish ladder. I turned into the next corridor and almost fell over Becca James sprawled on the floor. She cradled one elbow, wincing, cane just out of her reach.

I made like a human traffic cone to keep people from running into her. "Are you okay?"

"Yeah."

I handed her cane over. "You got rid of your crutches." On the last day of school, her leg had been in a cast after a fall ice skating.

"I switched last month."

Becca was as quiet as her two older step-brothers were wild. If their names were in the news, you could count on four other words appearing nearby: *known to the RCMP*.

Becca gripped the cane and took my outstretched hand to stand. She looked over my shoulder and I turned to see Rawdon, her biological brother, standing behind me, eyes narrowed.

Rawdon sported tattoos on his arms (none of them the kind that middle-class kids who want to be edgy get) and piercings. He had a pack of smokes in a T-shirt pocket, hidden well enough under a flannel shirt for teachers to pretend not to see. He always had cigarettes, even back in grade school, when he sold them to other kids. Rawdon should have graduated last year, but he had to repeat Grade 12. I'd never seen his name in the paper, though.

He looked from me to Becca. "You okay?"

"I'm fine," she said. "Go on. Don't be late because of me."

I retrieved her bag from under the row of lockers next to me and handed it to her.

"Thanks."

Rawdon caught my eye and gave me a chin lift, then headed for Building Construction, where I needed to be before the bell rang too.

"You okay now?"

Becca smiled. "Yes, thanks again. And you look really nice today."

AFTERNOON CLASSES PASSED at a glacial pace. I stood at my locker after last bell, the halls already emptied.

"You look good." Aidan had slung his ever-present messenger bag and a backpack over a shoulder.

"White pants are hard to keep clean."

Aidan quirked his lips, like he understood what I was trying to say. "What are you wearing tomorrow? Back to Henleys?"

"I don't know."

"I'd recommend the dark blue and black plaid short-sleeved shirt with a black T. Roll the sleeves a turn or two and wear it out over the indigo chinos. And those biker boots you have. Might as well keep the fashion momentum going."

I couldn't think of anything clever to say.

"Well —" he said, just as I said "I —"

Aidan gestured for me to go first.

"I got compliments on my clothes. So thanks."

"You're welcome." He was about to say more, when a commotion caught our attention. Loud laughter, trash talk. Brody, Ryder, Levi, and Caleb rounded the corner.

Brody slowed as he approached us, the other three following his lead. I pushed my backpack into my locker to leave my hands free.

Up close, his brown eyes were bloodshot, the circles under them more pronounced. His dishwater-blond hair was cut military short. Reverend Gilmore's idea, not Brody's. He was a bit shorter than me, and lean. I'd always thought he'd be better off playing soccer than football. He'd probably spend less time on the bench.

"Interesting look, Tryggvason. It's …" Brody paused, his expression suggesting he smelled something bad. "You. Yeah, it's definitely you."

A cold stare was my only reaction, so Brody turned his attention to Aidan. "What the hell is that on your pants?"

Aidan's face was all planes, as if he had stainless steel bones under his skin. Somehow he managed to sneer without moving a muscle.

"It's a traditional French toile print in cranberry on cream fabric. The pants are my own design." Aidan scrutinized Brody, not like checking him out but assessing and finding fault. "I'd be happy to help you with a wardrobe makeover. I won't even charge for my time and expertise."

Brody's lips twisted. "You fags make me sick."

"I prefer gay," said Aidan, giving the impression of looking down his nose at Brody, though he was the shorter of the two.

I tensed, ready to run interference if Brody went for Aidan, but just then, Mr. Lloyd, the head custodian, turned the corner and headed in our direction. Brody glanced over his shoulder.

"Come on, dude, we'll be late." Ryder pushed past Brody, and then the four football players were leaving, Brody's gaze holding mine until he turned to catch up.

Brody must think that Aidan and I were friends, and I was worried about what that might mean for Aidan. Bad enough that Brody was so homophobic — after lunch today, it was clear where he learned to be that way.

I retrieved my backpack and slammed the locker door. "Be careful around him."

Aidan regarded me and didn't say anything, like he was waiting for me to say more. Awkward.

"I've got to get a ride from my mum. See you around."

The expression on Aidan's face looked almost like disappointment.

Catastrophe
(Second Day of Classes)

DAY TWO OF incarceration passed in geologic time, except for Phys Ed and lunch. In the cafeteria, Brody looked worse than he had yesterday, his face drawn as if he hadn't slept at all. When your dad is getting trashed all over the media, it must feel lousy. Things were probably tough at home.

Beside me, Jason retrieved his phone and thumbed it on, then turned it to face me. "Have you seen this?"

A CBC news headline blared, "Controversial Pastor Fred Gilmore Withdraws as MLA Candidate."

Clusters of students leaned in, their faces avid as they talked. Every so often, they'd burst into laughter and look at Brody. Some bloggers were treating Pastor Gilmore the way Brody and Ryder and their crowd treated a lot of people at school. How did it feel to be on the other end?

Finally, last bell. Staying awake in English had just about killed me. The halls emptied fast, and by the time I headed toward the old building to catch a ride home with Mum, there was no one around.

Her classrooms were in the original high school building. Leaving the newer addition, I pushed through double doors into the narrow hallway with checkerboard floor tiles. The old building is creepy when you're by yourself after school — like the set of a slasher movie, as if bloody teenagers with bad eighties hair or nineties grunge-wear might appear around the nearest corner, pursued by someone named Freddy or Chucky. So when footsteps pounded, echoing in the hall, my heart sped up, even though it was stupid.

Wes, a Grade 11 player on the football team, charged up, panting. "They're killing that new guy from Toronto in the mop room."

"Who is?"

"Brody and some others. I'm getting a teacher."

Wes raced away, and I set off toward the mop room at a dead run, our footsteps echoing the length of the hall. I knew of only one new guy from Toronto.

The mop room was a custodian's storage area where Mr. Lloyd kept cleaning supplies. When I yanked the door open, Levi and Caleb had a tight grip on Collier, who was struggling to get free. Brody had Aidan's head submerged under filthy water in the deep floor-mounted mop sink: Ryder twisted Aidan's right arm behind his back. Aidan thrashed and fought, but Brody bore down with all his weight, yelling, so incoherent that I couldn't tell if he was issuing orders to Ryder or screaming insults at Aidan.

I took all this in for a split second that seemed to go on forever.

Brody looked at me over his shoulder, but before he could say anything, I was there.

I can't remember how I got to him with no time passing at all. I was in the doorway, and then I was beside Brody. I hauled him off Aidan and threw him into a row of battered steel supply cabinets so hard that one of them toppled with a crash.

Ryder jumped up, hands at chest level, palms facing out, total white-flag surrender. Levi released Collier's arm, allowing him to jerk free of Caleb's grip. Aidan hung over the mop sink, gasping for air and retching. Water streamed from his hair. He sounded like a malfunctioning air compressor every time he sucked in a breath.

I needed to move. Something was building inside of me, and I needed to get it out.

Scraping, gasping to my left. My head turned, slow, deliberate, as if someone controlled it with a joystick. Brody struggled to his feet, and I crossed to him in three strides and slugged him in the jaw so hard he rebounded off the lockers and fell to the floor. He didn't get back up.

I turned to Levi and Caleb, and Levi took a step back.

"Gunnar." Collier knelt on the floor by Aidan. "He can't breathe."

I crossed and dropped to my knees beside Aidan. His lips were blue, and he worked to pull air into his lungs with long, wet, rattling breaths.

"Where's his bag? He has an inhaler."

Collier lunged across the floor and tossed Aidan's messenger bag to me. Aidan wheezed with every inhalation and exhalation, struggling more each passing second.

I dug into the bag, found two small canisters at the bottom, and held them both up. Aidan reached for the one in my right hand, his arm shaking, his fingertips dead white. I put the canister into his hand and helped him draw it to his mouth, my fingers over his. I squeezed, and in a few seconds, his face gained a bit of color, so he was getting more oxygen than he had been. It wasn't enough. He was in a full-blown attack. He had to get to a hospital. That much I recalled from First Aid training.

Coach Mac knelt beside us. I hadn't even heard the door open. The vice principal, Mr. Clyde, was behind him, talking to someone on his phone.

"Hang on. We've got an ambulance on the way," said Coach Mac. The station was just a couple of blocks from the school. Aidan's eyes closed as he concentrated on breathing.

Reality clicked into place, like when you leave a theater after watching an intense movie. Mr. Clyde knelt beside Brody. Ryder sat on the floor, back against the wall, watching with a calculating look. Levi and Caleb stood to one side, expressions a mix of guilt and fear.

Only then did I see the red pool on the floor. Brody lay on his side, eyes screwed shut, mouth open, the angle of his jaw all wrong, blood and drool dripping out. He moaned, a continuous low sound like something out of a zombie flick.

Gurneys rattled in the hall. The principal, Mr. Kernes, entered, followed by an EMT who came straight to Aidan. A second EMT knelt beside Brody.

"Gunnar, Collier, Levi, Caleb, Ryder, collect your things and come with me." Mr. Clyde stood aside as we filed into the hallway and stopped beside the gurneys, unsure what came next. "Are any of you injured?"

My hand hurt, but I said, "I'm good." Levi and Caleb looked at the ground and mumbled "No," and Ryder shook his head, expressionless.

"I've got a few bruises," said Collier, with a direct look at Caleb and Levi. "But nothing serious."

"All right. We're going to administration." Mr. Clyde gestured for us to walk on, and I grabbed my backpack, still in the hall where I'd dropped it.

Collier and I walked side by side. His normally perfect hair was a mess, and his shirt hung loose where the top two buttons had popped off. He had the beginnings of a black eye and a fat lip, but he walked with his chin up, defiant.

IN ADMINISTRATION, MR. CLYDE ushered us through the reception area into a large meeting room. Wes was already there.

"Take a seat at the table, keeping at least one empty chair between you and the next person." That didn't sound good.

"Turn off your phones and put them away. Leave your backpacks on the floor."

Mr. Kernes strode in, Coach Mac following, and took Mr. Clyde to one side. While they spoke, Coach Chenoweth entered, scowling. He always looked mad: like a great horned owl, it was his natural expression. But that meant that when he was pissed off for real, he looked like the devil himself. This situation was looking worse by the minute.

Mr. Clyde approached us. "Mr. Kernes will contact your parents or guardians so they know where you are, and will arrange times for conferences with them tomorrow. Coach MacKennon and I will take statements from each of you. Coach Chenoweth will remain here until we finish the interviews. Bring your things when we call you. Questions?"

No one spoke. Caleb's eyes squeezed shut for a minute, and he exhaled and slumped into his chair.

Wes was called first and followed Mr. Clyde and Coach Mac from the room.

Time had crawled during the school day, but it was nothing compared to this. We shifted in our chairs, sighed, drummed fingers on the table, stared at the ceiling. Or the carpet. Or the walls. Or the tabletop. Ryder glared at me. Collier curled his lip whenever he looked at Levi and Caleb. My stomach growled and I turned red, but no one even looked. One after the other, my fellow detainees were called away. Collier, Ryder, Levi, Caleb. Me.

Coach Mac and Mr. Clyde waited in the small meeting room that opened off the principal's office. Mr. Kernes was speaking to them. When I came in, he slipped into his office.

"Have a seat, Gunnar." Mr. Clyde flipped a page on a legal pad.

"Is Aidan okay?" I had to know.

"Mr. Kernes was just giving us an update. He's stable, but he'll have to stay in the hospital overnight. He inhaled some of the water in the mop sink. Since he's an asthmatic, he has a higher chance of getting aspiration pneumonia, so he needs to be under observation."

Mr. Clyde cleared his throat. "Gunnar, we're trying to establish what happened this afternoon. How did you come to be involved?"

I took a breath. "I was going to catch a ride with Mum and I saw Wes running toward me."

"Where was this?"

"The long hallway in the old building."

Mr. Clyde nodded and made a note. "Go on."

I related the sequence of events as I recalled them.

Mr. Clyde tapped his pen against the legal pad, frowning. "Tell us about pulling Brody off Aidan again."

"I pulled Brody off Aidan and he fell against those metal cabinets along the wall."

"There's quite a distance between the mop sink and the cabinets. He fell that far?"

"Well, I mean …" I shifted. Why did I feel like I was on trial here? I didn't hold anybody's head underwater. "I guess when I pulled him off I sort of threw him away from the sink."

"Ryder says you forcibly propelled Brody into the cabinets."

Coach Mac's silence was putting me on edge.

"I wasn't trying to make him crash into the cabinets. I just wanted to get him off Aidan."

Mr. Clyde made more notes.

"What happened after Brody fell to the floor?"

"He got up, and I punched him to keep him down."

Mr. Clyde looked up. "Can you say a little more about that?"

"There were four of them, and the others do what Brody tells them. I thought he might make them go after Aidan again."

"Ryder, Caleb, and Levi all said that they didn't think Brody was going to fight further."

"They didn't say it then. I don't read minds." Coach Mac pinned me with a look, and I got the message: *Drop the attitude.*

"Yeah, okay, he looked like he'd taken a hit, but he was getting up. If somebody gets up, they're still fighting." I looked to Coach Mac, hoping for some sign of support, but he was blank-faced.

Then I realized what I'd said. *Oh shit.* I wasn't supposed to fight. I hadn't thought twice. I hadn't thought at all. But it wasn't fighting. It was defending. Not fighting.

"Ryder says that there was an incident between you and Brody in the summer and that you had it in for him."

My mouth fell open. "That's bullshit."

Mr. Clyde gave me a warning look that might as well have had flashing red lights and a loud siren accompanying it. *Walk it back.*

"Sorry," I said, not sounding sorry.

"The incident didn't happen?"

"It happened, but I didn't have it in for him."

"Ryder also said that Brody believed you and Aidan to be boyfriends."

I went red, hot from hairline to collarbones. My mouth was dry. "We aren't boyfriends." What else should I be saying? "He's friends with Elin."

Coach Mac and Mr. Clyde exchanged a look. They'd heard what I didn't say: *I'm not gay.* Well, I'd probably outed myself with these two. How far would it go? Would Mum and Dad figure it out? *Crap. Crap. Crap.*

Ryder had made it seem like I punched Brody because I wanted to hurt him or make him pay for something. Something like trying to drown a boyfriend. My jaw clenched. My eyes went cold. And that would make them think Ryder was right. *Breathe. Breathe. Breathe.* I stared at my hands, fisted in my lap.

Time to play some offense. "Why would that even matter? Why are you asking me this stuff?"

Mr. Clyde sighed. "Brody has a shattered jaw. He's going to be eating through a straw for weeks, maybe months. He also sustained contusions from hitting the cabinets."

He shouldn't have gone after Aidan.

"Is there anything else you would like to say, Gunnar?"

Anything else I could say might dig a bigger hole, so I shook my head no.

Mr. Clyde accompanied me into the reception area, where Mum stood with Mr. Kernes.

"We're done here, Sigrun. We're asking that students involved in this afternoon's incident refrain from discussing it with anyone other than immediate family until after tomorrow's meetings. No social media. We want to keep rumors to a minimum. Also, Gunnar won't be able to have his phone with him tomorrow while he's in the admin area."

Mum nodded.

Mr. Clyde rested his hand briefly on my shoulder. "Gunnar, you may have saved Aidan's life. Helping him was the right thing to do. Thank you for that."

WHEN MUM AND I arrived home, Elin and Tor met us at the door.

"Did you get in a fight?" asked Tor. "Stacy said you were fighting and there was an ambulance. And football practice got canceled."

Elin just watched me. She knew something bad had gone down by my face. We could always tell with each other.

"Wait." Mum held up a hand. "None of you can discuss this with anyone. No posts, no texts. Don't respond to comments or questions."

"What happened?" asked Tor.

"Brody and Ryder were holding Aidan's head underwater in a mop sink. I pulled Brody off and he got up and I punched him."

"What were the ambulances for?" asked Elin.

"Aidan had a serious asthma attack," said Mum. "Brody ..." She glanced at me. "Was injured too."

Elin went up in flames in front of me. "You should have kicked Brody's ass."

"Sounds like he did," Tor said.

DINNER WAS GRIM. Elin served split pea soup, roasted beets on fresh greens, and baked sweet potatoes in jackets with butter and cinnamon and maple syrup. I usually ate two, but tonight I had no appetite.

Gary gave me sympathetic glances: Elin must have given him a heads up when he got home. We all told a little about our day, but it was one of those self-conscious conversations where everyone is pretending to be normal and everybody acts like they believe it, but it's just really fake. Finally, we were done.

Dad's expression was scary serious. "Gunnar, your mother and I want to talk to you in my office."

"I can do your cleanup," said Elin. Any other night I would have been ecstatic to hear those words.

Delaying strategy removed, I climbed the stairs as slowly as I dared.

Dad's office had a small sitting area. He and Mum each took an armchair and I sat in the middle of the old couch retired from the living room. They both looked tired. My grandma used to say "every family has one." One family's "one" was the family drunk and another family's "one" was the guy who never moved out of the basement. I'm pretty sure I'm my family's one.

Dad ran his fingers through his hair, something he did when he was feeling frustrated. This probably wasn't a good sign. "What happened today?" Dad's hazel eyes watched me — his truth-finding eyes, Gary and Elin and I called them, because you couldn't look at him and lie without it being written all over your face.

When I finished telling, Dad and Mum looked at each other, wearing matching unhappy expressions. They were probably thinking about what happened in June.

"You can't get into any more fights," said Dad. "Today used up all your strikes and then some."

"I know." If I got into another fight, I would be in deepest, darkest shit.

"You did the right thing," said Mum. "Just maybe not in the best way."

"All right," said Dad. "There's nothing we can do now but get some sleep and meet with Mr. Clyde and Mr. Kernes tomorrow."

"Don't forget," said Mum. "No texting. No communication at all about today."

Back in my room, I pulled my phone out and stared at it. I couldn't reply, but I could look at my messages. Did I want to?

Without turning it on I shoved it into a dresser drawer and slammed it closed.

That Day in June

MUM AND DAD were worried. I'd scared them this summer. I'd scared me too.

In early June, Gary, Sam, and I went to Medicine Hat to pick up a tractor part for Dad. The store was in an old part of town, and on a late Saturday afternoon not many people were around. We were walking to an ice cream place a few blocks away, when Sam pulled Gary into a tattoo and piercings shop to look at designs. Sam wasn't sure about getting inked, but he liked the idea of it enough to window shop.

Instead of following them, I knelt to double-knot a boot lace that had been untying itself all day. Footsteps approached, but I didn't pay much attention. Not until people started talking.

"He must think he's Thor or something."

"Yeah, or maybe he's just a fag, eh?"

I stood and turned to face the speakers, taking my time — five guys about my age. The leader had to be the big one in the middle.

"What's with the gay hair, dude?" said Leader Boy. His friends snickered.

I just stared at Leader Boy until he flushed and clenched his fists. He looked familiar. I knew I had seen him before, but where?

The bell on the shop door behind me tinkled, and then two pairs of boots clomped in my direction. Gary and Sam stopped, one on either side of me.

Leader Boy tried to stare Gary down, which I could have told him was a waste of time. Then he glanced at Gary's "Valgard Vikings Wrestling" shirt, and just like that, he deflated. I remembered where I knew Leader Boy from: a wrestling tournament held last school year, where the Valgard High team dominated — make that humiliated — the Northwestern High School team.

"You ready to go, bro?" said Gary.

"Yeah," I said.

Leader Boy's eyes flicked over to Sam and noted the unmistakable fox red hair of the best wrestler on last year's team. He hadn't known me because he'd never seen me without a hair slicker. He scowled, turned his back on us, and stalked away with his cronies.

"I remember that guy," said Sam.

"Yeah, me too," said Gary. "He's a dick." Then he looked at me.

"What did they say before we came out?"

"Just some bullshit." I never told Gary and Sam when someone used the "f" word on me, because I didn't want them thinking too hard about it.

"Why didn't you go inside the store?" asked Gary.

I just stared at him. Okay, if I'd turned my back to them, maybe they would have jumped me and maybe they wouldn't, but I didn't want to give them the chance. Or the satisfaction of being able to say *Queer boy bailed*.

"That guy would have backed down anyway," said Sam. "He was backing down before we came out."

"What if Gunnar had been alone and the guy didn't back down?" Gary gave me a serious-big-brother look.

"Then Gunny would have gone all Viking on their asses." Sam winked at me.

Gary shook his head, and we fell into step in the direction of the ice cream parlor. "Next time walk away if you're alone and there's five of them."

In the store, Gary and Sam finished before I did. Sam decided he wanted one more look at a couple of the tattoo designs, so he said he'd meet us. Gary would get the truck and pick us up in front of the shop. I stayed to finish my ice cream. Then I tossed my trash, exited the store with a jingle of bells, and started up the sidewalk.

I was half a block from the tattoo shop when five guys boiled out of an adjacent door under a weathered canopy that read Dave's Liquor. A gray-haired man stood in the doorway and jabbed a finger in Leader Boy's direction.

"You may be eighteen, knucklehead, but there's no way all of you are. You could get me shut down. Don't come back." He disappeared inside. Leader Boy stood red-faced, fists clenched, totally shamed in front of his gang.

And then Sam stepped out of Tatts in the Hat. He saw them, but he played it cool, kept a poker face and looked up and down the street, making it plain: waiting for my friends.

Leader Boy said, "Hey."

I walked a little faster.

"Hey. You. You got a problem?"

Seriously? The guy in the liquor store embarrassed you and you're going to take it out on an innocent bystander? Except that wasn't exactly right. Sam had been on the team that humiliated North-western, and I had a feeling that was playing into Leader Boy's anger, even though he might not know it.

Sam turned and looked at Leader Boy. His stance seemed casual, if you didn't know him. He laughed.

Leader Boy looked uncertain. This wasn't how the script was supposed to go.

Meanwhile, Sam scoped out where the other four guys were. He was wound up like one of those Roman siege machines that threw boulders at the enemy.

Two of the guys didn't want any part of this. I could read it in how they stood, how they shifted from foot to foot and fidgeted. The other two were all in.

"Are you laughing at me, asshole?" Leader Boy shoved Sam.

I skirted the edge of the sidewalk to get past the four guys with Leader Boy. They were watching so intently they didn't even notice, but Sam saw me, and in the second he was distracted, Leader Boy sucker-punched him. It was a bad hit. Sam went down and Leader Boy drew back a foot to kick him, but by then I was there.

I'd never felt rage like that, like my blood was at a rolling boil and my head was on fire. A second later Leader Boy was on the ground, and the two buddies who were cool with piling onto one guy decided to take their shot.

One put me in a choke hold. I turned into Choke Boy to keep my air coming. Because I did, I caught his friend's fist on my shoulder instead of where he'd aimed it, and in the interests of time, I punched Choke Boy in the nuts. I wouldn't usually do that. But Sam was down and couldn't defend himself, and I didn't have time to fight like a gentleman. With Choke Boy on the ground, I parried a swing from the buddy and hit him. He staggered back, swiped his face, looked at all the blood from his nose, and was done. He and his friends may have been wrestlers, but they weren't boxers.

Sam was struggling to get in air but pushing to his feet anyway. Leader Boy was up, his leg already rising in a ridiculous fake ninja kick that was going to leave him wide open and off balance when it connected. Sam turned away from the kick, but Leader Boy's foot sank into his gut.

I don't remember much after that. Not until Gary and Sam were yelling my name, and they'd twisted my arms behind me, and I was breathing like I'd done fifty wind sprints all at once and Leader Boy looked like someone had used his face for a bongo drum. The friends who hadn't wanted to fight were gone. The buddy with the bloody nose was pulling at Leader Boy, urging him to leave. Choke Boy led the way, walking like a man who'd been punched in the nuts. I would probably go to hell for the stab of happiness I felt seeing that.

A couple of shop owners stood in the doorways of their stores. One was holding a cell phone like he was debating whether to make a call. But when he saw we were all on our feet and moving out, he just shook his head and went back inside.

"Come on." Gary and Sam half-dragged me to the truck. Gary had left the driver's side door open. The truck was still running. What had felt like hours must have only taken seconds. I hauled myself up onto the bench seat, and we were gone.

"Holy shit, Gunnar. You were like a machine. I thought you were going to kill that guy." Gary peered at me in the rearview mirror.

I scrubbed at my face with both hands. My knuckles ached.

Sam twisted. "Are you okay?"

"Yeah," I rasped out. I cleared my throat and tried again. "Yeah, I think so."

Sam's face twisted. "Asshole sucker-punched me."

Fights in real life are never like the movies.

"I didn't even get one hit. You did everything."

I was shaking. It was normal after a fight, but I was still embarrassed. I never wanted to be that out of control again.

TAP TAP TAP at the door. Elin entered, quiet as a cat on a hunt, and sat on the bed. "Is your phone blowing up?"

I shrugged.

Tap tap tap. Gary slipped in. He wrapped one arm around my shoulders. "You okay?"

"I don't know."

Gary perched on the bed beside Elin, and I scooted down to make room. Before I could say more, the door of the bathroom connecting my room and Tor's creaked and Tor's head poked through.

"Can I come too?"

At my nod, he came in and climbed onto the bed with the rest of us. I gave them a quick account of the events in the mop room and after.

"Are you in trouble? Are Mum and Dad mad?" Tor asked. At eleven, pissing off parents was still the worst thing he could imagine.

"They seemed worried more than mad." And that scared me.

Gary and Tor stayed a few minutes longer. Gary hugged me again before leaving, saying it would all be fine.

After they left, Elin crossed her arms. "Okay, what else happened?"

How did she always know?

"Ryder told Mr. Clyde and Coach Mac that Aidan and I were boyfriends and that I broke Brody's jaw because of that."

Elin could have passed for a Valkyrie. "That ass-kissing suckup."

"I told them we weren't boyfriends. But I didn't tell them I wasn't gay." I flopped back onto the mattress.

So much for staying under the radar.

Consequences

WEDNESDAY MORNING. MUM, Dad, and I waited in a small conference room in administration. When the door swung open, I jumped. "Mr. Clyde and Mr. Kernes will see you now." Mrs. Blevins stood aside to let us by.

"Sigrun. Trygg. Gunnar. Please sit down." Mr. Clyde and Mr. Kernes waited until we sat and then took their seats. Mr. Clyde folded his hands and rested them on his desk. He had dark circles under his eyes. So did Mr. Kernes. How late had they stayed up last night?

"We're handling yesterday's incident on school grounds internally. The purpose of this meeting is to review with you the decisions we've made." Mr. Clyde paused, as if he expected us to interrupt. Maybe the other parents had. "Two students, Levi Moreland and Caleb Green, have in-school suspension for the rest of the week and are barred from playing sports."

Levi and Caleb were off the football team.

"Ryder Buell and Brody Gilmore have in-school suspension for the rest of the week and are barred from sports, as well as all extracurricular activities."

So were Ryder and Brody.

"That brings us to Gunnar. Gunnar came to Aidan's defense,

which is admirable. It's what we want our students to do. Bullying will not be tolerated. But —"

I didn't like the sound of that *but*.

"Gunnar threw Brody into steel cabinets hard enough to cause a number of contusions, including a cut that needed stitching. He also struck Brody and broke his jaw. Gunnar said yesterday that he sincerely believed Aidan was in a life-threatening situation. An argument can be made that in the heat of the moment, fearing that Aidan might be seriously harmed, Gunnar instinctively used a level of force in excess of what was required."

I shifted in my chair. All my internal alarms were going off.

"Even if the force used to separate Brody from Aidan could be construed as reasonable under the circumstances, shattering Brody's jaw was far in excess of what might have been necessary to prevent further attacks. The force used was inappropriate and punitive, whether Gunnar thought it was or not."

Mr. Clyde paused. "Gunnar, you'll be on in-school suspension the rest of the week and you'll be barred from sports for the rest of the school year."

I couldn't have understood Mr. Clyde properly. What he'd said made no sense.

Mum asked, "Has the fact that Gunnar may have saved Aidan's life been taken into account?"

Mr. Clyde nodded. "It has." Then he looked me in the eye, and I got a glimpse of the person behind the principal mask. "Gunnar, thank God you were there, because the outcome might have been much worse. But —" And then the principal was firmly back in place.

Is he going to tell them what else Ryder said? Is he going to say Ryder accused me of hurting Brody to punish him for attacking my boyfriend? *Be calm. Air in. Air out. Slow.*

Mr. Clyde continued. "Gunnar, you're a big guy, a trained athlete."

Calm. Air in. Air out.

"You have been given the gift of physical size and strength and athletic ability, but with that comes the duty to use it responsibly. You can do greater harm, so you must take greater care. What if Brody's neck had broken when he hit the lockers? What if he'd become a paraplegic or suffered brain damage? The fact that you were defending someone would not be a defense." He looked at Mum and Dad and then me. "Do you have any other questions or concerns?"

Mum and Dad looked at each other, talking without words. Mum spoke for both of them. "No." I shook my head. Even if I did have questions, I couldn't have gotten any words out.

Mr. Clyde stood and shook hands with my parents, and Mr. Kernes ushered us out. I couldn't look Mum and Dad in the eye. I couldn't look anywhere except the floor. Dad gave my shoulder a gentle squeeze. My eyes got hot. *Breathe.*

Please don't make a big touchy-feely deal out of this. If you make me cry in public, I'll have to change my name and move to the Yukon.

Mum must have read my mind, because she only rested a hand on my shoulder for a second and said, "I'll see you after school." Then she and Dad left administration. I had never felt so thankful to have sensible parents who didn't make scenes or humiliate me. And I was a little ashamed that part of me didn't want them to go.

Mrs. Blevins was waiting. She walked me to my conference room prison cell, made sure I had no way to connect to the Internet, and said she'd check back before lunch.

Mrs. Blevins left, and Mrs. Chan came in and took a seat. "All right, Gunnar. We need to find you a replacement class for Phys Ed."

"Wait, what?"

Mrs. Chan stared at me with that teacher expression that says *Excuse me?*

"Sorry," I said. "I don't need to drop Phys Ed, right? I mean, I don't want to."

Mrs. Chan's gaze softened. "I understood Mr. Clyde to say that you did. Let me check. I'll be right back."

Five minutes later, Mr. Clyde came into the room. He closed the door with a gentle click and then slid into the seat Mrs. Chan had vacated. He clasped his fingers on the tabletop. "Gunnar."

This wasn't going to be good.

Mr. Clyde's jaw tensed. "Coach Mac feels that having you present when you can't participate in sports could lead to … morale problems. With the wrestling team."

"I'm not going to cause problems."

"I believe you wouldn't intend to, but Coach feels that … problems might occur."

I didn't have any leverage. Phys Ed 30 wasn't required for graduation. Would I even be able to appeal something like this? Who the hell was Coach Mac to ban me from Phys Ed? But what would happen to Mum if I fought the decision? It could get ugly and messy. I was graduating, but she still had to teach here.

And I had a feeling that Coach Mac's opening move would be to out me. No point in kidding myself. He didn't care about morale. He just didn't want a gay guy in his locker room — one he knew about anyway.

I sagged against my chair. "Fine."

Mr. Clyde nodded once. "Thank you, Gunnar. I'll send Mrs. Chan in." Did he suspect why I gave in so fast? I thought maybe yes.

Mrs. Chan returned. She looked at her tablet for a long time, swiping and poking with a stylus in Valgard High colors. How could it be this hard to find a replacement class? Maybe it was because I was on the dumbass track (okay, officially, the student retention initiative, but nobody called it that). Would life as a dropout really be that bad? It was looking better all the time.

"You could switch to Mrs. Young's English course in block two, which would free your block four, and you can get into Math 30-3."

I couldn't handle a third class where I'd have to sit still the whole time. "There aren't any other Career and Technology classes I could take instead?"

Mrs. Chan tightened her lips and jabbed at the tablet again. "Foods 30 in block four has space, but Foods 10 is a prerequisite. You haven't had Foods 10."

"I know all the stuff Foods 10 covers. Mum made us all learn basic cooking."

"You realize that if you have gaps in your knowledge because you haven't had Foods 10, you'll have to find a way to catch up."

"I can do that." Mum taught Foods 10 some years. She could show me stuff if I needed help.

"All right. I'll arrange the transfer and I'll bring you the assignments for Foods 30 and Mrs. Young's course."

After Mrs. Chan left, I pressed the heels of my hands into my eyes. *I'm not on the wrestling team anymore. I'm not even in Phys Ed.*
Hold on.

After school I could go somewhere I could be alone and grieve. Grieve like at a funeral. Because the one thing I was looking forward to at school just got taken away, and I didn't know how I was going to make it through till graduation.

Barn Therapy

I CLOSED MY bedroom door, tossed my backpack on the bed, and changed into work jeans and an old long-sleeved T-shirt.

I could hear Elin and Tor in the kitchen. They'd arrived home earlier on the bus. I crept down the stairs in my sock feet, dodging creaky spots. In the basement, I donned my work boots and a hoodie and ran to the barn.

Deck, Mackie, and Bonza were grazing in the pasture and raised their heads to watch me crossing the corral. I whistled, and after a few snorts, skin twitches and hoof stomps, all three horses crossed the field in a ground-covering fast walk. I slipped a handful of parched corn into the hoodie pocket and grabbed grooming tools from the tack room while I waited.

I rubbed all three horses around the ears and sweet-talked them, and then I hooked Mackie's halter to cross ties and groomed her. She didn't object when I rested my face on her neck. If it got a little wet, she didn't mind, and she'd never tell. Finished, I unhooked her halter, let her lip some parched corn off my hand, and then slapped her on the rump in dismissal. She stepped aside, tail swishing, and I tugged on Deck's halter to move him into the same spot. He was interested in investigating my pocket, so I pushed his head away, but gentle, not mean. By the time I'd finished brushing all three horses and giving them a second round of treats, it was dinnertime, and I could face my family without embarrassing myself.

Inside, I scrubbed arms and hands and face and neck to get off all the dirt and horse slobber and raced up the basement stairs. I took my seat as Gary took his.

Gary's sympathetic expression almost made me lose it, but I focused on my plate and regained my composure. Conversation flowed. Normally I'd be right in it, but not tonight. I couldn't spend every afternoon with the horses. I should get a project or find something else to do.

"Dad," I said into a momentary lull.

Five faces stared at me. "Remember Parker and Derek wanted some help and I told them not until spring? Could I start now?"

Dad and Mum exchanged a look.

"Why don't you check with Parker and Derek and see if they still want help, and how many hours a week," Dad said.

"Okay." I looked at Gary. "I'll still help you with the house."

He quirked his lips. "Definitely in your best interests." Mum and Dad had given him the okay to renovate the old farmhouse that used to belong to Great-uncle Gunnar. When he moves in, I'm getting his apartment. I didn't even have to fight Elin for it. Mum and Dad said we could flip a coin, but Elin preferred her bedroom.

I willed someone else to talk. Tor obliged by asking if he could go to the movies on the weekend with friends, prompting the usual parental inquisition: What movie? What is it rated? Who else is going? How are you planning to get there? (Meaning hell no, you aren't going with a new driver in a car full of teens and tweens.) What time is the show? When does it end? Are you going somewhere after? Will you be able to make your curfew?

Tor cleared the dinner plates, and Elin served mint Nanaimo bars.

My favorite. I could eat a pan by myself. She handed me a dessert plate with a bar that was twice as big as the others she'd cut. Tor sucked in a breath to make an eleven-year-old brother comment, but nothing came out. Elin must have kicked him under the table.

After dinner, Mum came into the kitchen as I finished scrubbing the counter — the leftovers stowed, the dishwasher humming, and the hand-washing in a rack beside the sink. I hung the dishrag over the sink divider, and Mum wrapped her arm around my waist, giving me a squeeze. "Nice job."

I ducked my head.

"How are you feeling?"

"Okay."

"If you need extra help in Foods, I want you to tell me."

"Okay."

"You know a lot already, but if there are things you haven't learned, we can get you caught up."

"Okay."

Maybe I should try sounding a little more grateful. After all, Mum and Dad could have piled on punishments at home. "Thanks."

Mum squeezed me again. "Your dad and I love you very much." She stood on tiptoe, kissed my cheek, and headed to the living room, which was good, because I couldn't have said anything with the lump that was in my throat.

Layers and Layers of Misery Cake

THE NEXT MORNING, I slipped into the school through the back door to administration from the teacher's parking lot. I was early, because Mum needed time to prepare for class, so I made it into my conference room without seeing Brody, Ryder, Levi, or Caleb.

Mrs. Chan came in just after the first bell. I traded my completed assignments for more paperwork from my teachers. There was something else I needed to do.

"I need to clean out my gym locker." I couldn't go anywhere on school grounds alone while I was on in-school suspension. "It's just my stuff." No school property. Nothing to be checked off returned against an inventory list.

I tried to decipher Mrs. Chan's thoughts by the minute changes in her expression, the way Neo read the scrolling green digital rain in those old Matrix movies. *Come on, come on.*

"All right. Now's probably the quietest time. We'll go straight there and back."

I paced beside her as she clop-clopped down the hall past the closed doors spaced along both sides.

The gym was empty. Mrs. Chan stopped in front of the men's locker room door, still propped open from the previous day's cleaning.

"I'll wait for you out here." She was already thumbing her phone as she walked to the nearest bleacher.

Inside was so quiet I felt as if I were walking into a church instead of a locker room.

Rustle rustle. Click. Jingle. Familiar noises — but who was here during block one? I rounded a wall and saw Caleb, his back to me, dressed only in jeans. He took a shirt from his open locker. On the bench behind him sat a gym bag, a bottle of water, and a plastic container of generic painkiller.

His back ... Tor used to bring home finger paintings covered in horizontal lines and irregular splotches in shades of violet and fuschia. Just like Caleb's back. I couldn't make sense of it. Not tattoos. Not some kind of airbrushed temporary decoration like you could pay to get at a fair.

My heart rate shot up as I figured it out. Someone had painted all right — with fists. Or maybe a belt or worse. For one second, I thought *Good, now you know what it feels like*, but then I was ashamed.

"Who did that to you?" I asked.

Caleb turned, his face flaming, fabric gripped in two fists. Raw red lines curved around his sides. "Get out!" From the way he winced, moving hurt. "Go on, get out!"

My feet felt like they were cemented to the floor. "Did you tell anybody?"

"Why do you care?" He spat the words at me.

"Nobody deserves to get beat up."

"Didn't stop you." The words felt like a punch.

Caleb began easing on the long-sleeved T one painful inch at a time. Shirt on, he lowered onto the bench as if his upper half were encased in a body cast. He slid his right foot into a shoe. Then his left. He grimaced, reached for the pill bottle, shook out two tablets, swallowed them with a couple of swigs of water, and wiped his mouth with the back of his hand. Then he glared at me. "You still here?"

"Who did that?" I repeated.

"My dad, not that it's your fucking business."

"Because of what happened with Aidan?"

"Because I got kicked off the football team." Caleb's mouth twisted. "If it hadn't been that, it would have been something else."

"He's done this before?"

Caleb rolled his eyes. "What planet are you living on, Tryggvason?" He leaned forward, slowly, like he was eighty-eight instead of eighteen, and tied his right shoe. "Anyway, he won't do it again. I'm out of here." He glanced up at me. "That should make you happy."

"It doesn't make me happy that your dad beats you up."

Caleb stared at me. Maybe he saw I was telling the truth. He bent to tie his left shoe.

"What will you do?"

He eased upright. "I'm going into the Forces. I applied the second I turned eighteen. I'm staying with my brother till it's settled."

"But you haven't graduated."

"I finished Grade 10, and that's all you need for what I'm going to do." He stood slowly, like he was being winched up, zipped his gym bag, and lifted it by the handles. He wouldn't be using the shoulder strap for a while.

Behind him, his locker door stood open, the space empty. "I'm not —" His knuckles were white where he gripped the bag. "I'm not like that."

"Like what?"

"Like — that. Like Brody. What happened that day — that's not me."

But you did it. So it was you. Caleb must have read my expression. He flushed. "I didn't know he was going to do it. And then it went too far too fast."

Kind of like me hitting Brody.

From the gym bag's side pocket, a muffled ring tone sounded. Caleb fished out a phone and glanced at it, then shoved it back in. "My brother's here."

"Good luck. With the Forces and everything."

Caleb gave one short nod. He took a step and stopped. "Your friend needs to watch his back. So do you."

Seriously?

"It's not Brody you need to be worried about. It's Ryder." He walked past me and was gone.

I RODE HOME with Mum after school. Tor and I had dinner duty. Usually I could lose myself in the cooking, but images of Caleb kept popping up in my brain like alerts on a smartphone.

I couldn't forget his words: *What planet are you living on, Tryggvason?* And the comment about Ryder.

That night at dinner, everyone was trying to act like things were normal. The harder they worked, the more uncomfortable I felt. Lucky for me, Tor came to the rescue. Not that he was trying to. "Stacy said Levi's going to Faith Academy starting tomorrow."

"How does Stacy know that?" asked Elin.

"Her best friend Trina is Levi's sister."

I already knew it was true by the way Mum's lips had tightened. When you teach where your kids go to school, you always have to watch your words so you don't tell something you shouldn't. I have to do that twenty-four/seven, so I know what it's like.

"Stacy said Trina said their parents tore Levi a new one."

"Tor." Dad gave him a dose of those truth-finding eyes. "Not dinner table conversation."

No one said anything about Caleb dropping out, but I didn't mention it. I'd have to tell how I knew, and I wouldn't be able to hide what else I'd learned. Caleb's private life was his. He should be able to decide who found out about it. I hadn't thought we had anything in common at all, but I was wrong.

I WAS AFRAID to see my friends. What if everyone thought what I'd done was awful? What if they thought I was the bad guy for breaking Brody's jaw and getting banned from sports? The wrestling team had a great big gaping hole in it now because of me. If my friends weren't already furious at me for getting booted off the team, they had to be pissed at being ignored.

Elin didn't get why I wouldn't even check my messages, and I couldn't explain it. I saw a coyote once, dead in a culvert. It got hit by a car and crawled in there to be alone to die. That was how I felt.

Friday night, I lay on my bed, a book open, staring at the same page I'd been looking at for twenty minutes. The wrestlers always went for pizza the first Friday after school started. Tonight.

Someone knocked on the door. I didn't say anything. The knob turned and the door creaked open. "Gunnar?"

"I'm busy."

Elin entered and slammed the door. I didn't move.

"Damn it, Gunnar. This self-pity bullshit needs to stop now."

I rolled over. "What is your problem?"

"My problem is this poor-little-me crap you've been putting us all through. You got kicked off the wrestling team. Worse things happen to people all the time. You're punishing Myk and Jason because they're still on the team. You won't talk to Aidan. Way to make him feel like shit."

"You made your point." I rolled away and picked up my book like I was actually going to read it now.

Elin gave an exasperated sigh, and the door banged. I lay my head on my arm and stared at the wall. I didn't know how to do this. How to make things okay again. How to stay friends with my friends when everything had changed.

Someone knocked on the door. I should have locked it.

"What?"

The knob turned and the door creaked open. "Gunny?"

An instant later, I was hugging Sam, a full-on body hug. I released him before it got too awkward. He smiled, but his eyes were worried.

"I thought you weren't coming home for a while," I said.

"I heard what happened. And I needed to get some stuff anyway, so I came." He put a hand on my shoulder. "You okay?"

"Yeah." I smiled, the first time all week. "Yeah, I'm good." I wanted to put my hands on either side of his face and kiss him, but if there was anything that could possibly make this week worse, having Sam shove me away in revulsion would be it. "It's good to see you."

We sat at the kitchen table, Sam telling me all about his time in Calgary so far. "It's kind of weird living alone, but I like it. My aunt is nice." His classes were good. He wished he'd asked Mum for cooking lessons because he was eating too much crap. He'd applied to volunteer at Foothills Hospital Emergency Room because everyone said it looked great on a resume and he'd get to know EMTs.

Tor was at the movies, and Gary was out with friends, but Elin, Mum, and Dad popped in to say hi. When a plate that had been piled with cookies held only crumbs, Sam rested his hands on the table and scooted back his chair.

"I should go, Gunny. I've got to head back tomorrow early. I met a couple of guys in the Paramedic program. We're going running in Nosehill Park."

I smiled, masking my disappointment, and followed him onto the front porch.

"Listen." Sam squeezed my shoulder. "It sucks that you got kicked off the team, but your friends think it's bullshit and they don't think you deserved it."

I didn't know that. Because I'd been hiding from my friends all week.

Sam hugged me again, a hetero guy hug, with back slap, short and sweet. "Come and see me. I mean it. My couch is your couch."

"Samwise."

He paused, mid-turn. I couldn't say it.

"Thanks for coming."

Sam jogged down the porch steps. He waved as he headed his truck up the drive, and I waved back, then went inside, lost in thought.

I went to my room and fished my phone out of the drawer where I'd shoved it. I plugged it in, dug out my earphones, and then started going through the messages and emails, oldest to latest. At the end, I fell back on my bed and stared at the ceiling. It hadn't been as bad as I'd feared. Most of the haters and likers would have shown up on social media, but I wasn't on any, so I missed all the loser rants and the likes and supportive comments.

Jason had texted today after school, before the team had pizza. *How are you?*

Myk's last message, sent a couple of hours ago, said *Sucks that you aren't here* and had a pizza slice emoji.

Would Myk and Jason want to keep up our standing Sunday workouts now? Would it all be too weird? Only one way to find out. I thumbed my phone to life and sent a text to both of them.

Gunnar: *I'm still on for Sunday if you are.*

In Which Riding Saves Everything

SATURDAY MORNING AT the dining room table: Mum and Dad reading the paper, a bleary-eyed Gary drinking coffee to wake up, Elin quizzing Tor about the movie he'd seen, and me. We'd all stayed up late, so breakfast was dragging on longer than usual. When the doorbell rang, everyone looked surprised.

"I'll get it." Elin ran to the front door. The house was weirdly quiet until the muted thumps of four feet sounded outside the door.

"Come on in," said Elin. Aidan stood in the doorway, circles under his eyes, hair a mess, dressed in old blue jeans and a wrinkled T. He seemed thinner.

"Good morning, Aidan," said Mum. "Would you like some breakfast?"

"Hi, Mrs. T. Actually, I came to see Gunnar." Aidan looked at me, his eyes fierce yet tired at the same time. "Can I talk to you for a minute?"

I shoved my chair back, tossed my napkin on the table, and gestured for Aidan to precede me into the living room. I leaned against the stone fireplace surround, arms crossed.

The look in Aidan's eyes reminded me of the little, male red-tailed hawk that hunted the fields behind our house. "Look, I know you hate me, but I wanted to say thanks. I know that doesn't make up for what happened."

What? "I don't hate you. Why would you think I hate you?"

A glimpse of the old Aidan appeared when one eyebrow shot up.

"Um — you don't take my calls. You don't answer my texts."

"I wasn't taking anybody's calls or texts."

"Why not?"

I exhaled, stared at the ceiling, looked at the floor, glanced out the front window. "I don't know. Because."

Aidan's lips quirked. "You really don't do touchy-feely conversation, do you?"

"I didn't want to talk to people." *Because they would ask me questions I don't know how to answer, just like you.*

Aidan's face closed again. "Yeah, well, I get that. I didn't want to talk to people either." He shoved his hands in his pockets. "I couldn't blame you if you did hate me. I'm sorry you got barred from sports because of me."

"It wasn't your fault."

"That's not how it feels." He dropped his gaze.

I had the feeling that what I did or said next was important. Like it would make a difference for both of us.

"Can you ride a horse?" I asked.

Aidan's forehead wrinkled. "I took lessons for a couple of years."

"Want to go riding?"

Aidan didn't ask questions. He thumbed his phone. "Dad, I'm at the Tryggvasons. I'm going horseback riding with Gunnar, so I won't be home till later today. Yeah, I'll text before I leave. Bye."

Aidan shoved the phone into his messenger bag. "He worries now if he doesn't hear from me every hour on the hour. Drives me crazy."

Aidan followed me into the kitchen, where he made Mum happy by drinking a glass of milk and eating a muffin while I packed some food and bottles of water. I led him to the basement and had him test the fit of my old ropers. They weren't even that worn, because I'd bought them at the beginning of a growth spurt.

I took two brimmed hats off pegs, handed one to Aidan, and grabbed a couple of old flannel work shirts to throw into the saddle-bags along with our other supplies. September breezes can run cool on the plains.

We got leads from the tack room and went to the pasture to catch Mackie and Bonza. I kept an eye on Aidan. While attaching the lead rope, he was calm and confident, even when Bonza was pushy and crowded him to get his scent.

"This is Bonza," I said. "You'll ride her today." An Australian exchange student at school had used the word the way we used *awesome*, and I liked it. Bonza ran the way her name sounded, flowing across the prairie.

"Hey Bonza." He patted her neck. "She's beautiful. What is she?"

"Leopard Appaloosa."

"I didn't know Appaloosas could have spots all over."

Aidan didn't even freak when she snorted and blew a big wad of snot on his shirt.

"It's official," I said. "Welcome to the herd."

Aidan gave me a snarktastic look as he cleaned his shirt, and I laughed.

I saddled the horses, and then we mounted up. Mackie and Bonza walked side by side along the edge of the field in the ruts left by our farm truck. Shelterbelt trees rustled in the breeze on our right.

"Why do I see straight rows of trees everywhere? In the middle of nothing."

"Shelterbelts." I nodded at the double row of trees we rode along-side. "The trees and bushes in back of our house and along the two sides are shelterbelts too, just different kinds."

"What are they for?"

"Sophisticated city boy like you doesn't know what a shelterbelt is?"

"No, country boy. Enlighten me."

"They're windbreaks. They prevent soil erosion. That's pretty important. You know plants grow in dirt, right?"

Aidan snorted, sounding so horse-like that Bonza's ear swiveled to listen.

"They're snow fences and wildlife habitat."

"How come some trees are big and some aren't?"

"They're a mix of ages. The first shelterbelts on our land were planted in the late 1800s, but trees don't live that long here. Every year, we remove anything that's dying and plant replacements."

We rode straight north until we came to a fence with two gates, one wide enough to accommodate farm equipment. I dismounted and led Mackie to the smaller gate, pulling out my keys.

Outside the gate a farm access road ran east-west, disappearing into the horizon in both directions. The remains of the summer grass alongside it were higher than the wheat stubble in the field we'd just left. Harvested fields lay as far as the eye could see, the land dipping and rising, never perfectly flat, like batter poured into a cake pan, before you smooth it with a spatula.

We led the horses across the road to another gate, and then we rode north, angling to the east across acres that had been cut for hay and into wild uncut summer grass.

Mackie knew where we were going and pointed her nose toward the small rise in the distance. The ground was rougher here, and the horses had to pay attention to the footing. Aidan looked at everything with wonder — the coyote that broke from the cover of brush and trotted away as we neared, the prairie falcon that flew over us with something furry in its claws.

We reached the top of a small ridge and rode down the other side toward a patch of wind-sculpted cottonwood trees. I swung Mackie wide into a bowl depression, Aidan following.

We were in a small flat space, a creek ahead, invisible until you were right there. On the other side, a ridge running alongside the banks protected us from the full strength of the wind. The cotton-woods further downstream were a giveaway that water was nearby, since they need plenty to survive. You could stand where the cotton-woods grew and not see this spot.

"Let's sit for a while," I said. We dismounted, led the horses to the creek for water, loosened the girths, and picketed them nearby. Aidan and I cleaned our hands in the creek, and I led us to a level section of ground, saddlebags over one shoulder. The sun washed across my face, gentle and warm. We should make the most of it, since winter was closing in.

"Hungry?"

"Yeah."

We both finished off a sandwich before we spoke again.

"When did you go back to school?" I asked.

"Thursday." Aidan shook his head and frowned. "Bad enough to be the out new guy from Toronto, but now I'm the out new guy from Toronto that Brody Gilmore nearly offed." He picked at something on his jeans only he could see. "I was glad you broke his jaw until I heard what they did to you."

Aidan fished another sandwich from the pack. "I didn't see anything that happened after you pulled Brody off me. But Collier said when he saw you standing in the door of the mop room, he knew how the Irish monks felt when the Vikings raided their monasteries. Except that in this case, he and the Viking were on the same side."

I laughed at that image and said, "Collier fought too."

"Yeah," said Aidan. "He's a good guy. He tried to stop Brody." Then his smile vanished, and his shoulders tensed. "There's something you should know. Ryder told Mr. Clyde that you broke Brody's jaw because we're boyfriends. Mr. Clyde asked me about it when I was in the hospital."

"Yeah. I already knew. He asked me too."

Aidan glanced at me, his expression cautious. "What did you say?"

"I told him we weren't boyfriends. What else would I say?"

Silence.

"What?"

Aidan shook his head and gave me a look I didn't understand. Somewhere between exasperated and pitying. "Nothing."

"No, say what you're thinking."

"You could have said you weren't gay. That would be the normal thing to say in that situation."

I picked at the crust on my sandwich. *Crap.* My life was moving like a runaway train, getting faster by the minute, and I had no brakes. What had happened to my plans? My coming out schedule? *I'm not ready for this.* I took a breath. Released it. "You know I am."

Aidan took his time chewing and swallowing a bite of peanut-butter-banana sandwich. "I didn't know for sure. I thought you might not know yourself yet."

I wasn't sure my face would ever return to its normal color. "I didn't want to come out until after graduation."

Aidan threw back a third of a bottle of water. When he set it aside, his face was hard. "I don't get people like you. You look like Butch Brawny, Ace Superhetero. Nobody's going to beat you up for walking down the street. Your parents are cool, so you're not going to get kicked out."

I had no idea what to say.

"Shit." Aidan lowered himself onto his side and propped his head on his hand. "Does anybody know?"

"Elin does. And I think Mr. Clyde and Coach Mac guessed. Coach was there when Mr. Clyde asked about us being boyfriends."

He looked me over, his expression speculative. "Have you ever had a boyfriend?"

"No. There's someone I like, but he's straight."

"That guy I met? Sam?"

I nodded.

"Yeah, I didn't get a gay vibe from him." Aidan watched me a moment. Then he sat up and wiped his hands on his jeans. "I'm sorry about giving you a hard time. Come out when you're ready. I was out of line."

"It's okay. I know I should."

"Don't do it because you should."

I bit into another sandwich. Aidan retrieved a fat spiral-bound sketch pad the size of my palm from his pack, followed by a flat metal case filled with colored pencils. He turned to a clean sheet, selected a pencil, and stroked the lead along the paper side to side, making a long rectangle of color. He chose another pencil and repeated the action.

"What are you doing?"

"I'm making notes. The color palette of this landscape is amazing. It's giving me ideas for my portfolio." He mixed two shades to create the silvery sage color of a nearby bush and scribbled a note beside it. Then he flipped to a new page and sketched.

"It's funny how those stones are in circles," he said, biting his lower lip as he concentrated on drawing them in proper perspective.

"They're tipi rings."

Aidan's eyes went wide.

"This was probably a campsite on the way to other places. I found a couple of arrowheads over there. It's a perfect location — plenty of hunting, water close by, sheltered."

"How did this survive?"

I shrugged. "This quarter section and the adjoining one were homesteaded by Olafur Tryggvason, and he died before he could plant more than he needed to prove his claim. Olafur's family went back to Iceland, but they didn't sell the land. They didn't do anything with it either. So most of the land stayed virgin prairie." Never plowed, never planted. Mum and Dad wanted to keep it that way too, to my relief.

"Your family has been here a long time."

"Yeah." Long for immigrants to Canada anyway. It probably wouldn't have seemed long to whoever left those tipi rings.

"Do you mind if I ask how much land you have?" Aidan looked up from his sketching.

"My great-great-great-great-great-grandfather Torvald Tryggvason came here from Iceland with his five sons and their families." I named them off: "Hannes, Gunnar, Trygg, Ragnar, and Olafur. They homesteaded twelve adjoining quarter sections, and we still own all of them."

I started packing the lunch remains.

"Is Gary the only one of you without an Icelandic name?"

"Gary's real name is Ragnar Petur, but when Elin was little, she couldn't pronounce Ragnar." It somehow came out sounding like "Gary" and before long that's what everyone called him.

"So how did your mum end up here?" Aidan put away his pencils and *snick*ed the case shut.

"My dad's family was in Toronto on holiday and they went to a social at the Icelandic Canadian Club. Mum was there."

Aidan looked up from stowing his gear. "That is so random."

Isn't everything? If you really think about it.

A few minutes readying the horses, and then we mounted up. I guided us to the east, toward the property line, so Aidan could see the contrast between our neighbors' cultivated acres and the untouched prairie. Shelterbelts lined field perimeters like soldiers on guard. East of us, silver silos perched on spindly legs dotted fields like tiny Monopoly playing pieces.

"This land across the fence is part of Sam's family farm." I pointed to hayfields in the checkerboard of fields in the distance. "Those hayfields are part of Brody's family's place."

"I thought his dad was a preacher."

"He is, but they farm too."

Aidan's lips tightened. "He was at the hospital emergency room. My dad got into a shouting match with him, and they had to call security."

I couldn't envision Mr. Standish yelling at anyone.

"Dad threatened to go after him in civil court."

"Why doesn't he?"

Aidan didn't look at me, his jaw muscles tight. "Gilmore said he'd go after you if we went after Brody." Bonza stamped a hoof and shifted.

I couldn't breathe for a second, as if I'd been slammed to the mat by a takedown I hadn't seen coming. Finally I said, "I'm sorry."

"Nothing to be sorry for." Aidan rolled his shoulders, and Bonza relaxed. "Anyway, Dad called Mr. Gilmore a — and I quote — 'hate-mongering bigot who instigates violence against people who have done him no harm' and Brody's dad said he had every right to preach the word of the Lord."

Funny how the Reverend Gerald Pindar and the Reverend Cinda Lynch at the Valgard United Church managed to preach the word of the Lord without including any homophobic rants.

"I like your dad."

Aidan's smile was sad. "Yeah, he's okay. But now Mum's worried that she made a mistake saying I could finish high school here."

We chirruped to the horses and rode northwest, making a wide arc that took us past the first of a series of prairie potholes, this one a big marshy circle with clumps of grass poking from the water. A few ducks flew away as we approached. They'd be migrating any day now.

"Do you think you made a mistake coming here?"

"I don't know.

We rode in silence, gradually angling south until we were headed back home. Bonza and Mackie picked up their pace as the gate came into view. We retraced our steps across the road and rode west along the fence line. The horses wanted to go directly to the barn, but I took a different way so Aidan could see more.

We rode another full minute before Aidan spoke again. "Elin and I made an appointment to meet with Mr. Kernes about starting a Gay-Straight Alliance. We lined up two advisors." Mrs. Young was one of the GSA faculty sponsors and — even more jaw dropping — Coach Chenoweth was the other.

Mackie and Bonza had drifted so close to each other that Aidan and I rode with legs nearly touching. Intimate. "Would you join?"

We rode a few more seconds before I replied. "I'm not much of a joiner."

"Um, wrestling team?"

"Sports are different."

Aidan looked at me sideways. "Elin says you transferred to Foods."

"Yeah, Foods 30."

"Interesting."

"What? Lots of guys take Foods." Didn't they?

Aidan laughed. Our eyes met and held, and he shook his head and looked away, still smiling.

Wrestling with Nanaimo Bars

SUNDAY MORNING. NO homework: a first. Mum, Dad, and Tor had gone to church. Elin was working on a sewing project, and Gary was checking moisture levels on some fallow fields we planned to bring into the planting rotation in the spring.

I'd already set aside clothes for Monday. I wasn't in the mood for reading, and I couldn't watch television. I never can, doesn't matter what it is: five minutes in and I'm jittering in my seat.

What else could I do? I was hungry for mint Nanaimo bars. In the walk-in pantry, I grabbed graham crackers and mint chocolate chips.

Might as well make lunch too. While the bars firmed up, I put a bag of frozen whole wheat hoagie rolls on the counter to thaw, and I made a batch of chickpea salad, which is like tuna salad except with cooked chickpeas (mash them but leave chunks). I remembered to write mayo on the grocery list since the jar was low, and then I added butter blocks, graham crackers, and mint chocolate chips.

I checked the bars, and they were ready for the next step.

When I'm juggling prep for different foods and remembering to do stuff like update the shopping list and it's all coming together, I feel like an air traffic controller. I wouldn't say that out loud because I'd feel stupid, but it's awesome when everything comes out just right.

Platter with pickles and carrot sticks and olives. Cheese board with a wedge of Oka and a block of cheddar. Washed grapes in a serving bowl. Elin walked in as I put the hoagie rolls on a plate. "Wow, looks awesome."

She opened the fridge to take out the water jug and spotted the mint Nanaimo bars. "You got ambitious." She cut a piece to sample. "Yum."

I cut a test bite for myself. Wow. For a wrestler, I'd made some seriously good Nanaimo bars.

I WAS DOING floor stretches on a mat when a knock sounded and the basement back door opened. Myk and Jason entered carrying work-out gear, which they deposited on the couch by the door.

"Dude," said Myk, as he removed his shoes. "Do you know how rude it is to ignore people?"

Jason rolled his eyes. "Myk."

"Just saying."

Jason sat cross-legged by my mat. "You okay?"

I pulled my knees up and wrapped my arms around them. "Yeah."

Myk joined us on the floor. "Brody's a prick. We should hunt him down and smash him up good. Maybe break some bones. Oh wait —"

I couldn't help it. I laughed. Myk was so over the top. No shame. No taste. My friend.

I told them how the EMTs and Coach and Mr. Clyde descended on the scene that day. About suspension. Dropping Phys Ed for Foods 30. They winced.

"A lot of people think what happened to you wasn't fair," said Jason.

I nodded, words stuck in my throat, my eyes dangerously hot. Lucky for me, Gary pounded down the stairs from his apartment. "Oh hey, Myk, Jason. You guys here to work out?"

And with that we fell into our usual routines.

When Jason grabbed water from the beer fridge, I followed him and leaned against the wall. "Coach Mac pick a captain yet?"

Jason tensed all over, but he looked directly at me, not being a wuss. "Yeah. I'm it. But it should have been you."

I shook my head. "You deserve it."

"I was hoping we would be co-captains."

"Me too. But I screwed up. Not your fault. Enjoy being captain. You earned it."

Jason's face lost the tightness around the eyes.

I'd wanted to be captain. Badly. I wasn't big enough to be selfless about getting kicked off the team, but I could pretend that I was. I could give that to Jason. And somehow, acting as if it was okay loosened something in me.

Good smells had been drifting down the stairs, and an hour into our workout Elin brought us a plate of cookies. "Mum wants to know how many for dinner. Everyone's welcome to stay. Nothing fancy, just burgers on the grill, roasted veggie kabobs, baked beans, and salad."

"And dessert?" Myk asked.

"And dessert."

Later we took turns showering and played blackjack at the dining room table. Like old times. Good times.

The New World

MONDAY MORNING, I put on one of my favorite new outfits, and the onyx and tiger's eye bracelet. My new clothes felt like a disguise: I was still trying to be the guy who dressed like this for real.

At breakfast, Elin said, "You look hot."

Block one. Social Studies. Ms. Gupta launched into yet another lecture on identity and ideologies. I kept my eyes on my desk and took notes.

Block two. English. When I got to the classroom, Mrs. Young directed me to an empty seat at the back of the room, next to Cari Van Pelt. I opened a notebook and pretended to be busy. When I risked a sideways glance, her pink face was ignoring me as hard as I'd been ignoring her.

We had to read an assigned novel and so far I wasn't into it, but thanks to suspension, at least I was caught up. Toward the end of the class, Mrs. Young reminded us about writing book reports for our portfolio. It sounded like a lot of work for something that was only going to be fifteen percent of the grade.

WHEN THE BELL sounded, I packed my things in slow motion, waiting for everyone to go. People crammed their stuff into backpacks as quickly as possible because no one wanted to stand in line forever for lunch. I'd eat in this room.

Mrs. Young left. Two students followed her, and then there was me and one other person still in the room. Cari. *Crap.*

"Gunnar."

"Yeah?" I risked a look. Her face was pale, but her cheeks were splotchy red.

"I'm sorry about the party." Cari's fingers lay tangled in her lap. "I'm sorry I didn't say so before."

"It's okay," I said.

"Are you going to lunch?"

"No. I mean I have stuff to eat."

"Where will you eat? You're not staying in here, are you?" From the look on her face, she'd figured out the problem. "Come eat with me." Cari stood and motioned for me to get up. "Come on." She smiled. "I won't try to kiss you."

When I didn't move, her eyes went flat. She picked up her books and turned.

"Wait." Had Elin been right? Did I want to sit in here wallowing in self-pity? "Don't you want to sit with your friends?"

Cari gave me a look that told me I'd said something dumb. "My so-called BFF Jessica posted pictures of me puking. My friends are the reason I shut down my accounts."

"You need better friends."

She laughed, hard and short. "Yeah, I guess. I understand if you don't want to be seen with me."

"I don't mind being seen with you if you don't mind being seen with me."

"Why would I mind being seen with you? You're looking stylish these days."

I shouldered my backpack, and we walked to the cafeteria. We'd both brought lunches, so we went directly to a table, a long one by the back wall, away from the popular places to sit. At one end, a couple of guys played chess as some of their friends watched. The geek squad, that's what they called themselves.

Cari and I sat at the opposite end, and I faced the wall, my back to the room. I didn't look for Elin. I didn't look at the tables where the wrestling team and the other athletes ate. I'd see Myk and Jason in the halls if at all. I'd not gone through a day of school in past years without seeing both of them in — well, ever. But I couldn't bear to look.

AFTER LUNCH, BLOCK three, Building Construction. I shared a work table with Eric Stetle, who was friends with Brody. Eric pretended I didn't exist. Fine by me.

Block four, Foods 30. Cari waved at me from the far side of the room. Everyone else stared at me as if they were waiting for me to figure out I was lost.

Mouths fell open when Ms. Freiberg directed me to the one open work station in the room — next to Becca James.

"Hey Becca."

"Hi Gunnar." Becca ducked her head, and her thick, shoulder-length auburn hair fell forward. She wore no-name jeans and a white oxford shirt. No makeup. Gold stud earrings. Her cane was propped against the table. She sat on a tall stool, and I took the matching one next to her.

Ms. Freiberg carried a stack of handouts to the nearest table and instructed the students there to take one and pass the rest on. "I promised last week to discuss your big project today. You can see the options for this year on page two. For example, you could choose a midday meal for Chaucer's pilgrims. You'd need to create a menu that would be typical of that period during the Middle Ages and find or create recipes for each dish. Of course, you'll show your sources and write up the research you did." Groans sounded.

Mindy raised her hand. "How would you ever find a recipe for the Middle Ages?"

"Make soup," said one of the guys in the class. "How hard is that?"

Ms. Freiberg smiled. "What would you put in your medieval soup, Joseph?"

"Uh. Carrots. Potatoes. Peas?" He looked around for help.

Ms. Freiberg crossed her arms. "Well, no, you wouldn't put in potatoes. Who knows why?" One hand rose. "Becca."

"It's a New World crop," said Becca.

"That's right. It's a New World crop. No potatoes in Europe in Chaucer's time. You could use turnips or parsnips instead. To get back to your question, Mindy, every option on this year's list is doable and you can find resources. So don't worry about that."

Next Ms. Freiberg lectured on pre-ferments.

Time to go hands-on. I pulled on a chef's coat, and then clubbed my hair and donned a white chef's skull cap. Not wearing a hair net. Just. No.

Becca and I mixed our poolishes, covered them, and set them aside on the bottom shelf of our work station for the next day.

"All right, everyone," said Ms. Freiberg. "Clean your stations, and you can have the rest of the class time to talk to about your projects."

From the way people were talking in groups, it looked as if most of the teams had already formed. "Are you on a team?" I asked Becca.

"No."

Great. In sports I was always one of the first guys picked for teams. Here I was one of the leftovers. I understood why I was, but from what I'd seen of Becca's skills so far, she was competent and efficient. "Do you want to be a team? With me, I mean?" I said.

She nodded. "Okay."

"I'll do my fair share." I didn't want her to think she was getting stuck with a lazy ass. Partnering with someone who didn't know much was bad enough.

Becca smiled. "I wasn't worried." She opened her booklet. "What project do you want to do?"

"Not a medieval lunch."

Becca laughed. I read through the project categories. "What about this one?" I pointed to Healthy Dinner on a Budget.

"I like it. But we have to do something to make ours stand out." Becca read through the project description, chewing on a nail. "Family of four … two working parents …"

I thought of Aidan. "What if we made it vegetarian?"

Becca nodded. "Not using meat is cheaper."

"Gunnar." Cari gripped my arm and pulled me a short distance away. "Do you have a partner yet? Mindy and I want you on our team."

"Thanks, but I'm partnering with Becca."

Cari widened her eyes. "Are you sure? She's a little … weird." I wished she would lower her voice.

"Yeah. Thanks anyway."

At the work station, Becca was staring at a page in the handout, but her eyes weren't moving. "It's okay if you want to change teams."

"I don't." She still hadn't looked at me. "I want to be on a team where at least one person knows what a New World crop is."

Becca didn't look up, but she smiled. "Okay."

AFTER SCHOOL ON the bus, I checked messages. I'd let Mr. Simmons know that I needed off at Parker and Derek's farm. We had agreed that I would do two afternoons a week and a few hours on Saturday. Elin and I shared a seat. Tor was several rows in front of us with friends.

Myk: *You and Cari? What's up with that?*

Elin leaned and read. "That's what I'd like to know."

Gunnar: *Nothing*.

I turned off the phone and stuck it into my backpack. "She apologized for what happened at the party. We ate lunch. That's it." I kept my voice down so no one else could hear.

The bus stopped at our driveway, and Elin and Tor got off. The next stop was Derek and Parker's place.

Possibilities

I FOLLOWED A footpath that wound through shelterbelts protecting the farmhouse. Parker waved at me from the doorway of the storage building that doubled as a workshop. "Gunnar. Good to see you. Come on in."

He led us inside. "I thought we'd start here, and work on the equipment shed when Derek is available. He's planting winter wheat today." I nodded. Dad and Gary were doing the same thing. Parker looked me over. "You don't want to work in those clothes, do you?"

I shook my head. "I brought some work clothes."

Parker pointed to a door in the back. "Washroom in the corner."

When I'd changed and rejoined Parker, he nodded at a ladder leading to a loft, where I could see boxes stacked in rows. "My goal is to clear that space. My shoulder isn't up to all the lifting and carrying yet, so if you don't mind, you can start with that first row of boxes.

Parker was already working when I set down the last of the boxes. "These are all from my mom's basement. We were ordered to get our stuff so she could sell her house." He grimaced. "I doubt there's much worth saving. Why don't you open a box and start sorting. Let me know if you have questions. Stuff that's worth keeping or donating stays in the box. Trash goes in the bin."

I grabbed a box cutter and opened a carton. Stacks of rubber-banded Valentines rested on top, but the bands had shrunk and broken over time. Under them, papers, drawings — a box of school-work. Parker groaned.

"I can't believe my mother kept this stuff. Even worse, I had to pay to get it to Canada."

I brought the next row of boxes, and we made steady progress. Parker swiveled to dump a stack of books into the trash (we were on our third bag by now) as Derek came into the storage building and clomped toward us in his heavy farm boots, looking tired.

Parker smiled up at him, but Derek was already reaching for the books in his hands. "Don't you dare throw away your yearbooks!" He placed them on a nearby shelf.

"And — my God — you're going to toss your baby book?" Derek plucked "Baby's First Year" from the trash bag and flipped it open. "This is priceless. You can't throw this out."

Parker rolled his eyes and winked at me. "This is why I'm not unpacking these with him." I grinned, basking in the warmth between them. I wanted what they had.

Derek won and carried off yearbooks and baby book. Parker dropped me off at the house a few minutes later. "Good start. See you Wednesday?"

"Sure."

A familiar truck sat in the front drive. When I went through the dining room, Dad was talking to Mr. Glasgow, Sam's dad, over coffee at our big oak table. They were taking a break, but they'd both be back in the fields later. I lifted a hand and said hello.

Mr. Glasgow gave me a short poker-faced nod. He was nothing like Sam.

I continued into the kitchen and removed my lunch things from my backpack for washing.

"Gunnar's doing some work for Parker and Derek," said Dad.

"Is that a good idea?"

I froze, waiting to hear what my dad would say.

"Not sure what you mean."

"Come on, Trygg. You're not worried about your teenaged son working for those two?"

"No. Not any more than I'd be worried about him working for you."

"As long as you're sure." Mr. Glasgow sounded as if he thought Dad was letting me work for serial killers.

AFTER DINNER I went to the basement and punched the heavy bag, trying not to think about wrestling. A sparring session with Gary would be even better than a solo workout, but he and Dad were doing equipment maintenance so they could plant more winter wheat tomorrow.

Elin bopped down the stairs, dressed to work out, as I toweled off sweat. Way too chipper.

"You're in a good mood." I glowered as I tossed the towel into a hamper.

"Obviously you aren't." Elin grabbed two 3kg dumbbells and sat on the weight bench to do wrist curls. "Talk to me while I exercise."

"You should use heavier weights for those."

"You're really fun this evening, Gunnar."

"Sorry." I poured a glass of water from the pitcher in the beer fridge and downed it.

Elin exchanged the 3kg dumbbells for a 5kg pair. "What's bothering you?" She glanced at me and caught my *are you kidding me* expression. "Okay, what else is bothering you?"

I told her what I'd overheard Sam's dad say.

"Don't worry about what some crabby old guy thinks." Elin paused between sets. "Go with me and Gary and Dad to the Calgary Farm and Ranch Show. You could use a break from Valgard. First weekend in October. Mark it down."

"Yeah, okay." Maybe a weekend away would be a good idea.

Discoveries

TUESDAY I RODE home on the bus and started preparing dinner, back on the weekday cooking roster since I wouldn't be playing sports.

Elin came in an hour before dinnertime and sat at the kitchen bar while I worked.

"First GSA meeting this week — Thursday flex block. We're putting up signs tomorrow. Will you come?"

"I can't." I was the world's biggest chickenshit excuse for a brother. But I couldn't. If it was anything else, I might have said yes, but this hit too close to home. Elin hadn't said anything. "Are you mad?"

She shook her head, still watching me.

"You are mad," I said.

She'd had my back with Mum and Dad countless times.

"I'll think about it." One small problem — I couldn't bullshit my twin.

Elin's lips formed a thin line. She pushed back from the table. "Okay." A second later she was gone. Asshole of the year. That was me.

I WAS HAVING trouble finding a book I liked enough to read all the way through for a report for my English class portfolio. On Wednesday, I stopped to talk to Mrs. Young at the end of class.

"Can we read a book for a book report that isn't on the list you gave us?"

Mrs. Young looked surprised. "You don't like any of them?"

"Most of them are like … some kid hates high school and just needs to survive until university, like real life doesn't start till university. And like everybody goes to uni." There were many books like that on the list — all the characters would be fine once they graduated high school and went to uni. I wasn't going to uni. "High school is real life too. And I don't like all those end of the world books."

Mrs. Young looked thoughtful, and then she bent and pulled a book out of the backpack she used for her classroom stuff. "Did you look at a copy of this book?"

I read the cover. *Aristotle and Dante Discover the Secrets of the Universe*, by Benjamin Alire Saenz. "No. They were all checked out."

"That's my personal copy," said Mrs. Young. "Why don't you give it a try? If you hate it, bring it back and we'll find something else."

Fair enough. "Thanks. I appreciate it."

I spotted one of the GSA club posters on the door as I left. Cari waited for me outside the classroom. We passed Coach Mac on the way to lunch. Before I could say hi, he cut his eyes away like he didn't see me. It felt like an actual physical blow. He liked me before. Was this because he thought I was gay?

Aidan waved at me across the cafeteria, but he spent the rest of lunch deep in conversation with the people at his table. Probably talking up GSA. I was kind of relieved he didn't come over.

IN FOODS, BECCA rounded a ball of dough on her bread board, quick and efficient. "Do you want to meet during flex block next week?"

That would give us a full week to come up with ideas for dishes to serve at our healthy dinner, and then we'd make a plan. "Sure. Thursday?"

Becca paused. "Tuesday is better if you can meet then. Thursday I'm going to GSA."

Seconds ticked by before I could get my hands back to kneading. "Yeah, sure. Okay, Tuesday."

I HOPPED OFF the bus at Parker and Derek's. An hour later, we'd finished working through the boxes from Parker's mum and were into boxes Parker had brought when he first came to Canada.

"What do you think, Gunnar?"

Parker held a pair of faded bell-bottom jeans, each of the enormous bells sporting a band of red velvet at the bottom, embroidered with white, green, and yellow peace symbols.

I grinned. "Awesome pants."

"I loved me some elephant bells back in the day. But what to do with them now?" He set the pants aside and took out a funky paisley shirt in psychedelic colors with mother-of-pearl snaps.

"You don't want to keep them?"

"No, I don't see much point. Maybe a charity would take them."

"I know someone who might want them. He likes old clothes."

"He'd be welcome to them."

I opened a box that had a smaller box right at the top, a long, narrow one. Inside was something I recognized from movies.

"Parker, you got a Purple Heart?" His expression was like clouds passing in front of the sun, his green eyes somehow faded when he reached out for the box.

I placed it in his hand, moving as if it had nitroglycerin in it instead of a medal. From the look on his face, it might as well have. Resting under the space the box had occupied was half of a framed photo. I shifted it from under the folded bandana that covered the other half. Three soldiers wore dusty green-gray pants that bloused at the bottom over lace-up boots, and nothing but dog tags above the waist.

They stood with their arms draped on each other's shoulders, Parker in the middle, forty years younger and just as handsome. The three wore lazy smiles, the one on the left with an unlit cigarette dangling between two fingers. His lips tilted up on one side, and his chin was down so that he was looking up at the camera. You knew he was messing with the photographer; maybe he'd just finished saying "Hurry up so I can smoke my damn cigarette." The soldier on the right wore a boonie hat. Even though he was smiling, his eyes looked wary.

Parker stared at the photo. Wherever he was that second, it wasn't in the storage building with me. He jolted back to the here and now, his eyes snapping to mine. "Close that one back up, Gunnar, if you will." He returned the medal box. "I'll go through it later."

Nothing Blows Up

AT LUNCH THE next day, Cari and I sat at "our" table. So far, no one had contested us for the space. We were nearly finished when Collier sat next to Cari. Aidan slid into the chair on my left.

"Hey." We hadn't really talked since the weekend. I hoped he wasn't annoyed that I wasn't going to GSA. Deflect.

"I know where you can get boxes of vintage clothes if you want them."

Aidan looked interested. "Tell me more."

Before I could, Elin and her friend Katie Tran arrived and started talking about some movie that Cari really wanted to see.

"Gunnar, would you go see it?" Cari waited for my answer. Actually, everybody waited for my answer, and Aidan had that *laughing without visibly moving muscles* thing going on.

"I'd rather sit through a lecture on lentil agronomy." Based on what I'd heard so far anyway.

"Interesting kink," said Aidan, and everyone (except me) burst into laughter. I was trying to think of something witty to say when Myk dropped into the open seat beside Cari and grinned.

"What's so funny?"

"Gunnar. Lentil fetish," said Katie, deadpan.

"Dude." Myk leaned back in his chair, taking up space twice as wide as the actual seat he was on.

Katie took pity on me. "Gunnar doesn't want to go see *The Blue Castle.*"

"What's that?"

"It's a new movie based on a really awesome book," said Cari. "This woman Valancy thinks she's dying and she's always let her family tell her what to do but since she's going to die, she decides to do whatever she wants."

Elin chimed in. "And of course, she falls in love with a gorgeous man who has a cozy cabin in the woods where they have hot sexy adventures."

Cari sighed. "I just love the name Valancy. I'm going to name my first child Valancy."

I noticed Myk had the same goofy expression that she did.

"Even if it's a boy?" I said, but only Aidan heard me. He snorted.

"So, would you go see that movie?" Elin challenged Myk.

Myk didn't take his eyes off Cari's face. "Absolutely I'd go see that. Am I invited?"

What? Myk's usual two-part test for whether he'd go see a movie was 1) Does something blow up? 2) Does something else blow up?

"I'll bet Jase would like to go too." Now Myk looked at Elin, oozing sincerity.

Did Elin just turn pink? "Let's get a group together," she said.

I gave Myk a *Jason is going to kill you* look and he smiled like the cat that got the cream, as my grandma used to say.

"You know nothing blows up," I said, pushing back from the table. Myk lifted a hand to wave, middle finger slightly higher than the others, nothing a teacher lunch monitor could call him on, still smiling.

Malachite Dreams

SATURDAY MORNING, A little before noon, Aidan rattled up Parker and Derek's drive in his dad's truck.

"Why don't you have a look at the clothes first?" said Parker. "So you don't waste your time if you don't think you can use them."

Aidan knelt beside one of the stacked boxes, opened the top flaps, and lifted out suede bell-bottoms. "This is incredible." He pulled out the next item: a Jefferson Airplane T-shirt. "Oh. My. God. This is in perfect condition. No rips. No sweat stains." He looked up at Parker. "I'll take everything you've got."

Parker helped us load the boxes of clothes, and then Aidan gave me a ride home. Today he wore a pair of jeans in a deep indigo blue and a military green rugby shirt under a field jacket in the same shade. Hot.

"Are you going to the movie tonight?" I asked. Elin had wasted no time forming a group to see *The Blue Castle*. Mum was letting her drive the van to Medicine Hat. Katie was driving her parents' Murano. Between the van and the Murano, they could fit everyone in.

"Not really my thing." Yeah, well it wasn't Jason or Myk's thing either, but I suspected they had ulterior motives. "I told Collier I would though, so yeah, I guess."

I couldn't figure out Aidan and Collier's relationship. At first, I thought they were just friends, but now I wondered if they were more.

"Are you going?" Aidan asked.

"No way."

"I don't know, you don't sound totally convinced."

Was he kidding me? Yeah, actually he was. I figured it out a beat too late, as usual.

"So," I said, as he pulled into our drive. "Are those clothes a fashion story?"

Aidan gave me one of his sharp smiles. "More like a fashion freaking epic." He hesitated. "You sure you don't want to come tonight? Just to hang out, even if you don't care about the movie?"

Yeah, it was a group thing, but there were a lot of people going who were paired off or trying to get that way. I could see it already. A van full of people crushing on each other and me on the edge somewhere having to listen to people talking about what they were naming their first kid. And I wasn't sure I wanted visual confirmation of Aidan and Collier pairing off. It would seem … weird.

So I shrugged. "Maybe next time."

I waved as he drove away and then went inside to get ready to work on Gary's house.

TODAY I WAS going to work on closets. Great-uncle Gunnar's house didn't have storage like modern houses.

Gary showed up two hours later, dusty and sweaty from the fields. He removed his cap and wiped his forehead with the back of a wrist. "You got a lot done." He grinned. "You must really want to move into the apartment." He stepped forward and wrapped a hand around an upright, tugged to check that it was solidly in place and then ran a thumb along one of the smooth joins. "You always do good work." His eyes lost focus as he looked at something — or maybe nothing — outside the window. A lock of butter-blond hair had fallen onto his forehead. He and Elin shared the same shade of hair and the same blue eyes. Sometimes people thought they were the twins instead of me and her.

I shrugged, but I didn't reply. I was in no hurry to move into the apartment because I'd miss him when he was gone.

"I can clean up," said Gary.

I picked up the broom and began sweeping up dust and shavings. "It's okay." I wanted to ask him a question. Now would be a good time. "Have you talked to Sam about the Farm and Ranch Show?" A shadow crossed his face.

"He texted me that we could meet up. That's all I know right now."

I hadn't heard from Sam since his last visit. In a way, I wasn't surprised. After all, Gary was his best friend. But he'd been quiet on the subject of Sam lately.

"How's he doing?" I asked.

A moment passed before Gary replied. "I think he must be really busy. Looks that way online anyway."

MONDAY, END OF English. "Gunnar. Um. I'm going to sit with Myk today. You want to come too?" Cari turned pink. Sitting through a movie with no explosions had apparently paid off for Myk, although Elin swore he fell asleep at least twice. She didn't give any details about how things went with Jason.

"You go on. I have a couple of things to do first."

Cari bit her lip, but shrugged on her pack. "Okay. If you're sure. See you later."

A few minutes later, I sat at our — my — table, getting a nod from a couple of geek squad guys at the other end. I put on my glasses and kept working my way through *Aristotle and Dante Discover the Secrets of the Universe*.

I loved my glasses, even if I only wore them when I absolutely had to. They were D-frames in malachite, a swirly mix of rich greens, and they looked really good with my hair. They were way cooler than me. I was still trying to be the kind of person who could rock those glasses.

I plowed through my book, losing track of time, which I never do when I read. Even though it was about two guys in high school, it was good — better than the title made it sound. One of the guys gets into fights. And one of them doesn't like to watch TV. So I'm not the only one.

You could read it fast, but you shouldn't because it had layers. Like the baklava we made in Foods. I kept rereading parts because first I'd read it and think, yeah, this happened. Then I'd read it again and realize, but maybe this too, like the second or third time through my brain figured something else out. I almost never read anything that makes me feel like I'm reading a story and working a puzzle at the same time, but this did.

Aidan fell into the seat across from me. He stared.

"What?" I said.

"Those glasses. You look h— good. Really good."

Had he started to say hot?

Aidan propped his elbows on the tabletop. "There were great clothes in those boxes. Thanks again for thinking of me." He took a breath. "You know, you're welcome to eat lunch with me and Collier."

Collier and Aidan ate lunch most days at the queer, miscellaneous oddball, and artsy/fashion/theater types table. I couldn't see me fitting in. The conversation would fly at light speed, and I'd stay three comments behind, quiet unless asked a direct question, which would always be the kind that would make me look stupid trying to answer it. Elin said quiet could be mysterious and I shouldn't worry what people thought. But when I'm quiet, no one is thinking I'm mysterious — more like I'm the dim bulb on the string.

The bell rang, and when Aidan and I stood, I managed to glance at the wrestling table without being obvious. Myk and Cari laughed at something, and Elin and Jason chatted as they gathered their things. Maybe my getting kicked out of sports made dating him less complicated.

We joined the stream of students exiting. Aidan's can't-touch-me cool façade was back in place, but I knew him well enough now to know that the surface was a mask hiding something he didn't want others to see. I wished I knew what he was thinking.

Life Keeps on Keeping On

THE LAST SEPTEMBER days slogged by. Every day, Cari, sheepish, left after English class to sit at the wrestling table. The geek squad ignored me, used to my presence.

Elin reported that the GSA meetings were going well. Katie had been elected GSA president.

Becca and I were having fun looking up stuff for our Foods project. Sometimes Rawdon showed up at the end of class to help her carry her gear to their truck. He always nodded at me, but never said much.

Jason and Myk came by to work out, and we still practiced wrestling, even though I wasn't on the team. At least I could help them work on their moves.

Ryder ate lunch with Eric Stetle and Billy Soderquist and a few other buddies. Brody ate through a straw, head down, in a corner by himself. Ryder took up all the space at their table now, the center of the group and the focus of attention.

LUNCH ON FRIDAY, first weekend of October. A body fell into the chair across from me.

"Dude. You look a hundred IQ points smarter with those glasses on." Myk stretched and then slouched against the chair, arms loosely crossed.

"Maybe you should get a pair."

Myk relaxed into his seat and scrutinized my clothing.

The tension was killing me. "What?"

"You're dressing different."

Run interference. "Shirt, pants, shoes. Same old same old."

Myk shook his head. "No. It's different." His eyes narrowed. "You're trying to get laid. It's about time."

Ouch. About time for the dressing better part or the getting laid part? Same old Myk. Almost as filter-free as Tor.

Myk looked to his left and I followed his gaze. Cari navigated through rows of tables toward us. She smiled and waved, and I waved back.

I put on the blandest look I could manage. "Seen any good movies lately?"

"Asshole."

Cari wanted to know why I was laughing so hard, but we didn't tell her.

DAD AND GARY picked up Elin and me after school and we headed to Calgary. Weight came off my shoulders, like when I rack a loaded bar after doing squats. Good to be away from Valgard, away from opinions and judgments. I'd be another anonymous person attending the show. I hoped I'd get to see Sam, but he hadn't suggested that I join him and Gary, and I wasn't going to horn in. Sam was Gary's best friend and I knew — deep down, I knew — he really was the straightest straight guy in Valgard.

We checked into our hotel, a residence-style place, and over dinner at a nearby restaurant, Gary, Dad, and Elin strategized for the weekend. Gary and Dad would hit vendor booths and get info and prices on equipment. They were all going to a session on precision agriculture and the latest technological advances.

I wanted to visit the livestock exhibitions. After that, I wasn't sure what I'd do. Mostly I was going to enjoy being somewhere different.

The Show

AT THE SHOW the next morning, we agreed to meet at the hospitality court at lunchtime, and then split up. I headed to the livestock building, carrying the messenger bag Aidan had finally convinced me to try. It didn't look too much like a man purse, and it turned out to be exactly what I needed when I wasn't toting ten pounds of school stuff. I made a mental note to thank him.

I wandered through rows of penned alpacas, sheep, goats, llamas, miniature donkeys, and cows, walking faster when I got a good whiff of horse. I could have closed my eyes and navigated by smell. I wandered past draft horses, gaudy palominos and Paints, silky-maned Paso Finos. Near the end of one long row, I stopped in front of a blue roan quarter horse mare. She stretched her neck and bumped her nose against my hand.

"You're a beauty, aren't you?" Glancing over to see who the breeder was, I locked eyes with a guy leaning against the corner post of the mare's pen, at a table sporting a banner for Litton-Holmes Farm Registered Quarter Horses.

He had ice-blue eyes and tawny hair parted on the side and swept back. Eyebrows in the same golden shade arched above his eyes like horizontal parentheses, giving him a frank expression. He'd been in the sun. A no-nonsense straight nose topped lips that were an open dare. He had a rounded jawline with a dimple in his chin and he wore a dark blue, long-sleeved polo shirt, the collar turned up and sleeves pushed to his elbows with faded Levi's. Jaunty. Cool.

We'd been staring at each other too long, and I tore my eyes away and stroked the mare. When I glanced back, Ice-Blue Eyes was accepting a form on a clipboard from a man. As he thanked the man for stopping by, he looked in my direction. We locked eyes again, but he had to reply to a woman who had a question.

Shy, I turned away. What if I'd completely misread him? *Go talk to him.* People clustered around his table waiting their turns. It wouldn't be fair to bother him when he was so busy. I could wander through the livestock building again later, so I headed to the hospitality court to find a quiet corner and read.

In the men's room, I washed so I wouldn't smell like horse, found a coffee stand where I bought a latte, and carried it to a small café table in a corner.

"IS THIS SEAT taken?" Ice-Blue Eyes regarded me.

My heart rate spiked. "No. Have a seat."

"Thanks. This place is kind of full." He placed his phone and coffee drink on the table and lowered his Levi's-clad ass into the chair. I couldn't not look. "I'm Ty."

I didn't know if he was gay. Not for sure. All I needed was to flirt with a straight guy and start a fight. Dad would love that. "Gunnar."

"Hi." He slouched against the rickety metal café chair, smiled, and sipped his drink.

"Hi."

His tongue swiped away a stray bit of foam. "Hey, don't let me interrupt you." He was giving me an out. If I went back to reading, he'd play along, acting as if he'd simply needed a place to sit.

"No worries." I shoved my bookmark into the book and placed it on the table.

"I noticed you looking at Callie. I'd have come over to see if you wanted any info, but I had a lineup." I stowed my glasses in my messenger bag, safe in the hard-sided case.

"Yeah, I saw." Now I relaxed and gave my tablemate my full attention. "She's a beauty."

"You ride much?"

"We have two quarter horses and an Appaloosa. But we don't compete."

"Where do you live?"

"Valgard."

Ty nodded. "We're on the other side of Medicine Hat, outside Wheatville."

Valgard had competed against Wheatville's wrestling team the year before.

"You at university?" Ty seemed surprised when I shook my head.

"I'm in Grade 12. How about you?"

"First year pre-vet at U of C."

"That sounds intense."

Ty smiled. That upper lip. When he wasn't smiling, it challenged all comers, somewhere between pouty and feisty. "It's a big change from high school. I came to help Mum and Dad this morning — a break for them and me both."

"I'm kind of here for a break too. My dad and brother and sister are going to some of the seminars, but I'm going to bail after lunch, do some sight-seeing."

"What do you want to see?"

I shrugged. "Maybe Kensington. I've been before, but there's always new stuff."

"Ever seen U of C campus?"

"No."

"If you're interested, I could give you a tour."

I hesitated. "If you're not busy, that would be great." Could I do this without being all loser-y? "If you don't have plans with your girlfriend or something."

Ty sipped his coffee, giving me a mischievous look over the rim. Obviously I hadn't been smooth. "Nope, no girlfriend waiting on me. Is there a girlfriend waiting for you?"

I didn't look away. "No girlfriend here." Thankfully my phone buzzed. I would flush bright red if we kept our eyes locked much longer.

Elin: *Where are you?*

"Excuse me for a second," I said. "My sister's looking for me."

Gunnar: *Back of hospitality court*

Elin: *I see you. Who's the cutie?*

I pinked, turned off the phone, and placed it face down just in case any embarrassing follow-up messages arrived.

Elin wove through tables like she was navigating a slalom course.

"You missed a good session." She spoke to me, but gave Ty the visual third degree.

"On yield mapping? Doubt it. Ty, this is my sister Elin. Elin, Ty."

They exchanged greetings, and Elin informed me that I could have lunch with her and Dad and Gary if I was ready to eat.

"I'm not that hungry," I said, although if the room hadn't been so noisy, Elin would have heard my stomach growling. "I can pick something up later. Ty's going to give me a campus tour." I glanced at him. "Unless you need to eat right now. No rush."

He smiled. "I'm good for a while yet."

I turned back to Elin. "Can you tell Dad I'll meet you later?"

"Okay. Be back at the hotel and ready to go by 6:00." With a "nice to meet you" to Ty and a significant look at me, Elin left.

Ty smiled, slow and lazy. "So, you want to get out of here?"

A Guy with Ice-Blue Eyes

WE TOOK THE CTrain to Sunnyside station.

"If you're hungry, there's a good place a few blocks from here," said Ty. "It's not too pricey."

"Lead on."

From Kensington Road, we turned at 19 Street NW and headed to a little café where we both had a burger and fries. The menu had vegetarian and vegan choices that looked good too, if you liked that sort of thing. Aidan would go for this place.

Ty was easy to talk to. We took turns telling sibling stories. His little sister dreamed of being a barrel racing champion. I told him about Tor's filter problems. He described his pre-vet program. I talked about our horses. If going out for real could be like this, I wouldn't find the whole idea of dating so scary.

"Do you play sports?" Ty asked.

"I did." I hesitated. "I'm barred from sports this year." I couldn't leave it hanging like that or he'd think I was some kind of psycho. He might think that after I explained, but at least he'd have the facts. When I finished, he gave me a long look I didn't know how to read.

"So, you stopped a gay bashing."

I hadn't thought of it like that. "I guess."

"They should have given you a medal."

I shrugged. Ty reached across the table and squeezed my shoulder. "That sucks."

His touch sent a jolt through me, and I couldn't stop a smile. Ty returned it, his eyes going to my mouth and back up again. "Can I ask you something?"

"Sure."

"You have a boyfriend back home?"

"No. I'm not ..." This was embarrassing. "I'm not out. A couple of people know."

Ty looked surprised. I had to know. "Are you out? Do you have a boyfriend?" .

"I'm out. No boyfriend."

"Have you been out long?"

The waiter laid the bill on the table. "Any time you're ready. No rush." He left to clear a nearby table. Ty and I did mental arithmetic and reached for our wallets.

"Since I was fifteen," said Ty.

"I'm going to come out soon," I said, surprising myself. I was going to come out? Soon? That would blow up my plan to stay under the radar. Why did I say that? The waiter swooped in to take our money, and Ty told him we didn't need change.

We left the restaurant and strolled along the sidewalk. Ty said, "Make sure you pick the time and not the other way around. I came out because my four-year-old brother told Mum I was kissing a cowboy in the barn. Mum asked if he didn't mean a cowgirl, and Petey got mad and told her he knew the difference between a cowgirl and a cowboy."

"Holy shit." I laughed, but with a queasy feeling in my stomach like after a roller coaster ride. "What happened?"

"Things were weird for a while. It's all good now though. Most of my friends were cool. But there were a few assholes. You know."

As we walked, I spotted an interesting store. "Do you mind if we stop in here?"

"A consignment shop?" Ty looked dubious. The sign said EvLynn's and the front windows showcased hats, scarves, jewelry, and leather bags. And a pair of kickass chestnut-brown biker boots.

"Most of what I'm wearing came from one."

"Yeah? Okay, sure."

We stepped inside. A woman Mum's age, with bright henna-red hair, leaned on a small counter in the corner. "Hi boys."

"Hi."

"Been here before?"

"First time," I said.

"Everything men on that side." She pointed. "Everything ladies this side."

Ty went to look at the boots in the window. I scanned through the racks, wishing Elin or Aidan was here to find the good stuff, when I spotted a silk and cotton crinkled scarf in a golden-brown shade with a delicate paisley print in orange and lime green. The same colors as the socks Aidan wore the first time we met. And like the socks, brown was the primary color, orange and green the accents. Marked down twice already.

"That's brand new." The woman I assumed was EvLynn spoke from her counter. "If you like it, I could let you have it for eighteen."

I glanced at the price tag. It had started at $120, although Aidan said original prices were price tag theater in a lot of stores, and you had to see if there was a second markdown to know if you were getting any kind of real deal at those places. Still. Sold.

Ty and I resumed our way along 19 Street NW, the wrapped scarf tucked in my messenger bag.

"I never thought of shopping in a place like that."

"That's because you don't have Elin for a sister."

Ty laughed, and we saved our breath for climbing the steep hill that led to the North Hill Centre and Lions Park station. We caught the next northbound train, and as it arrived at Banff Trail station, I said, "This is the stop for where we're staying."

"Convenient for coming back." Ty gripped a vertical bar, the same one I was holding. The Saturday afternoon volume of passengers allowed us to stand closer than the usual hetero male social distance in public spaces. My hair drew looks, but people were mostly all big-city cool and didn't stare. Ty leaned in toward me, so subtle that only I could tell. When our eyes met, he smiled.

We got off at University station and started walking. Ty pointed to the two science buildings where he spent most of his time. We strolled through the Student Centre, which had a bookstore and food court. Next, Ty led us into a sports facility where I drooled over the Fitness Centre, which was hopping on this Saturday afternoon, ringing with the crashes and clunks of weights being returned to racks and the grunts of lifters throwing themselves into their reps. University might not be so bad if you could spend all your time here.

We halted in front of an ordinary white multi-story building with a sign in front: Rundle Hall.

"This is my dorm," said Ty. "You want to look around?"

I checked the time. "Yeah, I do, but I think I need to get back to the hotel to be ready for dinner." I had a long walk back to the train station, and even though the ride was a short one, I still had to shower and change when I got back.

Ty hesitated. "Would you want to go with me for coffee later?"

I didn't have to think. "Yeah. That sounds awesome."

Eyes like Mine

AT THE HOTEL, Elin fell onto the couch beside me and adjusted my black bead and onyx bracelet so that the tiger's eye was on top.

"You look nice. So tell."

"Nothing to tell. I hung out with Ty. We had lunch. He showed me the U of C campus." I hesitated. "We're going out after dinner."

Elin pulled me close and gave me a loud smooch on the cheek.

"Gross, Elin." I pushed her away, and she laughed, releasing me.

"I'm going to fix your hair." By the time Elin pronounced me presentable, Gary had left to meet Sam and Dad was ready to go out.

A little while later, seated in a nearby restaurant with our orders placed, I told Dad that I would be heading out with Ty after dinner.

"This is the boy Elin met?" Dad focused those truth-finding eyes on me.

"Yeah." I told him a little about Ty and Callie, the blue roan mare. "We hung out for a while."

Of course, Dad wanted to know where we'd be. When I said, "Marky's Place," the muscles around his eyes tightened.

"You'll call if you need a ride," he said. Meaning *you won't ride with someone who's had too much to drink.* It went without saying that I wouldn't be drinking. Mum and Dad let us have the occasional beer at home, but drinking anywhere else before we were legal and getting caught was a social life extinction-level event.

I didn't bother to ask about a curfew, already knowing the answer.

Gary didn't get any questions at all. He'd announced he was meeting Sam and would try to be quiet when he came in, but all Dad said was that we'd have an early wake-up tomorrow and would check out before heading back to the show. Gary was over eighteen: in Dad's book he was a grown man. But he didn't act any different, so did that mean he was grown up for his age when he was seventeen, or that I was immature? I felt nowhere near adulthood, but I'd be turning eighteen in three weeks.

Dad asked what else I'd done that day. I thought of what I'd said to Ty during our lunch. If I was serious then I had to stop hiding.

"I went into a consignment store. You would have liked it," I told Elin. Two pairs of eyes fixed on me.

"You went into a consignment store and shopped? Voluntarily?" My sister placed the back of her hand on my forehead as if she were checking for fever.

"I even bought something."

I showed Elin the scarf for Aidan, still stowed in my messenger bag. Elin stared at it. "What's the occasion?"

"No occasion. It has the same colors as a pair of socks he wears sometimes."

Dad had a strange expression for a second, but he didn't say anything.

I knew Dad loved me. I wasn't afraid of him suddenly hating me if I came out. What scared me was maybe having to live out the rest of the school year under a gaze filled with disappointment, from a pair of eyes that looked just like mine.

The Date

TY AND I entered a packed room that looked as big as a soccer pitch, and we pushed our way through the crowd to the back of the building. We passed through a heavy swinging door marked "IN" (to its left was one marked "STOP! OUT ONLY") into a much quieter space with two pool tables at one end and tables and chairs scattered throughout the rest of the room. A long oak bar stretched along the west wall, and two baristas worked steadily making drinks.

We sat at a table for two against a wall. I shrugged off my jacket and draped it on the chair back.

Ty had changed into chestnut-colored cords, a white oxford under a dark red sweater, and brown desert boots. It struck me that I was on a date with a university guy I'd met that morning. This. Was. A. Date. Wait till I told Aidan. Unless. What if it wasn't? How did you know the difference between a date and hanging out?

Ty leaned forward. "Is this place okay?"

"It's awesome."

"People are cool here. Nobody bothers anybody."

A petite server wearing a *Chelsea* name tag power-walked over, menus tucked under one arm. "Get you something?"

"Double Americano, cream and sugar," said Ty.

"Same here," I said.

Seven guys and girls, some of them in Queen Elizabeth High School shirts, occupied a nearby table. One of the girls elbowed the boy next to her and jerked her chin in our direction.

Chelsea returned with the coffees and waters. "Anything to eat? We have a special on our truffle plate this evening."

Ty and I looked at each other, and his lips turned up at the side, revealing a dimple to go with the one in his chin. "Up for truffles?"

"Sure." Chelsea strode away.

"Do you ever go to gay bars?" I asked.

Ty shook his head. "Not so much. If I do, it's always with friends. I like to dance, and that's more fun with a group. To be honest, it takes most of my time to keep up with classes, so I don't get out much. I managed to find a few hours this weekend to help my folks though." He gave me a smile that showed off all his dimples. "Good thing I did."

I ducked my head. "Yeah." *Stop acting like I'm in junior high.*

"Here you go." Chelsea set down a white plate with six different truffles and positioned small dessert plates in front of us, topping them with forks. Pointing to each truffle in turn, she named them: "Chocolate Mint, Butterscotch Mocha, White Chocolate Lemon Mousse, White Chocolate Strawberry, Dark Chocolate Strawberry, and Mocha Passion Fruit. Anything else? Enjoy."

Ty used his fork to split the Mocha Passion Fruit truffle. He speared a half and held it out to me. "Feel like some passion fruit?"

I couldn't look away from him. After a beat, I nodded. He leaned forward, putting the fork in range of my mouth, so I took the truffle half without slurping all over his fork. I closed my eyes, savoring. The truffle was delicious, but the delivery was better.

"Mmmm."

"Good?" Ty asked. I opened my eyes to see him smiling devilishly.

He popped the other half into his mouth and his eyes half closed. "Mmmm. Yeah. That is good."

We talked so long we ordered another Americano each. We had plenty in common: a love of horses and riding, working out, sports. But we were different too. Ty watched a lot of television before he left home, but now he didn't have time, so he'd binge-watch a season's worth of favorite shows when he was home for the holidays. He thought renovating a house sounded boring, not fun.

Chelsea left our bill, and I reached for my wallet, but Ty waved me off. "I asked you. My treat."

"Thanks. This has been great."

"Still interested in seeing the dorm?"

I was flushing. "Yeah, but …" *Crap*. The clock above the bar said 10:45. Ty followed my gaze. "I have a curfew. I have to be back by 11:30."

Ty sat back. "Right. Sorry, I forgot to ask. I didn't think."

"Sorry. I should have mentioned it."

"No worries. Another time. You'll be back."

I smiled, tentative. "I hope so."

As we passed through the heavy door leading into the main pub, we were laughing, close and intimate, and that's what Gary, Sam, and Sam's friends saw from their booth. Ty's gaze followed mine.

"You know them?"

"Two of them. Come meet my brother."

A hetero guy distance between us, we crossed the room, and I introduced Ty to Gary and Sam, who introduced three friends from his Paramedic program.

"You two are brothers?" said one of the friends, Ray. Gary and I grinned and looked at each other. We have the same smile.

"Okay, I guess I can see it," said Ray.

"You look good, Gunny. Usually I see you in ripped jeans and a

Henley." Sam's look made me jumpy and eager to go, and I didn't know why.

Trying to get to the normal I knew, I said, "Samwise, you should see the mare Ty's parents brought. Blue roan, purebred quarter horse. She's a beauty."

Sam and his friends relaxed. They exchanged amused looks. Gary's face didn't change. He sipped a beer and watched.

"These guys ride Harleys," said Sam, jerking a thumb at his fellow students.

"Yeah, twenty bucks says you'll have your own this time next year," said Ray. I was really starting to dislike him.

Sam didn't disagree, just smiled.

"Well, if you go to the show look for Litton-Holmes Farms," I said, pretending I didn't see his friends' raised eyebrows. Assholes.

Gary gave me an assessing look, and I breathed in deep and relaxed my muscles as I let the air out slowly, like before a meet. *Let the anger go*. Sam and his friends didn't seem to notice.

Sam seemed so … not remote exactly, because he was smiling, but the real-Sam warmth in his eyes was missing. He didn't ask me about anything that mattered. Not that I expected him to get into personal stuff, but not even one question?

Ty and I didn't linger, leaving with a round of "good to meet you" and my "see you in a while" to Gary. As we walked away, I wondered if his assessing look had been because he thought I was going to start a fight with one of Sam's jerk friends or because they'd told him what kinds of people hung out in that back room. My heart rate sped up. So much for my brave words earlier in the day about coming out.

Ty had parked in the furthest corner of the lot behind Marky's. The nearer we got to the truck, the harder my heart pounded. What was I supposed to do now? Would he try to kiss me? Should I try to kiss him? What if this was hanging out and not a date? Did that matter?

The truck's lights blinked and the locks disengaged with a thunk. I climbed in on the passenger side. Ty stretched one arm along the back of the bench seat facing me and made no move to start the truck.

"How long is your family staying tomorrow?" Ty asked.

"We're leaving after lunch." I angled toward Ty, so I could look at him while we talked.

"Too bad. I'm covering for my parents again tomorrow morning. If you were staying in the afternoon we could hang out." Ty's gaze moved to my hair and back to my eyes, his face visible in the dim glow from the light beside the back door of the pub and a security light on the other side of the lot. "Come by if you have time. I can take a break. If you want to, I mean." He smiled, looking bashful for the first time since we'd met.

"Yeah. I'd like that. I'll come by." My heart maintained a heavy, steady beat.

"You have the most awesome hair." Ty lifted his hand, stilled it. "Mind if I touch?"

"No."

Ty slid closer to me and threaded his fingers through my hair. "Nice." He leaned forward and breathed in. "Smells good." Could he hear my heart thudding? I could, so loud I didn't see how he could miss it.

I shifted nearer and kept my gaze on Ty's mouth. He licked his lips, and seeing it made me lick mine. His fingers rubbed the back of my neck, a gentle circling that made me tilt my head back, eyes closed in pleasure. I opened my eyes to find his face so close I could feel his breath.

"Can I —"

"Yeah," I said, leaning in and tilting my head left. Our lips met, tentative. He grazed his along mine and pulled back, holding my gaze, checking that we were good. I smiled, got an answering smile that put his dimples on full display, and he leaned back in, his lips on mine again, brushing them with gentle strokes of his tongue. It felt so good I did the same to him. Our tongues traced the shape of each other's lips. I hoped I was doing it right.

He ran his left hand down my arm and slid it inside my open jacket. I pushed closer, and he nipped at my bottom lip. I inhaled in pleased surprise, letting him slide his tongue into my mouth. I tasted coffee and truffles.

Ty made a sound like the one when he ate the passion fruit truffle and held me tighter. I ran a hand under his jacket and down his side, feeling muscles and bone, hard under my fingers.

I breathed faster, wanting more of my body against his body, wanting skin, when he pulled back. He buried his hands in my hair on either side of my face and rested his forehead against mine.

"As much as I'd like to keep doing this, if we don't leave now, you'll miss your curfew."

He dropped his hands and I came back to earth. "Oh." I checked the time on my phone. Crap. Twenty after eleven.

"Don't worry. We'll make it." Ty ran a finger down my cheek and slid behind the steering wheel. The hotel wasn't far, and a few minutes later we pulled in near the entrance.

I released the seat belt latch. "Thanks for a great day." *Man up*. I scooted across the seat and leaned in to give Ty a gentle goodnight kiss. He didn't want gentle though and ran a hand up my neck into my hair again, pulling me in for a quick, hard kiss.

"Goodnight," I said, sounding out of breath.

Ty grinned. "Goodnight."

ELIN WAS READING in pajamas, the murphy bed in the living area already down and made up. Her eyes rested on my face and my mussed hair, and I was glad the room lights were off except for her lamp. Darkness could protect and conceal.

Or not.

"How's that to-do list coming?"

I snorted and disappeared into the bedroom before she could apply her Elin interrogation skills and discover every single detail of my day.

"Good night out, son?" Dad was still awake, reading something on his iPad. Probably one of his agri sites. He looked at me over his reading glasses.

"Yeah," I said, knowing I looked guilty, because when I'm worried about looking that way, then I do, even when I haven't done anything. Kissing a guy ought not to count as anything.

If I really had done something, those truth-finding eyes would know.

I changed into sleep pants and a shirt, washed my face, and brushed my teeth. I'd shower in the morning. I didn't smell bad, so Gary couldn't complain. He was back when I left the bathroom, and went straight in, looking tired. Tomorrow I would ask how his evening went. I crawled in on my side of the bed and was asleep so fast I didn't hear Dad place his glasses on the nightstand or see him switch off the lamp.

Ty Day Two

ON THE WAY to the Farm and Ranch Show the next morning, Gary and I rode on the truck's bench seat. Elin rode shotgun and talked to Dad about their morning plans.

"What did you and Sam do last night?"

Gary glanced at me, his expression still tired. Or maybe troubled. "He wanted to meet at Marky's, and when I got there, he was already there with those three guys. They wanted to eat." He pushed his hair back. "The food's crap."

"The truffles are good."

Gary smiled, the first time all morning.

"What else did you do?"

The smile vanished. "We played pool and talked, mostly about paramedic stuff."

I read between the lines. It had been stilted and Gary had felt shut out.

"Weren't you going to some famous cowboy bar?"

Gary didn't look at me. "Change of plans." His voice was flat.

"Sam seemed kind of different." I was probing for more information. The Sam I knew would have asked about the horses at the exhibition. He would have wanted every detail about a beautiful blue roan mare. Since when would he rather have a motorcycle?

Gary's hands clenched on his thighs. "He's busy with a lot of new stuff."

"Did you tell him about the work on your house?"

Gary's jaw muscles tensed. After a long pause, he replied. "It didn't really come up."

Huh? Sam had been over to the house lots with Gary, back when he was planning all the changes. Did Sam not even ask? What had happened to put that troubled look on my brother's face?

Gary sighed. I don't think he even knew he did. He leaned closer and spoke just loud enough so I could hear. "Sam said to tell you that you might want to avoid that back room if you're ever there again."

"Why?"

"He didn't say much. Only that it was supposed to be —" He hesitated. Sam had told him the truth and he was looking for a way to soft pedal it. "A little off."

"It was fine when we were there." I faced forward again and fought the frown trying to break through. Gary watched me, so I closed my eyes like I was resting until we arrived at the Stampede grounds.

Once inside, I went directly to the Litton-Holmes booth. A crowd of people surrounded the table and the mare, so I couldn't get near. I texted from the food court.

Gunnar: *Saw you are busy. At food court.*

A few minutes later a text came in.

Ty: *Okay, see you soon.*

I read about Ari and Dante until Ty slid into the seat across from me.

"We can do better than here. There's an exhibitor's canteen." Ty displayed a laminated badge with an attached keycard. He led us into a warren of hallways off the food court to a door with a sign: "Exhibitors only beyond this point."

Bzzzz. Click.

WE ORDERED MADE-from-scratch shakes and carried them to a table.

"You looked busy," I said.

"Yeah, everyone wants to get out early so they're all trying to cram in everything they haven't seen yet. Mum and Dad are going to take lunch in shifts, and I'll cover while they're away."

I tried not to look glum. The magical hours we'd spent yesterday weren't going to be repeated. Not today anyway.

Ty told stories about some of the weirder visitors to their booth, and he asked me questions. It was easy to be with him.

"When do you think you'll be in Calgary next?" Ty asked.

"I don't know. I wanted to come after my birthday." I lowered my voice. "I want to go to a gay bar once I'm legal. But not by myself."

Ty licked the thick shake off his long-handled spoon. "I'd go with you to any of them you wanted to check out. When is your birthday?"

"October twenty-eighth."

Ty's phone buzzed, and he glanced at it. His break was nearly over, but it felt as if we'd only been talking a few minutes. We tossed our cups and headed back.

"Hang on." Ty looked up and down the hallway and then led me into a dead-end alcove. "I scoped this place out. Just in case."

Ten minutes later I lifted a hand when he turned to wave a last time, and then I darted into the nearby men's room. My cheeks were flushed, my hair mussed. If Dad got a look at me with those truth-finding eyes … I brushed my hair and stayed there until I looked normal. As normal as I could, anyway.

Life, Hurry Up

I WENT THROUGH Monday on autopilot, taking notes and turning in assignments, but not tuned in. Instead, I kept replaying the time with Ty, the kisses, all of it. I was tired of waiting for life to start — well, some parts of life anyway.

Ty hadn't made any promises. He just said he'd hang out with me if I came to Calgary. And that was actually nice of him, because — I had to face it — he was at university and I was in high school. Yeah, he was only a year ahead of me, but the distance between high school and university was huge. I would be happy if we could be friends if nothing else was possible. Did I want anything else to be possible? Yes and no. I wanted a boyfriend I could hang out with. Cook with. Ride with. A boyfriend in Calgary wouldn't be able to do any of that.

So maybe I just needed to take the weekend for what it was and be happy. Because in the end, it really had been a great couple of days.

TY'S TEXT WAS waiting when I checked my phone at lunch. My heart drummed, and my face got hot and then a minute later, cold and clammy. *Breathe*.

Ty: *Hey, Gunnar. Awesome weekend. You online somewhere?*

I had to concentrate to type something legible because of the adrenaline rush.

Gunnar: *Yeah, good weekend. Sorry, no social media.*

For the first time, I wondered if Elin had been right. Maybe I had made a terrible mistake.

Ty: *No worries. Just checking. Got a lab, so later!*

Gunnar: *Later.*

Shit.

AFTER I FINISHED eating, I tried to jot notes for my book report, but Mrs. Young's format made me want to bang my head on the table. Maybe the cafeteria wasn't the best place to focus.

"Hey." Aidan slid into the seat across from me.

I grunted.

Aidan eyed the scratched-out mess that was my first attempt at a book report. I had to type it up anyway once I figured out what to say.

"Someone having a grumpy day?"

I flipped the notebook shut and leaned back, crossing my arms. "What's up?"

"I was wondering if I could come by and show you some sketches and get your opinion. And if you'd mind trying on a sample so I can see how it looks on a real person."

"When?"

"Today, if that's okay. I can give you a lift after school."

I didn't have to work at Derek and Parker's today because they'd gone to Edmonton. And I could use some distraction. "Yeah, that sounds good."

Revelations

ELIN AND TOR both had activities after school, Mum wasn't home
yet, and Dad and Gary were in the fields, so Aidan and I were alone
when I let us into the house and led the way to my bedroom. He
retrieved a sketchbook and flipped it open to two facing pages of
drawings. The clothes were sophisticated, with an edge, but you
wouldn't get into a fight wearing them in public.

Aidan straddled a chair. "Well?"

"I'd wear some of this stuff."

A flicker of muscles in his face — I'd hurt him. I tried to fix it.

"I'd wear most of it."

Aidan stared. Okay, that was a fail.

"Look, I don't know much about fashion."

Aidan snorted.

"I'd buy these."

"You'd buy those."

"Well, yeah. If they weren't too expensive. If they were, I might
wait for a sale."

"Gunnar."

"What? What's so funny?"

Aidan's shoulders relaxed and he shook his head, still laughing.

He rummaged in his sewing work bag and retrieved a white garment. "This is what I want you to try on." He pointed to a drawing. "It's this pair of pants."

"Why me?"

"You're exactly the kind of guy I'm designing this line for."

I took the sample and started to strip off my pants, telling myself I shouldn't feel self-conscious.

Aidan turned and fussed with something in his bag. He was giving me privacy.

I put on the sample pants and bent to play with the zippers at the ankle. The pockets had zips too.

Aidan had me turn and sit and bend. He drew on the sample with a blue Sharpie, which was okay when he was down by my ankles, but the closer he got to my crotch, the more I twitched and shifted. When he wrapped a tape measure around my thigh, Sharpie clenched between his teeth, he ordered, "Ho hill!" I thought about what I'd cook for dinner and tried to recall all the ingredients in Nanaimo bars — anything to avoid humiliation.

Finally, he stood. "Can you take off your shirt? I need to check the waist."

I stripped off my shirt. Tight lipped, Aidan fussed with the waist and the pockets in front and in back. Why was he so tense? I was the one getting jabbed with a Sharpie.

"Okay, that's good. Thanks." Again, Aidan turned away until I zipped up my own pants. He took the sample, folding it with care and stowing it in his bag, along with his sketchbooks. He was quiet, and I regretted my earlier lack of enthusiasm.

"I like the pants," I said. "The zip pockets are sharp." In guy speak, even gay guy speak, that meant "I'm sorry for being kind of an asshole."

Now would be a good time to give him the scarf. "Hold on." I handed him the wrapped parcel from my dresser.

"What's this?" Aidan turned the package, the paper crinkling under his fingers.

"It's for you."

"What's the occasion?"

"No occasion. Just a thank you for the messenger bag you gave me. And for helping me dress better. I got it in a consignment store when we were in Calgary."

Aidan's eyes shot to my face, and then he pulled the scarf from the wrapping and examined the pattern. "This is great."

"It's okay?"

"More than okay. It's awesome." He looked at me, his face less closed off than it had been a minute ago. "What made you pick this one?"

"Your socks. The ones you wore the first time you visited. They have the same colors."

Aidan looked as if someone had whacked him out of the blue. "You remember my socks from that day?"

My face warmed. "Well, you walked up the stairs ahead of me and I noticed them." Not just his socks, but he'd probably figured that out because he smiled.

"Thanks. I love it. It's perfect."

"Can you stay for dinner?" I had dinner duty. It would be nice to have company.

"Wouldn't I be in the way?"

"Are you kidding? In this house?"

"Well. My dad's at a meeting tonight, so I was going to have leftovers. Yeah, I guess. If you're sure."

Downstairs, Aidan left his stuff on a dining room chair and followed me into the kitchen. "Give me something to do."

I tied on an apron and nodded at the drawer it came from. "Aprons in there." Hair back and secured and hands scrubbed, I grabbed a chopping board, chef's knife, and four onions from a nearby bin.

"That's the recipe." I indicated an open binder on the bar with my chin as I chopped. "You can do spices. I'm making a double batch, so measure two of everything."

Aidan didn't speak, efficiently spooning, leveling, and dumping into the prep bowl. A couple of minutes later, he placed the bowl at my elbow on the counter. "Now what?"

"In the pantry, there's a big jar of red lentils. Weigh out twice what the recipe calls for into a bowl. Rinse and drain." I pointed with an elbow. "Scale's in the top drawer."

I placed a big soup pot on a burner and measured in olive oil, letting it heat until it was shimmering. Then I added in the onions and stirred with Mum's favorite oversized wooden spoon.

Aidan placed the bowl of rinsed lentils near me, on the counter beside the stove. "I didn't know you could cook like this."

"I can't. I can do these recipes because Mum taught all of us to make them. It's just following instructions." Like making a birdhouse in Building Construction 10.

I dumped in the spices, stirred for one minute, and added lentils, water, and vegetable broth, scraping browned onion bits and spices off the bottom of the pot.

Aidan leaned against the counter. "You're good at this. Whether you think you are or not. Is there something else I can do?"

"In the notebook on that facing page, there's a recipe for focaccia. You can scale out the flours. Double everything again, because we're making two."

Aidan pushed away from the counter, his movements lithe and economical. While he spooned flour into the bowl on the scale, I mixed yeast and warm water to proof, measuring in brown sugar and olive oil. I liked cooking with someone else.

"Can I do the mixing?" Aidan said. "Mum and I used to make bread."

"Yeah, sure." I placed my hand on the small of his back as I passed him. "Behind you." I'd expected him to tense up, but instead he leaned into my hand, not a lot but enough that I could tell. Or was it my imagination?

I retrieved Mum's bread board and two pans from the cabinet where we stored all the big flat things. Carrying them, I passed behind Aidan again, touching his back with another verbal warning. "Behind you." Not my imagination. He pressed against my hand, such a gentle movement that if I hadn't been looking for it, I might not have noticed.

I leaned against the counter watching Aidan knead the dough, imagining what it would be like to rest against his back, my chin on his shoulder, my nose in his hair … Wait. Where did that come from?

A few minutes later I slid two pans into the proofing drawer under the oven, and we washed up.

Aidan flipped through the recipe binder at the dining room table. "Snack?" I said.

"Sure. So what's the deal with these recipes?"

"Mum uses those when she teaches Basic Foods. We had to learn how to cook all the recipes, so when it's my turn to cook, I make something in there."

"These are awesome." Aidan paged through the binder.

I placed a plate of oatmeal raisin cookies on the table, along with a teapot of Red Rose tea, and took a seat. Aidan was smiling, a teasing expression on his face. He never looked at me that way. What was up?

"How was your weekend in Calgary?"

"Good. I met a cool guy."

I'd managed to surprise Aidan. His face shuttered. "Really?"

I told him everything.

"Would you have gone back to his room if you'd had time?"

"I don't know." That wasn't quite true.

"He didn't want to show you his hockey card collection."

"I know that." *News flash. I already have a mum.*

"Was it weird seeing Sam when you were with Ty?"

"It would have been weird anyway." I told Aidan how Sam seemed so different, so unlike the Sam I'd known all these years.

Aidan looked away, lips twisted. "People can change. Believe me. People you think you really know …"

I waited for him to continue. Under the bar, his foot swung, something he did when he was tense. "I'm sorry I was weird when we first met." He sagged against the chair back. "I'd just been dumped. Brandon, my ex, started at U of C this fall. That's partly why I came here. I figured it would be good to be closer. Three weeks before school starts, he said we were over."

"I'm sorry." That didn't seem sufficient. "He must be an idiot."

"He didn't want to be tied down, especially to someone still in high school. I'm still glad I came." I didn't say anything. Aidan wanted to talk, and the smartest friend move I could make was to keep my mouth shut and let him take his time. Aidan reached for the scarf, resting on top of his messenger bag, and rubbed the fringe in his fingers, his face thoughtful. "This guy … Ty …"

The back door banged open. "We're home. Hi Aidan," Elin called from the mudroom. In the commotion of Tor, Mum, and Elin coming in, whatever Aidan had been about to say was lost.

Old Good Stuff, New Good Stuff

THE NEXT DAY in the cafeteria, Aidan fell into the seat across from me.

He wore brown cords, a burnt orange long-sleeved T-shirt with the sleeves pushed up, and the scarf I'd given him, wrapped in a loose loop around his neck with both ends hanging in front. "I came to say thanks again for the scarf. I really like it."

"You're welcome."

"Hey, why don't you come eat lunch with me? Us. Collier and me." He was pink.

"Thanks, but …" I held up my notebook. "Book report."

"Okay. If you're sure. You're always welcome to join us." He left, his shoulders not at their usual angle. I felt bad, like I hurt his feelings. But there was just no way I could fit in at that table.

THE WAY AIDAN'S shoulders had looked as he walked away at lunch still bugged me. I grabbed my phone between classes.

Gunnar: *Want to go riding this weekend?*

Aidan: *Ygritte*

Gunnar: *Is that how they say yes in Toronto?*

Aidan: *It is when they have an autocorrect fail and don't notice and hit send*

Aidan: *And Toronto jokes? Seriously?*

He added the emoji that looks like *I'm so disappointed in you*, and that made me laugh. I liked his sense of humor. I wished there were more reasons for us to hang out.

Gunnar: *Do you want to learn how to wrestle?*

Aidan: *Are you high?*

WHEN I GOT home from school, I changed clothes and went to the basement to work out. Tor was already there, reading his tablet on the beanbag chair.

Myk was always telling me how awful his little brother Oleksander was (you'd better call him Zander unless you want his fist in your gut), but Tor wasn't so bad most of the time, aside from the whole filter thing.

I dropped to the floor and started stretches. Tor left his tablet behind and sat on the nearest weight bench.

"Are you going to beat up Myk?"

Huh? "Why would I do that?"

"He stole your girlfriend, didn't he?"

"What are you talking about?"

"Wasn't Cari your girlfriend?"

"No, Cari was never my girlfriend."

He considered that and then continued the interrogation. "Would you beat up someone who stole your girlfriend? I mean, if you had one."

"You can't steal someone's girlfriend or boyfriend. People aren't property. And you don't beat people up. You shouldn't even talk about beating people up." *Look at me being the responsible big brother.*

"You broke Brody's jaw."

Ouch. "Yeah, but I didn't beat him up. I hit him too hard and now I'm barred from sports. If I'd beaten him up, I'd have been expelled."

My phone buzzed.

Just Myk.

"Why are you always checking your phone now?"

Had people noticed? "I'm not."

"You're always checking it." He gave me a knowing look. "Do you have a girlfriend?"

Could he get off the Gunnar-needs-a-girlfriend train already?

"Is Jason Elin's boyfriend?"

"Ask Elin."

"I did, but she got mad at me. Why is everyone so weird and touchy? If I had a girlfriend, I'd tell everyone."

We know.

AT DINNER, MUM zeroed in on Tor, bent over so he looked fascinated with his crotch. He probably was, but not right that second. "Torvald Reynir, if you don't put that phone away, I'll take it away." Gary's eyes met mine and we both worked hard not to laugh.

Tor scowled, but tucked the phone in a pocket. Elin carried on telling us about the GSA fundraiser she was helping plan.

I was going to miss this next year. Miss my brat brother? Seriously? Yeah, maybe. Next year, Gary would be in his new house and Elin would be at university. Where would I be? Would I have a boyfriend? Would I be out?

We'd all come back for holidays and visits, but it wouldn't be the same. It's not that I didn't want to grow up and move out and get to be the boss of me and do all the cool things that adults get to do — fall in love, have a real job, get my own horses. I did. I just wished you didn't have to trade in all the old good life stuff to get to the new.

Eighteen

IN BUILDING CONSTRUCTION, I was making an inlaid table for Elin's birthday present. The top would be about the size of a large pizza. My pattern had a border of ears of wheat, sort of like on the old American wheat penny, but with long stalks. In the middle was a sheaf of wheat, based on one I saw in a picture from the Middle Ages when I was researching.

The first Tryggvasons would have stacked a lot of sheaves. The current Tryggvasons were really happy to use a combine. Of course, the combine was also why the land that used to keep six families working full time could only support one now. Combines were efficient, but no one wanted a picture of one on a tabletop. Wheat sheaves though — still beautiful even if you never saw them in fields anymore.

Mum has some pottery decorated with ears of wheat and a cookie jar with a big raised wheat sheaf on one side. Alberta potters are crazy about maple leaves, Canada geese, moose, and wheat sheaves. It's so boring. The Greeks used to put wrestlers on their pots. Naked ones. Horses too. Why don't we?

ELIN AND I were turning eighteen next week.

At school, everyone talked about applications. University. Community college. Technology institute. Trades apprenticeship. Everyone seemed to have a goal and a plan. Everyone except me.

I had considered cabinet making. Or carpentry. Or being an electrician. I like working with my hands. Mum and Dad had insisted that Gary and Elin and I fund our education savings plan as soon as we got our first paycheck from working on the farm. My RESP had been growing and I had enough money to take classes somewhere like Medicine Hat College. Or SAIT in Calgary.

The future was looking kind of grim right now. I sure as hell wasn't going to university. Maybe I should just give in and stay on the farm. Except — no. Farming is one of those things you have to love in order to do it. Otherwise why would anyone put up with the grief, the uncertainty, the danger, and everything else that goes along with it?

ELIN AND I were turning eighteen on a Wednesday, so our birthday celebration was going to be low-key. One of those now-I'm-legal birthdays where you go out and get shit-faced was never going to happen anyway, not that drinking till you puke ever appealed to me.

We already knew our big present — a trip after we graduated. Gary took his birthday trip in Newfoundland. Sam went with him, and they hiked a long stretch of the East Coast Trail and then hung out in St. John's for a while. Elin was planning a trip to the UK, but I hadn't decided yet.

We received the rest of our presents at breakfast. Elin got me a new leather wrap bracelet. I gave her the table with the wheat sheaf. She adored it, and Mum loved it just as much. Good, now I knew what to give her for her birthday next summer.

Gary and Tor went in on an international travel voltage converter with four outlets and four USB charging ports for Elin.

Tor pushed a rectangular package over to me. "It wasn't my idea."

That didn't exactly inspire confidence. Behind him, Gary winked. I tore into the paper and lifted off the lid of the box inside. On top was a leaflet showing the contents: a chef's knife, a boning knife, a paring knife, and a bread knife. I extracted the chef's knife and removed the protective blade covering. It felt good in my hand, like it belonged there.

"It was my idea," said Mum. "You'll be setting up your own kitchen before long."

She sounded funny, and when I looked up, her eyes were moist. Huh? Mum never got weepy about anything. "If you don't like it …"

"I love it. It's great." I caught Gary's eye first, then Tor's. "Thanks. It's perfect."

That evening, from the smells coming out of the kitchen, Mum had baked our traditional cake: triple-layer dark chocolate with inch-thick fudge frosting. She'd left a pot roast and potatoes and carrots in the slow cooker all day — one of my and Elin's favorite meals. We had a big salad with it. I ate a lot of greens so I didn't have to feel guilty about how much cake I was going to put away.

After dinner, my phone buzzed in my pocket, so I checked it as soon as I left the table. Birthday or no birthday, if Mum saw me with my phone out at the table, I'd be in the doghouse. I had a message.

Ty: *If you are there, call me.*

I raced upstairs to my room, and then I had to wait for my breathing to slow enough that I could sound normal on the phone. Ty picked up after one ring.

"Gunnar. Hey. Thanks for calling."

Be cool. Be cool. Be cool. "What's up?"

"It's short notice, I know, but I'm going home Saturday to help my dad get a couple of horses on Sunday. I thought maybe we could hang out on Saturday. Unless you already have Halloween plans."

"No, that would be awesome. When would you get here?"

"I need to put in a few hours on class work before I leave, so not before four."

I gave Ty directions, and he said he'd stop and text when he hit Valgard town limits. After we said goodbye, I had to stay in my room a few minutes until I could get the goofy grin off my face.

Downstairs, Elin sat in the living room with Gary, Dad, and Tor. Mum rolled the tea trolley in and started serving cake and ice cream.

I waited until everyone was eating and mentioned that Ty from the Farm and Ranch Show was going to stop by on his way home Saturday. I had to explain who he was to Mum and Tor while trying to hide that I wanted to jump up and down and run ten miles and fist pump and scream *Yes!*

Wednesday. Three days to go.

THURSDAY AT LUNCH, Aidan slid into the chair across from me a few minutes before the bell, wearing a "GSA Today" button.

"I hear your hot boyfriend is coming to town."

Obviously Elin had spilled the beans. That's what I got for letting it slip that I'd told Aidan about Ty. I couldn't stop a big fat grin from spreading across my face. "We're just hanging out. We're not boyfriends." I kept my voice low.

Aidan seemed strange today. He leaned back, crossed his arms, and smiled, but it didn't quite reach his eyes.

"Aidan, you coming?" Collier called over the cafeteria din.

"Yeah," Aidan said over his shoulder. He pushed away from the table. "See you later."

"Later."

Collier's head tilted as Aidan neared, and he shot me a look I couldn't decipher before his gaze returned to Aidan. They left for GSA together.

Ty Arrives

SATURDAY AFTERNOON. 4:25. I paced my room, trying to decide if I wanted to change again. I wore olive chinos with a braided slate-colored belt and my silky V-neck sweater, my hair clean and loose, parted on the side. The charcoal leather bracelet with silver studs Elin gave me for our birthday was double-wrapped and buckled around my right wrist.

I was panicking. Ty was used to a big city and on top of that, attending university. Was he going to enjoy a small-town Halloween festival? When we texted he said it sounded like fun, but maybe he was being nice. Was this a date or just hanging out?

My phone pinged.

Ty: *In Valgard. Arngrim's.*

God. Okay. *Breathe*. Reply.

Gunnar: *See you soon*

Ty had texted from the parking lot of Arngrim's grocery store. He'd be here in fifteen minutes. I ran downstairs. Elin and Mum were in the kitchen.

"Everyone is on their own for dinner," said Mum. "There's plenty of stuff in the freezer."

"Ty and I are going to get a pizza before we hit the festival."

"Be careful and have a good time." Mum headed toward the stairs with a mug of tea.

Elin flashed around the counter, gripped my elbow, and steered me into the living room. She stepped back, hands on hips.

"You look good. Turn in a circle."

I followed orders.

"Lift your arms."

"What? Why?"

"Do it."

I lifted my arms. Elin surveyed my waist.

"What?"

"I'm making sure nothing shows that shouldn't when you flash skin."

Elin says anyone who inflicts butt crack on the world should have to pay a fine. Ditto for guys who show underwear publicly. Double the amount if they're doing it on purpose.

"You look nervous."

"I *am* nervous." I opened the closet door and shuffled through coats until I found my black leather jacket.

"Does Ty drive a red truck?"

I leaped to the window. "It's him." I shoved my feet into my black biker boots.

"I'll probably see you guys at the festival. Jason and I are doing a one-hour shift for the Food Bank at 6:00."

"Okay. Bye." I thudded down the porch steps as Ty stepped from his truck.

"Hey," I said.

"Hey." He smiled, all dimples on display.

"Did you find the place okay?"

"Yeah. Great directions."

I stopped a little closer than hetero guy distance, but not boyfriend close, and stuck my hands in my pockets. "Did you want to come in for something to drink or a washroom break?" *Crap, did I say washroom?*

"I'm good." Ty's eyes were smiling even though his lips were pressed as if he were trying not to laugh.

"Are you hungry?"

"Starving. Lunch was a long time ago."

"I thought we could get pizza if you're up for it."

"Always."

In Ty's truck, I gave directions to Ismet's Pizza and Donair. As he drove, Ty asked me about our horses and school, and I relaxed. I had to make myself look away sometimes so I wasn't staring at him nonstop. Every time he glanced at me and our eyes met, he smiled, and my heart rate jumped.

Even though it was only 5:00, the parking lot was close to full. Inside, Ty and I slid into a semicircular corner booth in the back. He sat to my left, close enough that we could talk, but not so near that it looked like two guys on a date. A tall divider hid us from the booth beside us, which was perfect. Myk hated the booths with dividers. People on dates, however, always preferred the privacy. Were we on a date?

"Smells great in here," said Ty.

I breathed in. Yeasty dough, broiling meat on the rotating spits for donairs, tomato sauce, mozzarella and provolone, garlic. We settled on a pepperoni and double-mushroom with double-cheese, and the server left a root beer for Ty and water for me.

Ty nodded at my glass. "You don't drink pop? I noticed you didn't in Calgary."

"Coach wouldn't let us while we were in training. It's habit now, I guess."

"You can order something harder if you want. After all, you're legal. And I'm driving."

But I didn't want any of tonight to be fuzzy later, especially when I thought about what we did in the front seat of his truck only four weeks ago. I might be hoping for a little more of that. Who was I kidding? I definitely wanted some more of that. I flushed. "That's okay."

Ty's lip quirked as if he'd read my thoughts.

Time for me to say something. "What did you have to work on this morning?"

Ty told me about his homework and segued into stories of his two afternoons a week with a lab partner who had no sense of humor and took everything literally, and a lab assistant who wanted to be a stand-up comic and practiced on Biology students. I couldn't stop laughing.

"You could do stand-up too," I said, as the server delivered our pizza.

Ty chuckled. "Yeah, no." Then he shifted, so subtly I almost missed it. He looked past me and I followed his gaze. Myk stood beside our booth giving Ty a visual third degree that even Elin might not have been able to match.

"Myk. Hey." I straightened and introduced Ty.

"You going to the festival?" Myk asked, glancing at me before giving Ty another intent stare.

Before I could answer, Cari appeared and gave Myk a playful hip bump. "Myky! Hi, Gunnar."

Myky? It must be love because he'd have decked me for calling him that.

After another round of introductions, Cari and Myk rejoined their group.

Strange watching them walk away. Had I ever been in Ismet's at the same time as Myk and not been sharing a pizza with him and Jason or a group of friends or the team?

At school, I felt older. Students in Grade 12 were the biggest and most physically mature. We were about to launch into the world. We could pass for grownups. If we had turned eighteen, we were adults as far as the law was concerned. Our first stage was almost finished. Why did I feel so unready?

"Do you like university?" I asked. "University" wasn't what I meant. More like being on your own. Being someone who was out in the world for real. Being gone from home. Being grown up. "I mean being out of your parents' house."

Ty lifted a slice of pizza onto his plate before answering. "Yeah. It's funny — some of the people in residence might as well still be living at home. You've heard of helicopter parents?"

I nodded.

"There are a few people in my dorm with spy drone parents. It's like they haven't figured out their kids are actually separate people. There's one guy in residence whose mother picks up his dirty laundry and drops it off clean. Ironed, no less."

I imagined the look on Mum's face if she heard that. We all do laundry, even Tor. Mum says by having us cook and do laundry and iron she's making sure we can survive in the real world. I've always thought I could function just as well in a wrinkled shirt as an ironed one, but Mum doesn't see it that way.

"It's different, for sure," said Ty. "You're the boss of you, but that means you actually have to be the boss of you. Nobody's going to stop you from skipping class. Or watching TV or playing video games instead of studying."

"Except the spy drone parents."

Ty laughed. "Except for them. Don't get me wrong," he added. "I keep up with a couple of shows. I have a social life. Within reason. Pre-vet is a time suck." He licked sauce from a finger. I swallowed.

"What shows do you watch?" he asked.

"I don't watch TV. I get antsy sitting still that long."

"How do you get through movies?"

"Movies are different."

Ty's eyes were laughing at me. "What about video games?"

"Gary likes them. And Elin and Tor. I don't play much." How to explain? "I like real things."

"Some of them are pretty real."

"I know, but … not the way I mean."

"You're deep, Gunnar."

I flushed.

"No, don't take it that way. It's a good thing. I waste way too much time on Halo, believe me." Ty fiddled with a straw wrapper. "Tell me some things that are real."

"Horses. Riding. Building stuff. Boxing and wrestling. Cooking." Unlike television, watching a horse — trying to understand what it's thinking and feeling and getting it to do what you want without scaring it or hurting it — was interesting. Real.

"No social media?"

I shrugged. "I tried a couple, but they all seemed stupid. Who cares what my favorite color is? Who cares what music I like?"

"Maybe your friends want to know about you."

"Your friends *do* know about you. All those kinds of sites — it's not the real you. You post what you want people to see." I flinched, hearing my own hypocrisy. How many people knew I was gay?

"What?" Ty's fingers touched my arm. When I didn't move away, he ran them along my sleeve.

"I guess in real life we do that too." I swallowed hard.

"You mean like not being out."

"Yeah."

Ty's fingers moved to my hand, and he ghosted the pads of his fingers from my wrist to fingertips, a touch so light and sensuous that I barely managed not to shiver. "It's okay to be private. It's okay not to lay everything out there for strangers. Even when you come out, you aren't going to walk around with a big sign plastered on your forehead. You get to know people. They get to know you. Eventually you tell them."

He removed his hand from mine and sat straighter, with a subtle shift away from me. The server placed a tray with a folded piece of paper and two mints on the table.

He's being careful not to out me in my hometown.

I pulled out cash to pay, and Ty tried to argue, but I overrode him. "Want to head over to the festival? We don't have to stay if it sucks."

A dimple appeared, and Ty followed me out of the booth. "Sounds good."

Treats and Tricks

INSIDE THE LEGION Hall, streamers hung from the ceiling, along with the usual fake cobwebs and plastic spiders and ghosts on strings. Across the room, "The Monster Mash" blared as the background for a cakewalk.

I leaned in toward Ty. "When you're ready to leave, we can go."

"No worries."

We walked a slow circuit of the booths.

"Hi Gunnar," said Katie. I introduced Ty as a friend from Calgary. We moved on, but we didn't get far before I was making more introductions. Ty was good at being pleasant but detached, and kept us moving. If you're that good looking, you must learn to deflect in self-defense.

I exchanged nods with several classmates and waved at Becca and Rawdon across the room where they were making a circuit. We finally got to the Food Bank's booth where Elin and Jason were selling spiced apple cider, and I introduced Ty and paid for two cups. Ty placed a five in the donation jar, which was nice, because he didn't have to.

The festival was so packed now that the ticket takers had people lined up, waiting on others to leave so they didn't violate the fire code. Kids with plastic pumpkins full of candy plowed through the crowd, shrieking in excitement, endangering seniors and bringing down the wrath of parents.

"Are you into this?" I said.

He grinned. "Ready when you are."

We headed for the door, tossing our cups into a nearby bin, and squeezed past the queue of people waiting, shrugging into our jackets as we went. Two people at the head of the line pushed in as we passed them. We'd gone a few steps toward the parking lot when we met Aidan, Collier, and Elliot. Elliot stopped dead. His expression of shock morphed to *OMG I don't believe it* comprehension as he looked from me to Ty and back again.

Aidan and I said "hey." I snuck a peek at Ty. His expression was calm, if rigid, and his body had tensed.

I jumped in with both feet. "This is my friend Ty. He's on his way to Medicine Hat and stopped by for a quick visit. Ty, this is Aidan, Collier, and Elliot."

"We know each other," said Elliot.

"Hi, Elliot," said Ty.

"Tyler," said Elliot.

Aidan and Collier stepped forward and shook Ty's hand. Now Collier leaped into the conversational chasm.

"Is the festival worth the wait?"

"It's okay," I said.

Aidan looked from me to Ty to Elliot. "We'd better get in line. Nice to meet you."

"Yeah, nice to meet you." Ty's gaze moved to Elliot. "Good to see you again, Elliot."

Elliot gave a curt nod.

Ty exhaled as we continued toward the parking lot. "Sorry about that. Elliot and I hung out this past summer. He was a peer counselor at the day camp my sister went to."

As we crossed the parking lot, I noticed several guys standing at the back of a pickup, one of them Ryder Buell. Two had played football for Valgard a few years ago: Trevis and Boone. Except for Ryder, they were older than us, maybe early twenties.

Ryder gave me a look that would blister paint and stared at Ty too long before he crumpled a beer can and tossed it in the truck bed. Then he wiped the back of his hand across his mouth. Someone laughed, low and throaty, a dangerous sound.

"Gunnar!" I hadn't seen Cari, hidden by the much bigger man in front of her. One of the men had hold of her arm, and she jerked free of his grip. He was unsteady on his feet and staggered.

"Hey, don't run off, you — girl —" He turned to his buddies. "What was her name?" His friends laughed. "Hey, we got plenty of beer."

One of his buddies laughed. "Let her go, man. She's probably jailbait."

The guy who'd had hold of Cari cursed his friend at length, which cracked up the rest of the group. Cari walked fast to me and Ty, her face scared. "Gunnar, if you're leaving, can you take me to my grandma's?"

Ty and I exchanged a look.

"Of course," he said. We continued toward the truck with Cari, and I kept a close watch on the guys.

"Where's Myk?" I said.

Cari ducked her head. "We had a fight. Mindy dropped me off. I was going in and Ryder said hi, so I said hi, and one of the guys with him went to school with my brother Baye, and he asked how Baye was. I wouldn't have gone over except for that, and then the next thing I knew he grabbed me."

We climbed into the truck, and I scooted next to Ty, letting Cari sit by the door. Cari clicked her seat belt into place and then huddled in her oversized zip-up Vikings hoodie, looking miserable.

As Ty drove past the guys and signaled a turn, raucous laughter and curses spilled out, and a bottle shattered on the pavement. Someone would have called the RCMP by now. People with kids were parking in this lot. Ryder stared at us, radiating hate.

Cari's grandmother lived near the Legion Hall. "Take a left here." Cari leaned forward. "You're Ty, right?"

"That's right." In the dark cab, Ty's thigh and mine pressed tight. I could have moved. I wouldn't have dreamed of doing so.

"Right here. The white one with the fence."

Ty rolled into the driveway of a bungalow.

"Thanks for the ride." The seat belt *sscchhhllloooppp*ed up out of the way, and Cari bit her lip, not quite looking at me, a hand on the handle. "Thanks for stopping." She walked to the house without looking back.

When Cari was inside, Ty backed the truck in one smooth motion and retraced our route toward the main highway. "Where now?"

"How much longer can you stay?"

"The night is young. You'd better move over though, if you don't want to out yourself."

I was still pressed against him. I slid to the passenger side. "Sorry."

"Not complaining, believe me." He grinned before turning his attention back to the road.

"We could go to my house and do something, or I could show you my brother's house."

"The one you're renovating with him?"

"Yeah."

"Okay."

Ten minutes later I directed Ty along the circle drive behind the house.

"I don't want anyone to see a strange truck here and call my dad or the RCMP," I said, as I led us in. "We'll have to be careful not to show any lights inside." The Valgard RCMP detachment showing up at Gary's house would be just as bad as me getting into a fight, as far as Mum and Dad were concerned.

I took a flashlight and led Ty through the downstairs rooms. "We haven't refinished the floors yet, but we got the carpet ripped out. It was nasty." Upstairs I showed him the walk-in closet and master bath Gary and I had framed up.

In the last bedroom, on the west side of the house in the back, a convertible futon squatted in the corner. Tonight it was opened flat into a bed from the last time I'd been there working and took a nap. Was it too suggestive? "Have a seat."

Ty stretched on his side, head propped on a hand. I lit the antique oil lamp in the corner and adjusted the flame. We still wore our jackets because of the cold, so I closed the bedroom door and turned on the propane space heater, using the highest setting. It wouldn't take long for the room to get toasty.

I sat on an oversized corduroy-covered cushion, putting our heads at the same level. If either Ty or I had leaned forward, our lips would have met.

"You never got to finish your story about Elliot," I said.

"Right." Ty unzipped his jacket, the room's temperature already creeping up. "I told him from the start that I wasn't ready to be exclusive with anyone. I was happy to have fun, do whatever we were both up for. But no commitments. Not going into first year at university. Especially not long distance. He said he was okay with that."

I nodded.

"But later he wanted more, and we had a conversation and it didn't go well. From tonight, I'd say he's still mad." He removed his jacket and stretched on his side again. "I probably could have handled it better. I'm not good at scenes. Or confrontations."

"Me either." Ty sounded like he was way more experienced than I was. Not that I could call myself experienced. "Have you had a lot of boyfriends? If you don't mind my asking. If you do, it's okay."

Ty shrugged one shoulder. "I had a boyfriend for part of high school. Just casual stuff since then."

I was getting warm, so I took off my jacket, suddenly embarrassed. What a crappy place to bring a date. What a high school maneuver. He was in university. He'd had a boyfriend. He'd gone on lots of real dates.

"What?" Ty's eyes were warm.

"I'm sorry I didn't have a better place to take you."

"This is fine." Ty smiled. "I've had a great time tonight."

"Me too." And it was true. Ty was so easy to be with that I'd hardly felt self-conscious at all.

Ty reached for my hair and stopped. "May I?" I nodded. He slipped his hand into my hair, caressed the back of my neck. "I really love your hair."

I couldn't stop looking at his lips.

He leaned in and then hesitated. "You're good with this?"

"Yeah."

We kissed, gentle at first, then harder, my hands on his face, his hand wrapped in my hair. Ty pulled back. "Come up here with me?"

One part of my brain said that I hadn't thought about limits or boundaries. How far I might want to go. But the other part of my brain was propelling me onto the futon alongside Ty and making me angle my head back as he kissed down my neck into the V of my sweater. He sucked on exposed skin, and I put a hand on his chest. He raised his face to mine.

"Not where it'll show," I said.

Ty smiled — what Elin would call a pirate smile. "Okay." He

fingered my sweater. "Can you take that off?" The sensible part of my brain said *whoa, wait, this is moving fast.* The other part had me dragging off my sweater and tossing it aside, grabbing his shirt and saying, "You too."

Ty yanked his shirt from his pants and I ran my hands up his chest under the fabric. The hair there was soft, silky. I wanted to see it, but he gave up on his buttons and pulled me in, one hand on my nape, the other sliding down my back to my butt. His lips tasted of cider.

OOOOOOOOOOOOOOOOOOOOOOOOOOOOOOO ooo ooo ooo

Ty's phone played the sound of a foghorn, long and low with a reverberating echo.

And again.

OOOOOOOOOOOOOOOOOOOOOOOOOOOOOOO ooo ooo ooo

"Shit. That's my dad. I've got to take it." His right hand slipped from my backside, and he stretched to fish the phone from his jacket. "Hey Dad … No way … Okay … Give me an hour … I will … Bye." Ty shoved the phone back into his pocket and sat up.

"I'm so sorry, Gunnar. Dad's pickup died on the way to Medicine Hat after a delivery and they're getting it towed to a garage. I've got to meet him to hitch my truck to the trailer so we can pick up the two mares tomorrow." He ran his fingers through his hair. Gave me a crooked smile. "Dad's timing sucks."

It sucked like a black hole.

"I still had a great time." I held his gaze for a moment, then retrieved my sweater and put it on, followed by my jacket.

"Me too." Ty tucked in his shirt and shrugged into his jacket.

I turned off the heater and extinguished the oil lamp flame, leading us by flashlight. How could I ask what I wanted to know without being awkward?

"So," I said, once we were in the truck.

"So?"

"Do you think ..."

He knew what I meant. "I think if you come to Calgary, we should go out again, if you aren't seeing anyone. And if I'm not, but I won't be. I'm not ready to get exclusive any time soon."

"Okay." I tried to sound confident, cool — nothing like Elliot.

"Come here." Ty cupped my face between his hands and proceeded to prove that you actually could kiss and make it better. Finally, he sat back. "I wanted to do that now, because I don't think you want me doing it in your driveway."

"Yeah. I mean no."

He chuckled. When Ty stopped in our front drive, it was hard not to kiss him again.

"When you come to Calgary, let me know."

"I will." I slipped out, pushed the door shut, and watched until his taillights disappeared.

Who was I fooling? I *was* like Elliot. I wanted what Derek and Parker had. I wanted someone who wanted to be mine and nobody else's. Chances were high we'd never have another date. What would have happened if his phone hadn't rung? If we hadn't stopped?

I needed to think. About limits. Conditions. Everything I hadn't considered before. Why had I been so oblivious and stupid? Why was life so complicated and messy?

Jet-Propelled

GARY AND ELIN were already home, relaxing in the living room. When I sat down, Gary looked up from his tablet, and his eyes widened. He snorted.

Elin raised a brow. "Enjoy your evening?"

"What?"

She mouthed *hickey* and pointed to her neck.

Crap. I yanked the sweater's neckline higher as Tor ran in, nearly knocking a lamp off a table.

"Where are Mum and Dad?" I asked.

"Upstairs," said Gary. "Disturb for fire and death only."

Headlights raced up our driveway, and Tor leaned forward and peered out the wide front window. "Who's that?"

"Someone's in a hurry," said Gary.

A silver pickup slammed to a stop. The driver's side door flew open, and Myk stormed toward the house. I shoved my feet into boots and jogged down the steps to meet him, flipping on the porch light as I went.

"What's up?"

"Fuck you, Tryggvason." Myk shoved me.

"What the hell, Myk?"

Myk's gaze dropped, and he saw the hickey. "You son of a bitch."

I saw the punch coming, but I had no time to react. My head snapped left, then right.

Myk breathed hard, fists up. He wanted a fight. I pushed my anger back down.

After a moment, his hands lowered, but they didn't relax open. He took a step back, still watching. And then it was like he crumpled somehow — on the inside. I couldn't really read his face, but his shoulders told me plenty.

"If you were more than friends, why didn't you tell me?"

What? Does he know about Ty? But we're not more than friends. Not really. "What are you talking about?" My lips were that kind of burning numb you get sometimes after a punch, and the words came out funny, like I'd had a shot of Novocain at the dentist.

"Ryder saw you and Cari leaving together."

"Yeah, to take her to her grandma's house. She asked for a ride."

"That was two hours ago. Neither one of you has been answering your phone. Why is that, huh?" Myk shoved a hand through his hair. "You said you were just friends. You knew I liked her. It's not enough that half the girls at school are after you?"

"Dude, I have not been with Cari. I told you. Ty and I dropped her off." There is no way this is ending well. No way. Maybe if we could both scrub our brains and forget this conversation.

"You and Ty?" Myk's tone called *bullshit*.

I wiped at something warm trickling down my chin. Black on my fingers in the moonlight. I looked Myk in the eye.

"Ty and I left Cari at her grandma's house before eight. We were never even alone. I haven't seen her since then."

Myk wanted to believe me, but he couldn't. Not yet. "Yeah right. You didn't have that hickey when we saw you at the restaurant. If it wasn't Cari, then who was it? Your friend Ty?"

He'd expected a denial. He didn't get one. Slowly he straightened, and I could almost hear his brain making the connections.

"No way." My best friend from kindergarten and I stared at each other. "You're a fag?" What was I hearing? Shock? Disbelief? Something worse?

The word hung between us.

I took a breath — and realized I'd stopped breathing. "I prefer gay."

Myk spun and strode away. The truck roared as he executed a three-point turn and shot up the drive, gravel flying. I watched his taillights until they disappeared, like Ty's earlier.

Ty had said, "Make sure you pick the time." Too late. The entire school would know by Monday.

I hadn't put on a jacket, and I was cold, but at least that helped numb my split lip. My cheekbone throbbed. I turned. Mum and Dad stood on the porch, Mum in a robe and Dad in jeans and a sweatshirt. I trudged across the yard and climbed the steps, and they followed me inside.

My whole family watched me.

"Myk seemed upset." Mum's voice was gentle in a way I usually heard only when I was sick and she was taking care of me. "Do you want to talk to your dad and me? Privately?" How much had they heard? Anything? All of it? I couldn't tell.

I opened my mouth. Nothing came out. A pulse was jumping in my throat. Dad's expression was even more serious than the day I broke Brody's jaw. And Mum was white around the lips.

Tor braced his hands on the arms of his chair and lifted his feet, dropping to his knees in the seat. He leaned forward, and everyone looked at him. "Is Cari your girlfriend now? Is that why Myk was mad?"

"No."

Tor fell back into the chair and pulled his knees to his chest.

"Cari is not my girlfriend."

I looked at Elin, and her expression said what I needed to know: *got your back*.

"I don't have girlfriends. I'm gay."

"You are not." Tor leaped to his feet, his face red, hands balled into fists.

"Yes, I am."

For a moment, Tor just stared at me. Then he pounded up the stairs, and a second later Mum followed him. I sank into an armchair.

"Can you give me a minute with your brother?" said Dad. Gary and Elin left, and Dad pulled an ottoman over and sat in front of me. I couldn't look up.

"Gunnar. Son." Dad rested his hands on my shoulders. "It's okay. It's going to be fine."

I was afraid to look into his eyes. What if all I saw was disappointment? Or worse.

"Tor hates me."

"No, he doesn't. He hero-worships you."

"You mean Gary, not me." Who wouldn't look up to Gary?

"No. Tor has always wanted to be like you." He squeezed my shoulders. "Tor has to learn to see people the way they are, not the way he wants them to be. When he thinks about it, he'll realize you're the same brother you were an hour ago."

Slowly, I raised my eyes and met Dad's gaze. What I saw wasn't disappointment.

"Trygg." Mum stood at the top of the stairs. "Can you come up?"

Dad pulled me into a hug. "Your mother and I love you and we will always love you. Don't ever doubt that."

After Dad had gone upstairs, my brother and sister came in from the kitchen. Gary sat on the ottoman and handed me an ice pack. "Put that on your cheekbone." He had a basin of warm water and a rag, which he used to clean blood off my lips and chin. The water smelled like medicine. "It's stopped bleeding, but it'll be sore for a while. Don't suck on any lemons."

Elin perched on the arm of my chair, watching Gary. When he was done, she passed me a second ice pack for my lip. "What happened?"

I gave a quick rundown on Ryder and Cari in the parking lot, and how Ty and I took her to her grandma's.

"Knowing Ryder, he made it sound like a lot more." Gary frowned. "Did Myk hit you because you told him you were gay?"

"No, he thought Cari gave me a hickey. Which is just gross."

Elin and Gary collapsed in laughter.

"What?"

"Oh, Gunnar," Elin said, when she could finally speak. "I do adore you."

"Whatever. Anyway, he figured out it wasn't Cari."

"I can't believe Myk would stop being friends with you because you're gay," said Gary.

He might have gotten over the gay thing, but I wasn't sure he could get past the fact that he'd let me see him vulnerable and insecure. Or maybe he'd believed he'd stolen Cari from me, no matter how much I said we were just friends, and he'd beaten himself up only to find I'd never wanted to be with her at all. Did he think I was sneering at him?

Elin adjusted the collar of my sweater. "You'd better wear a high-necked shirt the next few days."

Gary squeezed my shoulder and winked when Elin wasn't looking. "Why don't you make yourself useful and carry this water to the kitchen?" Gary said to Elin.

Elin looked from Gary to me and back. "Yeah, okay, give it here. I'm going to bed." She kissed my forehead. "I'm glad you're out. That was brave." Actually, it wasn't and I hadn't exactly had a choice, but it was still nice to hear.

When Elin was out of earshot, I said "Did you know?"

"No. I thought you were a late bloomer with girls. Except — you've had a bro crush on Sam that seems like more than that sometimes."

Crap.

"Does he know?"

Gary got that it actually had been more. He pursed his lips, thinking. "I don't think so. The bro crush? Sure. More? No."

Then Gary flushed. "He did say something rude about the people who hang out in Marky's back room. I should have pushed back. I don't know why I didn't."

Because Sam is your best friend, and Mr. Glasgow taught him to think that way, and we always just looked away. But now I have to see him the way he is and not the way I want him to be.

"Can I tell him you're gay?"

"Yeah, I guess. Why?"

"Because if he's got a problem with you, he's got a problem with me." Gary smiled, but his eyes looked sad.

Mum and Dad's slippers scuffed on the stairs.

"I'm going to bed now," said Gary. He squeezed my shoulder again and left for his apartment.

Mum lifted each ice bag, her lips tightening at what she saw. "This isn't quite the return I'd expected on our investment in boxing equipment."

I smiled, and that hurt my lip, so I winced.

"Gunnar." Mum looked at Dad, uncertain. "I'm not sure what we should do. What do you need for us to do?"

"You're doing it." I closed my eyes. I would *not* get weepy.

"Are you telling everyone or just us?" said Mum.

"Everyone. I'm out. All the way. It's not like I have a choice. Myk will tell Cari and everyone will know by Monday."

IN THE BATHROOM I shared with Tor, I hesitated, then crossed to the door that led to his room and knocked. "Tor?"

The lock on Tor's side *snick*ed. I brushed my teeth, my eyes hot. I stood under blasting water in the shower until steam filled the room and fogged the mirror, and wished I could wash away everything that hurt along with the sweat and dirt.

I donned my oldest, most comfortable flannel pajamas and climbed into bed. An hour ticked by. I rested on my other side, then on my back, then my stomach. I checked the clock. 2:00 AM.

Click. The bathroom door creaked.

"Gunnar."

I rolled over. "Yeah."

Tor closed the door and approached the bed like a death row prisoner on his way to the execution chamber.

"I'm sorry."

"It's okay."

"Everything's changing. I don't like it."

I knew what he meant.

"Can I sleep here tonight?"

"Did you watch another scary movie?" Tor couldn't sleep alone after watching something scary.

"No. I just want to."

"Yeah, okay."

Tor crawled in and lay on his side facing me. "I couldn't sleep."

Me either.

"I saw you and that guy."

I waited.

"Is he your boyfriend?"

"No."

"Did you hit Myk?"

"No." No, I didn't hit my best friend. We'd somehow managed to stab each other through the heart. But I hadn't hit him.

Moonlight shone through a gap in my curtains. Tor watched me. "How did you get to be gay?"

"I don't know. I just am."

"How did you know?"

"I just did. Even when I was little."

A minute ticked by. Tor said, "Stacy was at the Halloween Festival. She likes me better than Zander, but she won't be my girlfriend."

I hoped he wasn't asking *me* for romantic advice.

Tor didn't say anything else, and his breathing slowed, evened out, and segued into the rhythm of sleep. I was right behind him.

Reverberations

SUNDAY MORNING, I went to Gary's house, up to the bedroom where
Ty and I had been last night. I sat on the floor and leaned against the
wall, elbows on knees, hands dangling.

Banging at the back door. "Anybody home?"

"Up here."

Firm tread on the stairs. Aidan entered, messenger bag and a canvas carryall slung over one shoulder.

"Have a seat," I said.

Aidan raised an eyebrow. "I'm sure you have a good reason for sitting on the floor, but mind if I sit on the futon?"

I waved a hand, which he took as permission, plumping a pillow
and shoving it behind him.

"I hear you burst out of the closet last night. Or should I say you
were jet-propelled?"

I shrugged. "How'd you know I was here?"

"Elin. She told me about last night. You're not on any social
media, are you?"

"Nope. Not on anything."

"Now wouldn't be the time to join."

I let my head thunk against the wall. "Is there nothing more interesting in this town than my personal life?"

"Today? Not really. In a couple of days, sure. All you have to do is wait it out."

Aidan opened his carryall. "This is for you." He handed me something squishy, wrapped in plain paper. "Happy belated birthday."

Inside the paper was a pair of pants, silvery moss green with zips at the cuffs and angled zipped front pockets, from the pattern I'd tried on.

"They're awesome. Thanks." The fabric was soft, like jeans washed so many times you can almost see through them. Like a caress on bare skin. "I'll wear them on Monday." For courage.

"How was your date?" Aidan leaned back against the wall, one leg up, his arms wrapped around the bent knee, his gaze steady, clear, unreadable.

"Good."

"Do I hear a 'but'?"

"I hate being in high school." More silence. The propane heater clicked on and rumbled in the corner.

"I'm not sure," said Aidan, "but I think I'm finally learning how to translate this strange language called Gunnar. Let's see how I do. You and Ty dropped Cari off. Then you came here. Yes?"

"How did you know?"

"The pillow smells of men's cologne, and you don't wear any. And …" He plucked something off the futon and held it up. "Short blond hair."

I blushed. "Gary has short blond hair."

"His is wavy." Aidan dropped the hair into the nearby trash. "Now here is the part when I may lose the trail. It's embarrassing to bring a date back to your brother's house that's not even renovated yet so you can have some privacy. Especially a guy at university. But getting frisky in vehicles in October — or even July for that matter — lacks a certain *je ne sais quoi*. Given that you're in high school in a small town, you don't have many options. When you say being in high school, you mean not being the boss of you yet. How did I do?"

I shrugged. I wasn't going to give him the satisfaction of telling him he nailed it.

"Nice turtleneck, by the way."

Elin must have told him about the hickey. I glared.

Aidan held up his hands, palms out. "I'll stop teasing you. I came to leave your present, but I also thought you might want to talk."

His expression was guarded. Still — generous of him to come. There were questions I wanted to ask. I was afraid of the answers.

"If two people live in different places and they go out sometimes, but they know they aren't going to be exclusive and they aren't going to have a relationship, what would you call that?"

"If they have something physical going on, I call it friends with benefits. If they hang out and they know they aren't going to get romantic, sounds like plain old friendship."

That was what I'd been afraid he would say. I leaned my head against the wall and sighed. "I can't do that."

"Can't do what?"

"Friends with benefits."

"Elliot can't either."

Elliot must have said something to Aidan about Ty.

I'd lost a best friend, been ejected from the closet, and didn't even have a boyfriend to show for it. I closed my eyes. Sighed again.

"You okay?"

"Yeah," I said, because really, what choice did I have?

AFTER DINNER, I picked out clothes and made sure everything was ready for school the next day. I hadn't heard from Ty. Time to check in.

Gunnar: *I hope everything worked out with the horses.*

Ty: *Yeah, it's all good. Dad's truck is fixed. The horses are fine. I'm back at my dorm now.*

Gunnar: *Awesome. I had a great time last night. I'm glad you came.*

Ty: *Me too.*

Gunnar: *So, I'm out.*

Ty: *Congrats! That was fast. How'd it go?*

Gunnar: *Mum and Dad were great.*

I wasn't going to tell him everything. He might feel as if he was responsible. He wasn't. Not even a little.

Ty: *That's good. You happy you did?*

Gunnar. *Yes.*

There wasn't any other answer I could give.

First Day Out

I DRESSED FOR Monday morning in my new silvery moss green pants from Aidan and a favorite consignment store shirt and blazer. I wore a bracelet that Derek had discovered in the drawer of an old desk in the equipment shed as we worked — small glass beads no bigger than a grain of soft, white winter wheat in a repeating pattern: one bumblebee yellow bead with black stripes next to a light jade green bead with yellow stripes, followed by a black bead with jade green stripes. I liked it because it was from Derek, and because the colors reminded me of summer on the prairies.

My hair was loose, a honey-colored silk curtain, thanks to Elin's insistence on applying a heavy-duty conditioning treatment the night before. I agreed to it because she swore not to tell anyone, even if tortured or bribed.

Elin sat by me on the bus, and I got lots of looks. My lip was still swollen and kind of gruesome because of the cut. My cheek sported yellow, green, and purple bruises.

"You can't be paranoid," she'd said Sunday night. "Lots of people won't know or care about your personal life. Don't think everyone's staring at you."

Aidan waited by my locker. He appraised my face. "Better than yesterday."

I smiled for the first time that morning.

"Nice look," he said. "Can I see your bracelet?"

"Faggots," someone yelled.

Aidan turned the bracelet, admiring it. "Be as you wish to seem," he murmured. I relaxed, unlocking muscles that had tensed.

He accompanied me to my block one classroom. Some people stared at my face. Some ignored me in a way that let me know they were making a point. Rude, and so obvious that I smiled. It was kind of funny. Some people went out of their way to say hi, even a few people who wouldn't have usually. I was relieved that lots of people acted like normal. Some of them did it in a way that let me know they were working hard to seem "normal," but that was okay. It meant they didn't want to make a big deal out of whatever they'd heard.

"Thanks," I said when we arrived at my classroom.

Aidan gave me a lopsided smile. Barely moving his lips, he said, "Faggots got to stick together."

BLOCK TWO. CARI ran through the door as Mrs. Young was closing it, twisting her way through desks to her seat. She slid into her seat, and her eyes widened when she caught sight of my face. I wondered if she and Myk were still together.

After the bell at the end of class, Cari shoved her class materials into her backpack and slung it on her back in record time. She took one step toward the door and half turned.

"Thanks again for the ride Saturday." She gave me the worst fake smile ever, all lips and teeth, eyes impersonal. *Socially radioactive. That's me.*

I didn't bother saying anything. She joined the stream of students bottlenecking at the door.

In the cafeteria, my usual seat was occupied, plus another five or six around it. Ryder Buell and friends. If the geek squad had been role-playing-game characters for real, they'd have incinerated Ryder and his cronies with the looks they shot their way. Brody wasn't with them, but I hadn't seen him with Ryder since September.

I was already turning to leave the cafeteria when I saw hands waving. Aidan and Collier. Aidan pointed at an empty seat across from him. I crossed to the table slowly, thinking hard. There was no way I would fit in with this group. I hesitated, standing behind the empty chair. Maybe I should just go.

Elliot glowered. "Stop overthinking. Sit. Down."

I sat.

Collier turned to Elliot. "Thank you."

"You're welcome." Elliot's expression was so cold that if I'd spilled my water on the table between us, it would have flash frozen.

I glanced at my old table. Ryder smirked and raised a middle finger. I turned, controlled and deliberate. I wouldn't give him the satisfaction of jerking my eyes away or letting him know he'd gotten to me. But he had. In that moment, I couldn't think of anything I'd like better than a knock-down drag-out fight with him, throwing punches until I'd worked off all my anger.

Remember Brody crashing into the lockers. Remember Brody's jaw. Don't remember how it felt so good. Remember how I got barred from sports. Remember how my actions hurt Mum and Dad. Don't remember how Ryder twisted Aidan's arm as he spasmed in agony, terrified, drowning.

Ryder hadn't paid enough for that. Not nearly enough.

Remember what Mr. Clyde said about greater responsibility.

But it would feel so good to punch that look off Ryder's face.

"Eating?" Aidan nodded toward my unopened lunch.

"Yeah." I pulled out a sandwich.

I half-listened to the conversation. My seat gave me a view of the wrestling table. Myk sat by Cari, their backs to me. So they were still together. He and the guys at his end were cracking up. The worse Myk feels, the louder he gets, all in your face and making jokes and being crude. If you knew him, you could tell his fake good moods from his real ones. To me, he looked miserable.

Elin and Jason sat on the other side of the table from Myk, a few seats away. She glanced at him and Cari a few times, and when she did, her face got that same tight look Mum gets when one of us has gone too far.

Katie was on my left. She wore a silver double-headed axe pendant with savage-looking curved blades, on a delicate sterling chain.

"Awesome axe," I said.

"It's a labrys."

The way she said it made me think that maybe I was supposed to know what that was.

"The sacred double-headed axe of ancient Crete," she said.

Oh, well that explains everything.

"It means I like girls."

Oh. "I guess I won't wear one," I said, and Katie laughed.

"Why aren't you coming to GSA?" she asked.

"I'm not much of a joiner."

"Maybe you should be." Her gaze pinned me in place.

Elin said Katie wanted to go to law school. I could see her as a Crown Prosecutor. She shouldered her backpack and picked up her tray. "Gotta run. Later."

Jason dropped into the chair Katie vacated. His face was drawn.

"Hey, Gunnar." He glanced left. "Aidan."

"Hey," I said. Aidan nodded.

"Can I talk to you after school?"

"Sure." I'd already asked Derek if I could skip working Monday this week.

BUILDING CONSTRUCTION. ERIC Stetle glared at me, arms folded, and made no move to set up his workspace.

"Problem, Mr. Stetle?" Mr. Gilkie paused, clipboard in one arm.

Eric scowled. "I want to work at another table."

"As you can see," said Mr. Gilkie, "we don't have any open spots. The class is full. You've been working at that table all semester. What's the problem?"

By now, everyone in the class had paused to watch. Eric wasn't going to say he didn't want to work with the fag, because that would get him in trouble. Mr. Gilkie stared at Eric. Eric glared at me. Stalemate.

"Switch places with me, dickwad." Rawdon James paced over, carrying a plastic bin that contained his project in progress.

Eric, affronted, turned to walk away, mumbling something really rude about me and Rawdon.

Rawdon brought the room to a dead stop. No one could miss his words. "Eric. You're welcome. Did you see Gunnar's date at the festival? Pulling guys like that, what would he want with your pimply butt? I think your virtue is safe." Then not so loud. "Asshole." Most students in the room laughed, a few looked scandalized, and Mr. Gilkie had a convenient moment of hearing loss. Mum says that sometimes good teaching is knowing what not to see or hear. She doesn't mean not hearing what you should hear.

I nodded at Rawdon, meaning *thanks*, and he jerked his chin up, an acknowledgment. He didn't say anything else, and we both worked steadily until the bell.

IN FOODS, BECCA tried not to stare at my bruised face. "Hey Gunnar."

"Hey."

"You look nice today."

Across the room, Cari giggled with friends who glanced my way. Good thing I hadn't joined her project team.

AT THE END of the day, I wanted to tell Aidan how much it meant that he showed up at my locker that morning. But I couldn't find the right words. So I texted, trying to get it across without being touchy-feely.

Gunnar: *Pants are awesome. Thanks again.*

Aidan: *Welcome.*

He added a rainbow emoji, and I thought maybe he got it.

ELIN HAD TO stay after school for French Club, so it was me and Jase in his car. I led him to the kitchen and pointed to a bar stool. "Have a seat. Want some hot chocolate?"

"Sure."

Jason smiled, but it was a sad, weary one. His normal smile always made me think of the light that filtered through the cottonwood trees along the creek's banks at the old campsite on our land. Like a lot of the athletes, he'd added the school colors to his hair: azure blue and winter white streaks that reminded me of magpie wings.

"Hair looks good," I said.

"Thanks." Jason leaned his elbows on the table.

I dumped ingredients into a pan. "So, what's up?"

"Wrestling isn't …" He sighed. "There are a couple of real assholes on the team, but some of the other guys think they're hilarious. I don't enjoy practice anymore, and what's the point of doing it if you're not having fun?"

I could guess who one of the poisonous guys was. Billy Soderquist was a wrestler.

"I call them out if I hear trash talk, but a lot of the time, I don't hear it because they make sure I don't. And Coach doesn't say anything."

Did Myk hear it? Or worse, take part in it? I couldn't think about that.

I gripped the wooden spoon so hard my knuckles were white. "Not surprised. Coach Mac hasn't spoken to me since that day in the mop room. He won't even look at me in the cafeteria or in the hall."

Something occurred to me. "Aren't you supposed to be at practice now?"

"I skipped."

I stared at him. You only missed practice if you were dying or you'd told Coach in advance and had a really good excuse, like open heart surgery. Even if you were having an unplanned emergency appendectomy, Coach expected at least a text from your hospital gurney as you were wheeled into the operating room.

"I told him I had a dentist appointment." Jason grimaced. "I blew a test this morning." That wasn't Jase at all. "With everything that's going on — I just didn't want to be there." Jason cradled his mug in both hands, hunched, like he was cold. "I wish you were co-captain."

Gary had been an easygoing captain, but tough if he needed to be. Sam always had his back, but the guys causing problems this year weren't doing that last year. Being around some guys makes you want to be the best guy you can be. The best man you can be. Gary is one of those guys.

"Elin told me about Saturday night."

"Myk didn't?"

Jason shook his head. "I think he's still figuring things out."

"Are you?"

"I kind of thought you might be gay." He chuckled at my expression. "Dude, girls have been throwing themselves at you nonstop since junior high, and you're oblivious. It's like they don't even register."

We sipped, silent for the moment. It wasn't awkward. Jason and I are okay not talking. After a while, he said, "How was it today?"

I shrugged. "Not too many haters." I told him about Building Construction.

"I'd have paid money to see that."

"Rawdon's okay."

"Well." Jason pushed up from the bar. "Guess I'd better get home. I've got to study. Thanks for the chocolate. And … thanks." He didn't have to say for what.

ELIN SAT BESIDE me on a mat as I did bicep curls after dinner. "You want the bad news or the bad news first?"

I kept curling. "Tell."

"Katie heard Cari say that she always thought you must be gay because you wouldn't kiss her. She's trying to get back in with her old crowd, and she's using you for social capital."

"What does that mean?"

"Everyone wants to know what happened Saturday, so she's getting a lot of attention and she's milking it. I think she dated Myk because he's an athlete and she could improve her status. I predict she'll dump him as soon as she can replace him with someone more popular."

"Poor Myk." I worked my triceps.

Elin hugged her knees to her chest. "She's making it sound as if Myk hit you because you're gay. She even managed to suggest you were hitting on him. It's all innuendo. She doesn't tell actual lies."

There are lots of ways to lie that don't involve saying something untrue.

"Is Myk backing Cari's version up?"

"I don't know."

I put the dumbbells away and sank onto the bench. Had I never really known him?

Maybe he was asking the same question about me.

Reveal

I RODE THE bus to Derek and Parker's, changed into work clothes, and joined Derek.

"Hey Gunnar."

"Hey."

Derek got a good look at my face and didn't quite stop his eyes from widening.

I took a breath. "So, um. I'm gay."

Derek put one hand to the back of his neck and stared at me. "Parker and I are gay."

"I know."

"Then we're good." Derek watched me. "Aren't we?"

"Yeah." He hadn't asked about my face. Derek was officially one of the coolest people I knew.

A minute later, face masks on, we were back in the thick of rust, dust, and mouse turds.

When we finished, I met Parker at the truck. I could tell Derek had told him during one of our breaks. He smiled and said, "Hop in."

"Can I ask you something?" I thought of Tor's missing filters as I buckled the seat belt. "You don't have to answer if it's not my business."

Parker glanced at me, before pulling out of the driveway. "Of course."

"You and Derek ..." Hard to put the question into words. "They didn't make ..." *Crap*. "The American government wouldn't draft you if you were gay, right? I mean, for Vietnam."

Parker took a deep breath and settled back in the driver's seat, eyes on the road. "There's a long and complicated response to that question, but the short answer is that saying you were homosexual could get you out of being drafted if they believed you. There were people who claimed to be who weren't. It was risky to say you were. I had a gay friend who lost out on a couple of jobs when the employers called to check his draft status."

"You didn't tell them?"

Parker's knuckles were white on the steering wheel. "No. Derek and I didn't think there was anything wrong with us. We both agreed that if you used being gay to get out of service, then it would be hard to argue that being gay shouldn't be a bar to having all the rights of any other citizen."

"You didn't have all the rights of any other citizen."

"Well," said Parker, his voice mild. "That was something we hoped would change." He glanced at me again as he turned into our drive. "Derek and I both believed the war was wrong. Derek was braver than me and came here."

Didn't it take more courage to get shot at than to go to Canada? Maybe not. Maybe sometimes it took more guts to follow your conscience.

Alliances

THURSDAY FLEX BLOCK. I stood outside the library. A couple of people pushed past, giving me curious looks. I took a breath and shoved through the door, then stepped to the side so I wouldn't block anyone.

Three conference rooms opened off the library, accessed from a hallway at the back. All three were booked during flex block, and a steady stream of people disappeared into the corridor. I took a step and stopped. I didn't want to do this. Seriously did not want to. I took another step. I hadn't told Elin I was going to attend. I hadn't been sure I could force myself to go. I took a few more steps and then my knees locked.

Behind me, footsteps approached, punctuated with regular *tlocks*. "Gunnar?" Becca stood at my side, cane in one hand and backpack slung over a shoulder. She wore a puzzled frown. "You okay?"

"Yeah."

"I'm going to GSA, so I'd better get going. I'm running late."

When she neared the corridor, I forced myself to follow. Just as I reached the entryway, I glanced left. Brody sat at a study carrel, watching the students heading into the meeting rooms. When he saw me looking at him, he didn't glare threats. Instead, he turned red and stared at his tablet, his shoulders hunched.

I headed into the GSA meeting room and took a seat in the big circle of chairs. I didn't look up at the murmur that greeted my arrival.

Mrs. Young sat next to a clean-shaven man with short cropped hair the same dirty blond shade as her shoulder-length bob. He wore khakis with a tucked-in, long-sleeved, forest green polo shirt and by the way they fit, he worked out. He wore a wedding ring on his left hand.

Katie was in the middle of introducing the man as our guest speaker, Officer Seth Rourke, Mrs. Young's brother, a ten-year veteran of the Calgary Police Service and an LGBTQ+ Community Liaison with CPS.

Officer Rourke rolled up out of his seat and stood, relaxed, looking us over. He talked about his duties as an LGBTQ+ liaison.

While everyone was focused on the speaker, I looked at the faces around the circle. I wasn't sure who was what. Gay? Straight? Bi? Was anybody trans?

Collier and Aidan sat next to each other. Was he *with* Collier or were they just friends? Not knowing was really starting to annoy me. I wasn't going to be rude and ask, but if they were together, they should let people know. It's just common courtesy. Navigating social stuff was hard enough without stumbling across land mines like people's secret relationships.

Officer Rourke took questions, and then Katie wrapped up the meeting. I stayed seated while most of the other students filed out.

"You actually came," said Katie. "You didn't say anything at lunch." She, Aidan, and Elin faced me with crossed arms. Jason stood beside Elin, and Collier leaned against Aidan, elbow propped on his shoulder.

Yeah, well, I hadn't been sure I'd go through with it. I didn't know what to say, so I shrugged and stood.

"See you next week?" Katie inquired.

"Maybe."

Katie, Aidan, and Collier filed out and I fell in behind them. Elin walked alongside me, Jason following in our wake. "Well?"

"Well, what?"

Elin thumped me with a knuckle. "What did you think?"

"It didn't suck."

Elin rolled her eyes and strode away. Jason followed, but grinned at me over his shoulder.

THAT NIGHT IN my room, I pulled out my phone and thought about how I could find out what I wanted to know. First, make contact.

Gunnar: *Want to go riding this weekend?*

Aidan: *Wish I could. Big project due Monday.*

Seconds ticked by. I couldn't ask the question I wanted to, and I didn't know what else to say.

Aidan: *Glad you made it to GSA.*

Gunnar: *Yeah.*

More seconds ticked by. A minute. Two minutes.

Aidan: *Okay, so later.*

Gunnar: *Later.*

Sometimes I think I could do with a few less filters.

Rapprochement

ON SOME SUNDAYS, Lije, Sam's older brother, came and worked out with us — he and Gary drank coffee at Cilla's Café many early mornings, along with other farmers, and they were hanging out more now that Sam was in Calgary. Lije, Sam, and Gary had learned to box at Bo's Gym in Valgard, before Bo closed it.

Jason still practiced at our place when he could. It wasn't the same without Myk. Did he miss me as much as I missed him? Cari ignored me every day. At least she wasn't sitting by me anymore in English. I didn't know what Becca said to Mrs. Young, but one day she took the seat next to me and Cari occupied Becca's old seat.

At lunch, Cari sat with the girls she'd been with at the party where she tried to kiss me, and she seemed to be pretty cozy with Eric Stetle. Elin said she'd broken up with Myk.

On this Sunday, everyone was too busy to work out, so I drove to Gary's house with Tor.

"Here." I handed Tor the key. "Go ahead and unlock the door and I'll get the stuff from the truck."

I set a crate of supplies on the porch and went back for more, just as a silver truck turned into the driveway and crunched along the gravel.

"Tor, take the crate and wait for me in the house." For once, he didn't argue.

Myk slammed the truck door and scuffed through brown, dry grass. A few feet away from me, he shoved his hands in his pockets and rotated his shoulders the way he always did when he was uncomfortable.

"I'll give you two free punches." He turned red.

I shook my head. "I didn't even want to hit you that night." It hadn't been his fists that hurt the most.

Myk stared at the sky as if there might be some apologies-for-the-clueless cue cards floating overhead. "Can we sit somewhere?"

I jerked my head toward the house and led the way to the big front porch. I sat on the steps. Myk sat too, not as near as a friend, but not as far as a stranger.

He took a breath. "I'm sorry I hit you. I'm sorry I called you a fag. I still want to be your friend. I hope you still want to be mine."

"I never stopped."

Myk winced like I'd actually punched him.

I waited.

"I believed Ryder. Which was stupid, I know. I don't even care. I mean, I don't care that you are. I kind of cared that you never told me." He looked away, and I flushed.

I'd imagined a lot of reactions Myk might have. Hurt wasn't one of them.

"I'm sorry I didn't trust you," I said at last.

"I should have trusted you too." Myk tugged at a loose thread on his coat. "I know I sounded like a total loser that night."

This was the tricky part. He'd revealed far more than he'd intended and that was probably what was bothering him the most. Loser was code.

"You've never sounded like a loser. A dick, maybe. Asshole, yeah definitely." In guy speak, that meant *I'll never use that night against you.*

Myk didn't look at me, but his shoulders relaxed.

Tor poked his head out the front door. "Are we going to work or what?"

Myk and I had plenty to catch up on. We'd never gone so long without communicating. Did he want a real friendship with me or was he just looking for a truce?

"Wanna go riding?" I searched his face for clues.

Myk nodded. "Yeah."

At home, Mum and Dad did a fine job of wiping their startled expressions when Myk and I walked through the living room. They greeted Myk as if he'd been coming by regularly instead of being incommunicado ever since he punched me and stormed off on Halloween night.

"We're going riding," I said.

"Will you stay for dinner, Myk?" asked Mum.

"Is there dessert?" The same thing he asked every time.

Mum smiled. "Would I ask you if there weren't?"

I WASN'T EXPECTING it when Myk joined me at my adopted lunch table on Thursday. I couldn't help glancing at the wrestling table. Jason's face was drawn. His body language said *exhausted*.

"Yeah," said Myk, seeing where my gaze had gone. "Jase is running on fumes."

"You slumming?" said Aidan, across from us, Collier beside him.

"Gracing you with my presence."

I was taken by surprise when he leaned back, did that thing where he suddenly took up twice as much space as his body required, and rested an arm on the back of my chair.

Coach Mac gaped at the sight of Myk sitting next to me.

"Coach," said Myk. "How's it going?" Jaws dropped. What the hell was Myk doing?

Coach Mac flushed, nodded at Myk, and shifted his gaze immediately. He turned away.

"See you at practice, Coach." Myk couldn't have been more cheerful or friendly. Coach's step faltered, and then he continued his circuit. Myk removed his arm. "You're right. He doesn't look at you if he can help it."

I'd always respected Coach Mac. He was a good coach. He didn't spout stupid, meaningless clichés. He cared how we performed, but you never got the feeling he was worried about having a winning team so he'd look good. He came down on anyone being a sore loser, but he said not to be a sore winner either, meaning show some sportsmanship.

So it hurt that he never spoke to me now. If he thought I'd been the only queer kid playing sports at Valgard, he was dreaming, but I guess as long as we were in the closet, he couldn't be expected to know.

Myk hadn't finished generating shock waves. He tagged along with me, Jason, Aidan, Collier, Elliot, Elin, Becca, and Katie to the GSA meeting. He bought a fund-raising long-sleeved T-shirt from a stack on display. He listened, didn't make any wisecracks, didn't roll his eyes or exhale audibly or get twitchy in his chair.

After the meeting, Katie collared Myk. I waited by the meeting room door.

"Are you serious about joining or is this some kind of stunt?" Katie could have been practicing for her first trial as a Crown Prosecutor.

Myk leaned back against the wall and crossed his arms, no longer towering over the petite president. "I'm serious."

"If you're only here because you think it will look good on university applications, find some other group."

I didn't think Myk was going to be able to resist the impulse to say whatever had sprung into his head. His expression revealed the battle going on in his skull. He had the perfect comeback. It would make guys laugh their asses off. Probably not Katie though.

Somehow Myk fought back smart-ass in favor of smart. He smiled and brushed a lock of hair off his forehead. His naturally curly, dirty blond hair was longer, and he didn't look like a poodle: he'd turned into a chisel-jawed young man with the build of an adult athlete. I hadn't noticed — until now. That was so weird I had to look away.

"We'd better get to class." Myk peeled off the wall and sauntered toward me, leaving Katie standing, arms crossed, wordless. "See you."

I looked at him sidewise as we left the library.

"So you're wearing that shirt next week?" We'd wear our GSA shirts the following Thursday to publicize the group.

"Hell yeah."

I hoped I was there when Coach Mac spotted it. Myk wasn't the only one who liked to see things blow up.

Gift Exchange

DECEMBER PROMISED TO be an endurance event, like always. I'd wrapped up the work for Derek and Parker, a good thing, since now it was all parties and pageants and shopping and caroling — the usual holiday marathon.

Aidan came by to exchange gifts the day before he and his dad flew to Toronto. I liked that we were the kind of friends who exchanged gifts. I couldn't have imagined that at the end of August. He sat on my bed, the late afternoon winter sun low on the horizon. Dark comes early and fast in December.

"I didn't have time to wrap your present. Hope that's okay." He lifted something from his work bag and held it like a bullfighter's cape.

My jaw dropped. The shirt had copies of touristy postcards all over it. Life-sized postcards, in blindingly bright color. Long sleeves, button-up front, slits on the sides, the biggest lapels I'd ever seen.

"It's an authentic disco shirt," said Aidan. "Vintage. 100% polyester. What do you think?"

I didn't know what to say. I'd go naked before I'd wear that shirt. But Aidan looked so hopeful ... until his mouth twitched and he turned red and fell on the bed, snorting.

"Oh my god if you could see your face."

My brows contracted. If I'd been a cartoon, my ears would have been smoking. Aidan laughed harder. I launched a tickle assault.

"No, Gunnar stop! No!" Aidan curled into the fetal position, giggling, and fell off the bed with a thud. "Ow! Damn it, that hurt."

"Good," I said, checking to see if he showed signs of damage. I wished he hadn't fallen off quite so quickly so I could have gotten in more tickling.

Aidan sat up. "Does that mean you don't like it?" He cracked up again. I glared while he folded the hideous shirt and put it back in his bag. "It's from your friend's boxes."

"Parker wore that?"

"Nobody wore it, because it still has the price tags on it. I can consign it at a vintage store and sell it in a heartbeat."

No way. Who would pay money for that?

Aidan pulled out a parcel wrapped in plain tissue bound by a gold ribbon and offered it to me. He laughed when I looked at it with suspicion.

"Go on, it's safe."

I opened the package. A button-down shirt in cranberry red. It totally rocked, and I knew it would make me look good because Aidan made it. "It's great. Thanks."

I handed over my gift for him. I'd taken Mum's computer file of recipes for quick, healthy meals and printed all the vegetarian ones on creamy heavy paper, which I'd placed in sturdy plastic sleeves. The software automatically generated a table of contents and index, so I printed those too. I put everything into the nicest binder I could find and made a cookbook stand from cedar, one big enough to accommodate the binder or a big, heavy cookbook.

Aidan paged slowly through the binder. "I can't believe you remembered I liked these."

What I couldn't forget was how good it had been to cook together.

Break(s)

THE NEXT MORNING, Elin and I cleared the breakfast dishes, neither of us talkative. I'd left my phone on the table, thinking I'd text Aidan, and an incoming message buzzed.

Aidan: *At airport. Starbucks! About to board.*

Gunnar: *Have a good flight.*

Aidan: *Calling our section. Later*

I SPENT TIME with the horses. Their winter coats had come in thick and lush, and they enjoyed being brushed in the sun.

Gunnar: *Bonza misses you. Saving you a big wad of snot.*

Five minutes passed.

Aidan: *Mature as usual, I see*

He cracked me up.

GARY AND I worked on his house. We were moving fast now.

Gunnar: *Refinishing floors. Wish you were here.*

An hour later.

Aidan: *HaHa*

He must have been busy. Or distracted.

BEFORE SAM AND Gary graduated, Sam spent most of his Christmas break at our house every year. Video games, movie marathons — depending on the weather, sometimes we might ride horses or snowshoe or go exploring on our land.

The year I was in Grade 8, we had big snowfalls in December, and I trained Mackie for skijoring. It was amazing. Gary and Elin used skis we found in a storage room. Sam brought his snowboard. Mackie was okay pulling our old toboggan too, so we were even giving Tor little-kid rides, in between runs on our homemade course. After a while though, we wanted to try some of the fancy stuff we saw online.

One day, Mum and Dad pulled into our driveway just in time to see me on Mackie, riding at a dead run, Elin being towed on skis, launching off the snow ramp we'd built up in the front field that morning and landing a spectacular wipe-out that ended in a trip to the emergency room and a Christmas-colors cast. Mum was so mad, she took away all the privileges: phone, TV, movies, video games — if it was fun and it used electricity, it was off-limits. All we could do was play board games until the new year. We still thought it was one of the best Christmases ever.

Christmas wouldn't be Christmas without Sam around.

Working with Gary at his house one afternoon, I asked, "Is Sam back from Calgary yet?"

Gary's lips tightened, and he didn't answer until he finished seating another nail and tapping it home. "Yeah, he is." He placed the hammer on top of the workbox and then stood and stretched. "Let's take a break."

We sat in a pool of sunlight coming through a window, and Gary poured us both a mug of hot chocolate from Dad's old thermos. I cupped mine in my hands and savored the warmth, then sipped, watching my brother over the rim.

"We've been texting. I invited him for a workout. Or dinner. Whatever. He said he's too busy. Which was bullshit," said Gary. "We met up at Cilla's for coffee last night since he won't come to our house. I told him if he couldn't be cool about you, that wouldn't be cool with me."

How hard had that been for him to say? I didn't want to be the reason their friendship ended. "You don't have to stop being friends because of me."

Gary frowned. "I'm not. It's up to him. I told him to think about it and let me know." After a second, he looked up and held my gaze. "Are you leaving because of Mr. Glasgow? And Gilmore? People like that."

"No." It was true. "No, I have to find something to do. There's nothing here. I'm not running away."

"Okay," said Gary. "Because you don't have to. This is your home."

"I know." I knew what he was trying to say. He had my back. My family had my back. I wasn't leaving because of a few nasty people in Valgard.

"I'm sorry about Sam," I said, because I was.

"His loss."

But it was ours too. Sam might not want to be around me anymore, but I would still miss him.

TOR HAD HIS twelfth birthday December twenty-fourth. Seriously bad luck to be born on Christmas Eve, but it mostly worked out okay for him because we weren't allowed to combine his birthday and Christmas presents to save money.

Just before Tor's birthday dinner, I texted Aidan.

Gunnar: *What's up?*

My phone didn't buzz during dinner. Or present opening and cake eating.

At midnight, a message came through.

Aidan: *Merry Christmas!*

Gunnar: *Merry Christmas to you and your family.*

That was all.

I SPENT MOST of Boxing Day patching and sanding the house's old baseboards and base shoes with Gary. When I got home late that afternoon, I was filthy and tired. No messages from Aidan since midnight Christmas Eve.

I didn't text either. I didn't want to be that annoying guy who bugs you all the time.

Brandon

AIDAN AND HIS dad were flying back on Boxing Day. The day after Boxing Day, Elin poked her head into the living room, where I was reading. "Aidan is coming over to show me some of his thrift store finds."

Oh.

I was reading the book Mrs. Young recommended for my next report: *The Inexplicable Logic of My Life*, also by Benjamin Alire Saenz. This one had a guy who got into fights too. The chapters were short. The family in the book reminded me of mine. So far, I really liked it.

Elin ran to her room to change, and I tossed my book onto the couch and followed her upstairs. I checked my phone. No messages.

I threw on workout clothes and went to the basement, where I warmed up and then wrapped my hands before donning gloves. I punched the heavy bag, concentrating on my form, thinking about breathing and hitting. Not about why Aidan didn't bother to let me know he was back. Or say hi. He didn't owe me anything. What could I even complain about? *You fell off the face of the Earth after you left and it hurt my feelings? I thought you would text me and you didn't?* That sounded weird. Pathetic.

I slammed the bag until I was drenched in sweat, breathing hard, muscles burning — getting close to the wall. I threw a last round of punches and stepped back, catching my breath.

"Gunnar." Elin, Aidan, and another guy descended the stairs. I'd ponytailed my hair and clubbed it, so sweat ran down the back of my neck. I wiped my face with my arm, realizing too late that I'd flashed a big armpit sweat stain. "We have company."

"Hey," I said, and stripped off my gloves. "How was your trip?"

"Good," said Aidan.

I unwound my hand wraps, dropped them by the gloves, and looked the guy over. He was maybe nineteen or twenty, with black hair (from dye, not nature) tied back in a short ponytail. A few tendrils, streaked with red, hung in his face. He wore a poet shirt, jeans, Doc Martens, a rainbow-colored peace symbol on a leather thong, hoops in both ears, and a stud below his lower lip.

"Gunnar, this is Brandon. Brandon, Gunnar."

His ex? Maybe not so ex now.

I held out a hand, after I swiped it on my sweats. Brandon did a quick catch and release of a handshake. "Nice to meet you." His tone said it was anything but.

"Nice to meet you," I said, equally cold.

"Brandon goes to U of C," said Aidan. "He's visiting."

"Cool," I said, monotone, not caring if I sounded like a jerk. Brandon stared at me. I could tell he was speculating on what I was to Aidan. Or what Aidan was to me. "I should shower and change. Before my muscles chill."

I took my time cleaning up, but they were still there when I got upstairs. I slid into a chair across from Aidan and Brandon. Elin presided at the head of the table and pushed me a mug of coffee. They'd been discussing Aidan and Elin's post-grad plans.

"What are you doing after graduation, Gunnar?" said Brandon.

"I don't know yet."

"Anything you're thinking about?"

"Not really."

"Don't want to farm?"

Couldn't he drop it? "No."

Aidan's gaze moved from my face to Brandon's, back and forth like he was watching a ping pong match.

"I saw you were reading Benjamin Alire Saenz," said Brandon. "How do you like him?"

Damn. I'd left that book on the living room couch. "It's good so far."

"I've read a short story collection," said Brandon. "And a couple of his novels. Not any of his young adult books." His nose wrinkled when he said *young adult*. "I find his style down to earth. Not literary." He put "literary" in air quotes and said it in a fake British accent. "So much of his work focuses on identity. Kind of an overarching theme across everything he writes. Of course, that's just my opinion." He leaned back, crossed a leg over a knee, rested his arm along the back of Aidan's chair, smiled. "What do you think?"

"It's good so far," I said. "Hey Elin, do we have any cookies?" Out of the corner of my eye, I caught a movement — Aidan looking at Brandon. I couldn't make out his expression.

Elin disappeared into the kitchen and came back with cookies on a platter and a stack of dessert plates.

"Help yourself," I said, gesturing that they should serve themselves first.

Brandon smiled. "Watching my boyish figure."

"I'm not," said Aidan. He placed two cookies on a plate and gave Brandon a neutral look in response to his lifted eyebrow.

"Brandon was telling us about U of C," said Elin. "He's studying English Lit."

"Emphasis on creative writing," said Brandon.

"What do you plan to do with your degree?" said Elin.

"Write, presumably." Brandon spoke to Elin, but watched me. I pretended not to notice. "I might go to grad school. MFA. Something like that."

Aidan couldn't seriously be considering taking this guy back. Or had he already? He'd had all of Toronto to choose from and that was the best he could do?

Brandon broke off a piece of Aidan's remaining cookie and popped it into his mouth. Licked his lips and smiled in a way that was probably meant to be seductive. On the sexy smile scale, it didn't rate higher than a creepy. If a boyfriend of mine ever smiled at me that way, I'd either run screaming or projectile vomit.

Aidan tapped his arm with a loose fist. "Get your own."

Brandon's chin jerked up a millimeter, but it was enough to make Aidan drop his gaze. What the hell?

I wiped the scowl off my face. I had no right to be angry on Aidan's behalf.

Elin was telling Brandon about the post-grad trip she and Katie planned. "We're going to buy rail passes and hit as many places as we can. London and Bath first, then Oxford. We'll only take as much as you can fit in a backpack and stay in hostels."

I risked a look at Aidan, and he was watching me. We both glanced away. I didn't understand. Had I offended him? We were good when he left.

I couldn't take any more of this. I stood, something mean in me liking that Brandon flinched when I loomed over the table.

"I have chores to do, so I'd better get going. Enjoy your visit."

Brandon smiled. His eyes glinted. They said, *I win*.

"It's great to finally meet you. Aidan's told me a lot about you. He thinks you're a superhero. Always rescuing people."

"People have to rescue themselves."

Brandon's brows shot high. He turned to Aidan. "Should I ask for a translation?"

Aidan went ghost white. Whatever he saw on my face made him swallow. Brandon sat back, looking satisfied. I turned and went to the basement, where I sank onto the floor, back against the partition hiding the laundry nook.

I don't know how long I was there before footsteps sounded on the stairs. A second later, Elin sat beside me.

"What did Brandon mean with the translation thing?"

"Aidan was teasing me about finally figuring out how to translate stuff I say. He must have told Brandon."

"Aidan was acting like he'd been taken over by an alien or something. And that Brandon — what a pretentious shit. He was all but peeing on Aidan to stake his claim."

"It didn't look like there was anything for him to be worried about."

LATE IN THE afternoon, I read in my room, but I couldn't keep my eyes open and set my book aside to nap.

"Gunnar?"

Mum pushed my door open and poked her head in, and I sat up, rubbing my eyes.

"I'm sorry. I didn't know you were asleep."

"It's okay." I yawned.

"Aidan's here and wants to talk to you. Can I send him up?"

Crap. "Yeah, okay." I checked to make sure there was nothing on display that would embarrass me, like dirty underwear. A knock sounded.

"Come in."

Aidan slid through the door, pushed it shut, and stuck his hands in his pockets.

"I came to apologize. Brandon's gone."

"Sit." I scooted back to make room. He lowered onto the bed carefully, acquaintance distance. It felt like miles. It felt like months ago.

"I'm sorry about the translation thing. I told Brandon a lot about you, how you say quirky, funny things that I had to get to know you to understand."

"Stupid things, you mean."

"No." The word exploded from Aidan's mouth. "Not stupid. It's just sometimes you're five or six jumps ahead of the person you're speaking to." He touched the end of my foot, all he could reach. "You are not stupid, Gunnar. I'm the stupid one."

Aidan ducked his head. "My friends never liked Brandon. My dad couldn't stand him." He shook his head. "Stupid."

So why were you with him? I didn't say it aloud.

"Brandon came to see me in Toronto and begged me to give him another chance." Aidan's lips twisted. "I guess he didn't find anything better at U of C. He kept saying we shouldn't throw away two years."

WTF? "You were with him for two years?" I was stunned.

Aidan nodded, splotches of red on his cheeks.

"I said we could try again but we'd have to date. I hadn't realized how much I used to change my behavior to keep him from sulking. Or yelling. I hadn't censored myself for months, and all of a sudden I was having to again, and I hated it."

That explained the alien-wearing-my-body behavior. I thought of the flinch I'd seen earlier. "Did he hit you?"

"No. I wouldn't have stuck around for that." His eyes flicked to one side. "He could be handsy sometimes. Grabby."

You can be a physical bully without hitting.

"I told him we were done." Aidan looked self-conscious. "When you said people have to rescue themselves ..."

I waited.

"I translated," he said.

Signposts

THE FIRST DAY of school after the break, we were in the middle of an Arctic blast that was supposed to last at least a week. Headlights shone through the front windows as I passed by the living room on my way to the kitchen. Dad was plowing our drive. -20°C outside, -30°C with the wind chill. The sun wouldn't be up till 8:37.

I hate January. Except for the sunrises over snow-draped prairies. And trees wearing frost like sprayed-on crystals. Clear winter night skies like a black-lacquered platter sprinkled with silvery glitter. How amazing hot soup feels in my stomach on bitterly cold days when gusting winds fling clouds of snow. The way the horses nicker, welcoming me when I check the automatic waterer to make sure it hasn't frozen and put out more hay. Except for all that, I really hate January.

MS. FREIBERG ANNOUNCED THE five team projects she'd chosen to represent the school in the AHS Culinary Competition. No one gasped or looked stunned when Becca's name and mine were called.

Becca rode home on the bus with me so we could practice for an upcoming skills test. She had stopped using her cane and was getting around well now. In the kitchen, I hauled out Mum's cutting board. "Let's make *pommes frites*."

Becca peeled potatoes at light speed and couldn't stop smiling. She wanted to go to the Southern Alberta Institute of Technology culinary arts program. Our nomination would help her application.

"What do you want to do after SAIT?"

"I'm going to work in the best restaurants I can get into and I'm going to get my Red Seal cert."

Getting a Red Seal was intense, but once you did, you could work most places in Canada without needing extra licenses or certs from a province.

"When I've saved up enough money, I'm going to open my own restaurant."

Why did everyone except me have such firm plans for the future? "Where will you open it?"

"I don't know yet. Maybe here in Valgard. You could come after a long day of farming when you're too tired to cook." Becca placed the last peeled potato in the bowl of cold water and stood, drying her hands on her apron as she walked to Mum's pots and pan drawers.

Farming? Had we never discussed this? "I'm not going to farm."

She stared at me. "What are you going to do?"

"Don't know."

"Why don't you go to cooking school? You'd be great at it."

I had that same feeling I get when I'm working a jigsaw puzzle and press the last piece into place. Or when I'm solving a Sudoku and fill in the last empty block. That click of something fitting where it belongs.

"What?" said Becca, when I kept staring at her.

I shook my head to clear it and went back to slicing potatoes into thin lengths for *pommes frites*. "What if I didn't like it?"

"What if you did?"

THAT NIGHT AFTER dinner, I curled up on my bed with my laptop. First, I looked at the SAIT culinary program information. If Becca and I both attended SAIT, we could study together. I could go home some weekends and ride horses. The move would be easy. Life would be comfortable.

Should it be?

I leaned against the headboard and stared at the ceiling. I'd never eaten Indonesian food before. Or Turkish food. I hadn't eaten most of the cuisines that Aidan talked about. I'd never traveled further east than Manitoba except for a Grade 10 school trip to Montreal.

Our first day there we walked past an Ethiopian restaurant on Ste-Catherine and I breathed in scents I'd never smelled before. They hinted of worlds I hadn't encountered.

What would culinary school be like in a place like Toronto? I searched for programs and found Agnes Macphail College. I read the website: the classes I could take in the fall, the supplies I'd need for the courses, the residence I could apply to live in.

But would I like living in the middle of miles of concrete and asphalt in a big city? A place where you could go the rest of your life without setting foot on actual dirt?

I kept searching. Yes, there were places you could ride horses, even in Toronto. The college had two campuses. Two fitness centers. Two gymnasiums. Varsity and intramural sports. *Wrestling.* I could wrestle on a team again if I made the cut in tryouts.

I'd be the guy from the country surrounded by sophisticated people who consider Albertans hicks. What if everyone thought I was a big, dumb, farmer boy?

Aidan would say *You won't show up in overalls with straw in your hair. And you'll learn to navigate the city like everyone else who moves from a small town.*

What if I was lonely?

Aidan would be there.

I read down the list of course names. *Patisserie. Garde Manger.* They felt like treasure maps or presents to unwrap.

I'd be spending years far away from my family. I'm not ready to leave yet. I'm not ready to say goodbye to all the old good life stuff just to get to the new.

An application wasn't a commitment. I'd be figuring out the options, not signing a contract. I opened a tab for SAIT next to the one for Agnes Macphail College. I would do both. Options, not promises.

AIDAN AND I had lost the ease we'd had between us before his trip to Toronto. I missed the way we'd been. I missed him.

One afternoon, he was at our house getting Mum's help with his portfolio for fashion school applications, and when they wrapped up, he stopped by the kitchen where I was chunking up vegetables to roast in olive oil.

"Hey."

"You look good," I said. Dark teal, roll neck sweater over jewel-tone plum slacks. Slate blazer with a burgundy pocket square that had tiny polka dots in teal and white and light gray.

"Thanks." Aidan nodded at my chef's coat. I'd bought a second one to wear at home. "You look like a professional."

"Want something to drink? Can you stay for dinner?"

"I'll take something to drink. Too much to do tonight to stay for dinner. Thanks, though."

"Have a seat. Tea? Coffee? Hot chocolate?"

"Tea please." He watched me while I prepared the tea and a tray with mugs, spoons, and the rest of the works. I added a plate with cookies for good measure.

"You seem different," he said, reaching for a cookie.

"Different how?"

"I don't know. In charge. Competent." He took a bite. Chewed, wide-eyed. Swallowed. "This is incredible."

"Thanks. It's a chocolate chip cookie recipe with sea salt, the big flakes. The flavor really comes through."

"Yeah," said Aidan. "That's what I'm tasting. It kind of crunches when you bite into a flake. Like little bursts of salty. Outstanding."

Aidan closed his eyes in pleasure over another bite, and I enjoyed his expression. "How are your applications going?"

"If it weren't for your mum, I'd be losing my mind. What about you?"

"I applied to a couple of culinary programs." To my relief, Mum and Dad had thought it was a good idea.

"I can see you doing that." Aidan licked a smear of melted chocolate off a fingertip. "Where'd you apply?"

"SAIT and Agnes Macphail College."

"Agnes Macphail?" His gaze honed in on me like a laser. "That's in Toronto. What made you apply there?"

I shrugged. "I had to apply to at least two places. Agnes Macphail has a good rep." The truth, but nowhere near the whole truth. "It all feels kind of weird."

"Weird how?"

I couldn't find the words to say how strange it was that I wasn't just the farm boy wrestler who liked to ride horses, that I'd turned into the kind of guy who cooks for fun, that I was in GSA, that I knew what matchy matchy was and why it was bad, that I might cross the country to go to a big eastern city for school. So I refilled our tea mugs instead. Shrugged. Nudged the cookie plate toward Aidan. "Just weird."

He took another cookie. "You really don't do touchy-feely conversations." He bit and closed his eyes in appreciation again. "Mmmm."

He hadn't looked so unguarded around me since before Christmas.

"I wish it wasn't too cold to ride horses."

Aidan's look told me he'd translated, and he gave me one of those smiles where his face gets so — smart — like all his features get sharp and he's — beautiful is the only true word for it. I would never say that out loud.

Prairie Seasons

AIDAN WAS WAITING at my locker after school on a Friday in February. "My place tonight for pizza? I've got a favor to ask. Or do you have plans?"

"I have to pick up Tor from the Valentine dance at nine-thirty." Mum asked if I'd mind — one of those requests that's actually an order.

"Lucky you."

I snorted.

"Not a problem," said Aidan. "We'll make sure you're on time."

Hanging out with Aidan — I could get on board for that. Even if all he wanted was to ask a favor.

AIDAN HAD HIS door open before I climbed the steps to the porch. "I got the pizza. Dad's at the Legion for the Valentine's Day bash."

I removed my boots and followed Aidan to the kitchen. We talked about school and GSA until we finished eating, and then he pushed his plate aside and took a breath. "I need a model for Fashion Daze. And I'd like for you to be it."

Fashion Daze was a competitive, invitation-only regional show for up-and-coming fashion designers. Mum encouraged her best students to submit portfolios in the high school division. Aidan and Collier were the only Valgard students invited this year, but that was a huge deal for Mum, because the other students in the high school division were all from big schools in Edmonton and Calgary.

"I don't know how to model." I'd probably dislocate a hip if I tried to copy the models in the videos I'd seen online.

"It's not hard."

"What about Elliot?"

"He's modeling for Collier. And he wouldn't show the line to best advantage. Not like you would."

Aidan handed me copies of the portfolio drawings he'd submitted for Fashion Daze, and I paged through them. His figures were somewhere between London fashion week show models and Ralph Lauren ads that Elin sent me links for all the time. The models in those London shows were skinny. Pretty guys though. Most of them had prominent jaws and cheeks, like bone sculptures under their skin, with firm chins and wide mouths.

I wasn't skinny. Or pretty.

"I'm calling this line the Prairie Seasons Collection. I got the idea that first time we went riding. You're the perfect person to show off the clothes."

Aidan stood by me when I was outed. He'd taught me to be as I wished to seem.

"I'll try," I said. "But if you decide I'm bad at this, you'll replace me, right?"

Aidan smiled, and I could see his relief. "I won't need to. You're going to rock these clothes."

TIME TO GET the kid.

Tor clambered into the van.

"How was the dance?" I headed for home.

Tor lazed in his seat looking blissed out. "Would you slow dance with a guy you didn't like?"

"What?" My voice came out about an octave higher than normal. I forced my eyes back to the road.

"You know. Like some people will slow dance with somebody they don't like and some people won't."

"How do you mean *like*?"

"Like, *like like*."

And Aidan accused me of having my own private language. "Do you mean would I slow dance with somebody I wasn't romantically interested in?"

I could feel Tor's frown like a laser dot. "That's what I said."

"I don't know." I never thought about it. *Actually, I never slow danced before*.

Tor settled against the seat again and started playing a drum beat on his thighs with invisible sticks. "Stacy wouldn't slow dance with Zander." He slammed an imaginary hi-hat cymbal.

Did I dare ask? "Did she slow dance with you?"

"Yeah. And Zander lost a wristband." Every kid got two wristbands at the start of a dance, and if you were caught dirty dancing or doing anything else against the rules, the monitors took one. If you lost both, the school called your parents and you had to leave.

"Did you lose one?"

"No, *duh*." Tor's look was all offended innocence. "If I posted a picture of Zander handing over his wristband to Mr. Schmidt, that would be a DME, right?"

"No way." I should never have told Tor about dick-move exceptions. Usually being a dick is bad. But sometimes you can say or do something on purpose to be a dick and it's the right thing to do. Like maybe being rude to a bully to humiliate him when he's picking on someone. Thing is, if you're a dick most of the time, dick-move exceptions don't apply to you, and if you have to ask if what you're about to say or do is a dick-move exception, it isn't.

"Whatever." Tor popped in earphones and returned to drumming.

Just as we arrived home, my phone buzzed in my pocket, so I checked it after Tor headed into the house.

Aidan: *Have fun playing chauffeur?*

I sent a scowly-face emoji.

Aidan: *That good, eh?*

Gunnar: *Tor thinks there are two kinds of people — the ones who slow dance with people they don't like and the ones who don't.*

Then I thought that might not be clear, so I clarified.

Gunnar: *Like like, I mean. Tor's words.*

It was probably chickenshit to throw Tor under the bus like that, but I didn't want to sound freakish.

Aidan: *Which kind are you?*

Admit I'd never slow danced with anybody? No way. I sent a zipped-lip emoji.

Aidan sent me a rolling eyeballs emoji.

I jabbed at my screen and missed the emoji I was aiming for. An eggplant appeared instead. Oh well, I liked to cook. Maybe he'd think I had hidden depths. I hit *send*.

Aidan: *WTF? Are you serious with me right now?*

Crap. This was why I hated social media. Everything meant something else and I never knew what.

I sent him that emoji that looks like someone saying *Dude, what?*

Aidan: *Google is your friend.*

Maybe I could still salvage this.

Gunnar: *It doesn't mean the same thing in Alberta.*

Seconds ticked by. I snickered. Aidan was trying to figure out if I was bluffing.

Aidan: *YASFOS.*

The back entry light came on. I was about two seconds away from a parent coming to investigate why I hadn't come in. I didn't want to be found giggling in the minivan over my phone like a kid in middle school.

Gunnar: *g2g. Later.*

Then I added a sweet potato emoji just to screw with him and shut off my phone before he could reply. How long would he Google trying to figure out what that meant in Alberta?

Spring Is Coming

AIDAN STARTED SPENDING lots of time at our house. He took picture after picture of me in the clothes I'd be modeling, documenting all the production stages. He uploaded shots of me wearing different outfits and pics that were goofy and fun from when he and Collier marked out a fake runway in our basement for me and Elliot to practice.

The first day of practice, no one else was allowed downstairs. I was not doing this in front of a live audience yet.

Collier explained what he wanted. "Okay, so first, the feet go side by side. Only women do the scissorwalk."

Wait, what? Scissorwalk?

"You walk on the right side. At the end, you stop with both feet parallel in the center and pause three seconds because the judges will be sitting at a table facing you. But don't look at them. You can't make eye contact with anyone. Then you pivot — elegantly — and go back the way you came, on the other side of the runway. If you aren't the first in the category, you'll start walking when the person ahead of you reaches the mark." He pointed to a piece of tape on the floor about halfway down the runway.

Aidan held pages he'd printed off the show website. "And they'll photograph you in that three seconds, so your stance is important."

Collier continued. "Swing your arms, but not like a soldier on parade. And your expression needs to say *You want me, you really do, but since you can't have me, you should totally buy these clothes*."

Oh God.

"Elliot, you go first." Elliot strode with confidence, his expression haughty. His arms swung, hands relaxed, and his posture was good, upright but not stiff, like a confident man walking down the street. At the end of the runway, he paused three seconds in a comfortable stance, pivoted, and returned.

"Good," said Collier. "Gunnar, you're up."

My heart rate sped up. I took a deep breath and stepped out, swinging my arms, eyes straight ahead. At the end of the runway, I stopped and counted to three, spun, and returned to the starting point.

Collier and Elliot were frowning. Aidan gave me a tense smile. "Not bad. Just a few notes. First, can you lighten your gait a little? You're walking a bit — um …"

"Like a gorilla," said Collier, as Elliot said, "Like a wrestler."

"I don't understand."

"Think how Jason walks," said Aidan. "Jason's walk is self-confident, but low-key. Myk's walk is cocky, but not in your face. You need to aim for somewhere between Jason and Myk. Try again."

I took a breath and let it out. Walked. Paused at the end. Spun. Returned. Collier and Elliot were still frowning. Aidan gave me another tense smile. "Better." He tapped a finger against his lower lip. "Let's try this. Think of a guy you've seen who is graceful. Think of how he moves."

Rawdon, rolling to his feet out of a chair in Building Construction like a cougar unfolding itself from a recline, elegant, controlled.

Rawdon, padding across the room as if he were on paws, not legs. Rawdon, gliding like a big cat on the prowl for a meal.

"Try again," said Aidan.

I imagined a mountain lion prowling and walked. Stopped. Pivoted. Returned.

Aidan, Collier, and Elliot gaped. "Whatever you were thinking," said Aidan, "keep it up. That was perfect."

I'd work on muscle memory for this walk so it wouldn't desert me when I was under the lights on the runway.

People were reacting to all those pictures Aidan and Collier were posting on social media. Most of the comments stayed online, so I didn't see them. In Foods, Cari whispered with her friends over a smartphone, sending looks my way. After the first few times, I tuned them out.

"She's just jealous because she didn't get a Fashion Daze invitation," said Becca one day, her knife blade flashing up and down, leaving carrot coins in its wake. It took me a second to figure out what she meant. A piercing giggle clued me in. "And it drives her crazy that you aren't paying attention to her and her friends."

"Why would they even care?"

Becca shrugged and reached for another carrot. "I have no idea."

I thought I might. I was supposed to be paying a price for being different. Cari was "normal." Normal people were winners. Different people were losers. I wasn't cooperating though.

Cari and her friends wanted me to care what they thought. But unless they were giving away a free horse with every opinion, I couldn't be bothered.

Maybe that was why Coach Mac was so hostile. I wasn't acting the way he thought a queer guy should, like I should walk around looking all miserable, eyes on the ground, wearing a big scarlet Q on my chest to show I understood the school was doing me a favor by letting me be there.

Just by being alive, you bug some people.

AIDAN AND COLLIER had the order of the categories we would compete in from the event website, and we practiced quick changes from one outfit to the next. Every detail mattered — a bracelet, a scarf, the right shoes, a pocket handkerchief.

Aidan drilled me on what to do at the end of the runway in front of the judges. For one outfit, I was supposed to pause with my hands in the pockets. For another, hands at my side. For another, pop the jacket button and grasp the lapels. Anything less than perfection was not an option. I could have watched Aidan in his creative zone forever. He was like an athlete at peak performance.

Elliot and I paraded to the show playlist now, one the event organizers put together. I guess they thought there was no way eight high school fashion designers were going to agree on runway music, so they avoided problems by choosing a set of songs with a good beat.

Sometimes Aidan and Collier let loose and danced as Elliot and I practiced. They reminded me of the way our horses occasionally sprinted across the pasture in spring for no reason, like they got a whiff of green things unfurling, or maybe just for the joy of it. Running is how horses dance.

In the Headlights

A COUPLE OF days before the show, Alison, one of Collier's friends, came by during practice. "I'm here to do makeup."

"What do you mean, makeup?" I said.

Alison looked to Aidan.

"You need a little something so you don't wash out under the lights," he said. "Alison has generously agreed to do yours."

I frowned.

"You won't look like you have makeup on," said Alison. "But you'll look better." She took several photos of my face. Before shots. If I wouldn't look like I had any on, then why put it on?

I let Alison push me into a chair and put slimy, gross stuff on my face. "You have good bones," she said as she worked. "We just have to make sure they show up under runway lighting."

Elin came downstairs to watch. "You look great. You should wear that all the time."

Oh, hell no.

"Okay, look up, Gunnar. I'm going to put on a coat of clear mascara. Hold really still."

"Clear? If you can't see it, what's the point?"

Alison perched on a footstool, leaned in, and stared me down.

"One more complaint and I'll use the eyelash curler on something it isn't designed to fit. You get me?"

I got her.

Finally, Alison stepped back and Aidan moved in. "I like the hint of liner. His eyes really stand out. And look at those cheekbones."

Collier peered over Aidan's shoulder. "Cheekbones for days. Fantastic job."

Aidan pulled Alison into a sideways hug. "You did great. This is exactly what I want for the show."

"No worries." Alison took more pictures. Elin and Aidan did too.

"You're not posting those, right?" I said.

Alison gave me an eye roll, and Elin, Aidan, and Collier cracked up. Behind them, Elliot stood with his arms crossed, looking down his nose the way he usually did around me.

THAT EVENING I texted Ty.

Gunnar: *In Calgary on the weekend. You around?*

Ty: *Around, but I've got to study for an exam that's a third of my grade. Sorry! Wish we could hang out.*

Gunnar: *No worries. Next time.*

Ty: *For sure. Call me while you're here if you have a minute. I can take a break.*

Gunnar: *Okay, will do.*

THURSDAY AFTERNOON IN Building Construction, Billy Soderquist accidentally-on-purpose ran into me on his way to his workbench. He muttered, "Watch it, fag," but there was no question that he'd run into me, not the other way around.

He was trying to start something. Billy was Ryder's lackey. If I got into another fight, I might get barred from extracurricular activities, like modeling for Fashion Daze. And even if I didn't, I wouldn't be much good as a model with a busted nose or a black eye or broken bones or visible stitches. Aidan would be screwed.

"You okay?" asked Rawdon.

"Yeah, thanks." Our eyes met and held a moment before we turned back to our projects. Mr. Gilkie stopped by and spoke quietly with Rawdon. He was checking in a lot lately.

On my way to the scrap recycling bins, Billy shoved past me and tripped me at the same time. I stumbled, but stayed upright. Billy made a point of looking over his shoulder and smirking.

"Soderquist. My office." Billy half-strutted, half-slunk to Mr. Gilkie's office, trying to give off a *Teachers don't faze me* vibe. A few minutes later he reappeared, face red, and busied himself at his work bench, shoulders hunched.

Rawdon and I exchanged a glance, biting back smiles. Mr. Gilkie was pretty cool for an old guy.

Fashion Daze

AIDAN, COLLIER, AND Elliot picked me up early Friday evening, and we left for Calgary and Fashion Daze. Elliot drove his mum's van, and Collier was riding shotgun. There was just enough room on the bench seat next to Aidan for me and my overnight bag. Mum couldn't go because she had a big commission for a wedding dress with a tight deadline, but she and Elin saw us off, waving until we were out of sight. Alison's mum was driving her, and they'd stay with family outside Calgary and meet us in the morning.

Aidan smiled when I boarded, but the muscles around his eyes were tight. Elliot was telling Collier about some gig he was playing with his dad's band the next weekend. I didn't try to talk to Aidan over the noise of the van and the conversation in front of us, but I watched him when he wasn't looking at me. His body shouted "tense." I touched his hand.

Aidan looked at me, one brow lifted.

"You good?" I asked.

Aidan nodded and then relaxed into the seat. His second smile made it to his eyes.

We checked into the same hotel where my family had stayed for the Farm and Ranch Show. Collier's mum had sent a cooler with sandwiches and potato salad, but none of us was super hungry. I kept thinking about walking the runway in the morning with television cameras and a huge audience, and what little appetite I had vanished.

FASHION DAZE RAN all weekend; the high school competition was Saturday morning, and we arrived at the venue by eight.

Alison applied my makeup. "Stop scowling. I'm using a very light touch." Finally, she stepped back. "Here." She handed me a mirror.

I looked like me. A better looking me, with sharper cheekbones and hazel eyes with a little more woodsy green in them than they usually had. Good but not fake. There was nothing I could point to specifically to say *this, this is the reason*. Alison had told the truth. My face didn't look like it had been made up. "You're good."

Alison smiled. "Let's do your hair." First, she brushed it out from roots to ends. Next, she pulled a handful straight back and ponytailed it at the crown, leaving the rest loose. Last, she applied product to make it smooth and sleek. When she finished, she took pictures from different angles, tucked her phone away, and handed me the mirror again.

She made me look like a guy who could wear Aidan's clothes. And then it hit me: Alison didn't make me look like somebody else. I looked like me. I *was* the guy who wears Aidan's clothes.

Aidan and Collier were still assembling their outfits and accessories in the spaces allotted to them, doing last minute touch-ups with an iron. While I waited for the clothes to be ready, I had a look at the show program. It described how Alberta landscapes and lifestyles inspired Aidan's Prairie Seasons Collection and emphasized that every piece in Collier's collection was constructed from re-purposed clothing that would otherwise have been thrown out. I finally understood what Aidan meant by fashion narrative. He and Collier had to do more than just design great clothes to stand out from the crowd.

I set the program aside and stretched, then turned to find Aidan waiting, Alison next to him. "How does he look?" asked Alison.

"Perfect." He stared at me for a beat and then motioned me to a folding screen with a rolling clothes rack beside it. I'd read that at real fashion shows people just changed in front of everyone. I was grateful to have something to hide behind.

I put on my first outfit and stood like a horse being readied for the show ring while Aidan tugged, adjusted, and smoothed. Finally, he stepped back and looked me over. "You look amazing." He pinked. "You make my clothes look amazing."

I stared at the floor. What if I screwed up? What if I didn't make his clothes look good on the runway? What if I flubbed so badly that his future was torpedoed? Was that possible?

"Hey." Aidan stepped nearer and squeezed my wrist. "Thanks. More than you know." His hand slid into mine, and I glanced up to find him standing close to me. Really close. "You've got this," he whispered. Then he released my hand and stepped back.

We stared at each other. I wanted to say something, but I didn't know what. Or if I even could. My mouth felt as if it had been stuffed with cotton balls.

"Places, everyone." A woman carrying a clipboard and wearing an earpiece, dressed in a *Fashion Daze Staff Volunteer* T-shirt, motioned at the spot where the models were to line up. An announcer recited the names of the designers, their schools, and their collection themes. My heart beat faster; I took long, controlled breaths, grounding myself the way I used to before wrestling meets. *Control the fear. Focus.*

The first song in the playlist spilled out of the speakers, a sassy, jazzy one with a thumping bass beat at just the right pace for modeling. I knew it well.

Control the fear. Focus.

Eight students were participating in the high school part of the show, and the models went out in the same order for each category. I was third, Elliot fifth. As we stood in line for the runway, I visualized Rawdon and the cougar.

Control the fear.

Focus.

Perform.

When the model ahead of me reached the halfway mark, I stepped forward, and all the hours of practicing kicked in. I puma-prowled down the runway, focusing on a point in the distance. My pulse hammered so hard the whole world should have been able to hear it. *Don't rush. Don't stumble. Don't look at anyone. Glide like a big cat.* Having to look stone-faced and remote helped me hide that I was terrified.

At the end of the runway, I stopped, the way we'd practiced, held my pose for a three count, and then pivoted. *Eyes straight ahead. Glide.* Finally, I reached the end of the runway and swiveled to the right, disappearing behind the partition. Aidan was there waiting, and he hustled me to his clothes rack, shoving a water bottle into my hand.

"You rocked," he said. "I knew you would."

When I stepped out in the second outfit, I could hear the music front and center instead of dimly against the pounding of my heart. I padded like I was on paws. People whistled. *Face like marble. Be the cougar.* And then something in my head clicked and I was in match mode, tuning out distractions — the crowd, shouts and whistles, all of it. I was performing, and I was doing it well. I was in control. I was the guy who wore these clothes and it was … awesome. Amazing.

It's like wrestling. We're a team — but my battles are my own. So far I'm winning the mental game, but losing means something totally different here than it does on a wrestling mat. The challenge is to play my part and not let Aidan down.

Each time I came off the runway, Aidan led me to his space, where I changed as fast as possible.

"You're doing great," he said. And "You looked awesome." And "You're kicking ass." All the while, his fingers flew, buttoning, zipping, tweaking, adjusting, until the outfit met his standards. *In the zone.* Alison stepped up to dust powder on any shiny spots and smooth my hair as I took my place in line.

At the end of the show, the designers took their bows and the audience went crazy. I peeked out from backstage. Cameras from at least two television stations bobbed around the floor and panned the crowds and the designers. I was glad I hadn't spotted them earlier or seen how many people were there before I took that first walk down the runway.

The designers turned and beckoned the models. We walked out in our marching order, and we didn't have to stare into the distance this time. We could even smile. Aidan didn't take his eyes off me the whole way. When we lined up behind the designers, they bowed to the audience again, then turned and raised a hand to us, and the cheering got louder. More bowing. Finally, we exited in reverse order, to applause and whistles. As soon as we were offstage, Aidan threw his arms around me.

"Thank you so much."

My brain stuttered and before I could move, he had released me.

"You were perfect." He hugged me again, and this time I hugged him in return. It felt good. He stepped back first. "Thank you."

I was still processing how the hug felt. "Um. Sure. I was glad to."

Aidan gave me one of those sharp smiles. I hadn't been glad to at first, but he knew that. I thought he was about to say more, but Collier pulled him away to pack up.

WHEN AWARDS WERE announced for the high school competition, Collier's collection had earned the Green Earth prize, which was a thousand-dollar scholarship to be used for post-high-school education.

Aidan's collection won Best Regional Expression and a five-hundred-dollar prize.

Aidan and Collier were attending a lunch for the high school competitors. They'd get to meet some designers who were acting as judges and representatives from several design programs. I set off to find a quiet spot.

IN AN ALCOVE off a side entrance, I perched on a hard, plastic seat and called Ty.

He answered after two rings. "Gunnar. What's up? What brings you to Calgary?"

"I modeled clothes today at Fashion Daze."

"Like a runway kind of model? That's excellent."

I waited, but he didn't say anything else. "What's up with you?"

"I've been crazy busy with school." Ty paused long enough that I wondered if we'd been disconnected. "How long are you here?"

"Till tomorrow. We're going out to Hot Zone tonight."

"Good choice. My friend Nico likes to go there."

The way his voice changed when he said *friend* told me he'd scrapped his plan to avoid commitment and exclusive relationships.

And I was fine. Maybe even a little relieved. We talked about horses and his classes and the funny lab assistant that he had again this semester. I told him that I was applying to culinary school. When I sensed he was ready to get back to studying, I said goodbye, but not regretfully. Ty was a good guy. An awesome first kiss. A friend I hoped to keep.

Hot Zone

OUR CAB STOPPED in front of a building that looked like a warehouse, a windowless front stretching the length of the block. Above the door, orange and black pulsing lights spelled out Hot Zone.

We stepped into a foyer where warm air blasted from an overhead unit. A doorman in a black button-down shirt with the bar's name and logo on the pocket occupied a bar stool behind a high counter. To his left was a heavy steel door. In front of it was a grizzly of a man, arms folded, feet planted shoulder-width apart, wearing a black long-sleeved Hot Zone T-shirt tucked into sooty jeans, with biker boots. He had an earpiece, and a microphone clipped to the end of his sleeve. Beside him, screens displayed views outside the building: the back service road, the street on the west side, smokers clustered in an alley that ran along the east wall.

The doorman examined Collier's ID with a penlight.

"I'm eighteen."

"Don't push, sweetheart. I've seen it all — and you're not getting in if this is a fake ID."

Collier vibrated with indignation, but when the bouncer-slash-security guy glowered, he subsided.

The doorman decided Collier's ID was real, and Elliot stepped forward. He wore olive moleskin trousers with a dark, long-sleeved T-shirt under a black leather blazer and matching Chelsea boots, and he looked like someone already at university.

Aidan gave me a sideways look. "Did you call Ty?"

"Yeah. He's busy with school. And I think he's seeing someone."

Aidan's brows rose. "Really."

Before he could say more, the doorman beckoned me and took my ID.

"Nice hair." He handed it back, then took my cover charge and stamped my hand. Once Aidan's hand was stamped, Grizzly Man stepped aside, and I was inside my first gay bar.

Collier complained as we hung our jackets on the self-serve coat racks. "Gunnar looks younger than I do, and he didn't get the third degree."

Aidan laughed. "Gunnar does not look younger than you." He glanced at me, smiling, and his expression left me flushed. "He looks totally grown up."

Collier marched to the bar, the rest of us trailing in his wake, and we ordered drinks. He raised an eyebrow at my bottle of sparkling water and led the way to a tall table with a good view of the dance floor and the rest of the club.

As I scanned the room, trying to appear like being here was no big deal, a guy looked our way and did a classic double-take. He weaved his way to our table.

"Elliot!"

Elliot introduced us to Darren, a peer counselor alongside him the previous summer. They headed for the dance floor.

A minute later, a young woman channeling Audrey Hepburn approached our table, a cute brown-eyed, sandy-haired guy behind her.

"Can I ask where you got your jacket?" she said to Collier.

Collier leaped to his feet. "Like it?" He turned a full circle and gripped the sleek black notched lapels. "I took an old sport jacket I got for five bucks at Chichi's in the Hat and cut it down. Lightweight, summer wool with a bit of stretch." What he'd done was the clothing equivalent of starting out with a family sedan and ending up with a muscle car. Under the blazer he wore a tight, white T-shirt with a black bamboo print tucked into form-fitting, gray trousers with matching gray Converse sneakers.

As he explained how it came to exist, Brown Eyes inched up beside the girl, never taking his gaze off Collier. Aidan and I exchanged amused looks. Before long, Collier and Brown Eyes were on their way to the dance floor, while Wing Woman returned to their friends. Smooth.

"Don't you want to dance?" I asked Aidan.

Aidan turned his empty glass, staring into it as if it were a crystal ball. "Was that an invitation in Gunnar language?"

My face heated. I wanted to dance with him. *Does he want to dance with me?* Before I could find the right words, a tall brunet appeared at Aidan's side.

"Congratulations on your prize. I loved your designs." He must have seen the show. "Would you like to dance?"

Aidan gave him a smile that could melt chocolate and followed him onto the dance floor.

The pizza I'd had for dinner congealed into a lump in my stomach.

Aidan was exuberant and animated, still cresting on a Fashion Daze high. Brunet didn't hesitate to push close and follow Aidan's moves.

This was worse than seeing him with Brandon over Christmas.

The second I thought of Brandon, I saw him for real. He was on the opposite side of the dance floor from Aidan dancing with friends. At least I thought they were his friends. If they weren't, some nineties grunge tribute band was missing three members. Brandon danced like he had a battery cable wired to his dick and some evil villain was sending random jolts of electricity. *I hope he doesn't spot us.*

I returned to watching Aidan. But the way he was dancing with Brunet … A pulse pounded on one side of my head. *Why didn't I ask him sooner?*

More people moved to the dance floor, and I couldn't see Aidan or Brunet for the crowd. *Why didn't I ask him the right way?* I could sit here and have a pity party, or I could man up, find Aidan, and ask him to dance.

The beat sped up as the DJ transitioned into the next song. I shoved to my feet and started for the dance floor, maneuvering around tables and clusters of people.

A moment later I stutter stepped. Aidan and Brandon were off the dance floor, nose to nose in an intense discussion. Just a few minutes ago, Aidan was glowing with happiness and accomplishment. Now his face was pinched, his body taut as a wound-up spring.

As I neared, Brandon saw me and glared. Aidan followed his gaze and I couldn't read his expression.

"This is a private conversation." Brandon gritted out the words.

Aidan thrummed with tension, like a horse about to bolt. I didn't take my eyes from his. "Want me to leave?"

He shook his head no.

"Aidan, I'm talking to you!"

Aidan didn't look away from me. "Get lost, Brandon."

"Aidan, come on —"

"Everything cool here?" The grizzly-sized bouncer balanced on the balls of his feet, ready to intervene.

Brandon took a couple of steps back, his eyes fixed on Aidan's face. Whatever he saw there made him spin and lose himself in the crowd.

"We're good," I said. Grizzly Guy nodded and disappeared.

For a moment Aidan and I just looked at each other. Then he jerked his chin toward the exit. "Come with me." I didn't ask any questions. We retrieved our jackets on the way and headed outside, following voices to the alleyway where smokers congregated. Out here, the music was loud, but it didn't drown out the conversation and laughter. People clustered around tall, sand-filled pottery planters that had been repurposed as ash trays. A few security lights illuminated the area.

Aidan walked until he reached a shadowed spot under the metal stairs of the building's fire escape. He leaned against the weathered brick wall and shoved his hands in his jacket pockets. I faced him and waited. I couldn't read him.

"Were you coming to rescue me?"

"You looked like you were rescuing yourself." The muscles around his eyes relaxed. "I was coming to ask you to dance."

Aidan's mouth tilted up on one side, just as the music segued into a slow dance. He snugged a hand in my right trouser pocket and tugged. "Come here." We slipped our arms around each other's waists, under our jackets. His head rested against my shoulder, and my nose ended up in his hair. He smelled like the hotel's aloe green tea thyme soap and shampoo. *I guess we're dancing now.* Except we weren't moving.

My heart galloped. I might be the first person in the universe whose head exploded trying to slow dance. I took a breath and let myself feel the song playing for a moment. Then I eased into the music, the way you push from a pool's edge to swim, and Aidan followed me, into the rhythm.

I would never admit I'd looked up slow dancing on the internet. Mum and Dad did the kind of slow dancing where you had to know steps. They could do dips and twirls and all kinds of fancy moves. I didn't think I was ready for that.

There was slow dancing that looked like two people hanging onto each other and shifting their weight from foot to foot, which always reminded me of sleepy horses in the field on a sunny day. And then there was the kind that would get you kicked out of school dances if you didn't stop when the monitors told you to.

We slow danced our own way. We moved so smoothly together, it was like breathing, but when the song finally ended, Aidan stepped back and crossed his arms. *Why is he still putting up walls?*

Should I ask what happened? Was it my business? *I don't care if it isn't my business. I need to know.* "Brandon just wanted to dance?"

Aidan's chin tilted up. "No. But I'm not a fall-back plan. And I'm not going to be anyone's second choice." He watched me, his expression the careful one I remembered.

Sometime before Christmas, Aidan had turned into my only choice. But I hadn't understood. Over the past weeks I'd finally started to get a clue, but what if I was reading everything all wrong? What if *I don't want to be anyone's second choice* didn't mean *I want to be your first choice?*

If I told him how I felt, the words I got back might not be the ones I wanted to hear, but I had to know. So I took a breath. "I'm the second kind of slow-dancing person."

He blinked as he processed. "The kind who doesn't dance with someone he doesn't like?"

"Like like," I said, just to be clear.

"Me too."

I stepped into him just as he reached for me, and we ended up holding each other. Oh, I liked this.

"Hey, Gunnar." Aidan leaned back just enough that I could feel his breath on my face.

"Yeah?"

"Is it okay if —?"

I didn't even let him finish. "Yeah."

He ghosted his lips along my jaw until he reached my mouth, and then we bumped noses when it wasn't clear who was tilting which direction. We sorted that out, laughing at ourselves, and then we were kissing.

He buried one hand in my hair, which felt amazing, and I was working on my own strategic hand placement when someone coughed.

"Aidan."

Aidan and I jerked apart.

We turned to see Elliot with his friend. "You weren't answering your phone. Collier has food poisoning. We have to go back to the hotel."

Gentling

ELLIOT DROVE US back to Valgard the next morning. After he dropped me off, I went to Gary's and tried to work on some of the house's final details, but I was sleepy after being up so late and stopped for safety. Power tools and grogginess — good way to drill a hole through your hand or smash a finger. Or worse, cut one off.

I checked my phone one more time. Aidan and I hadn't had any time alone after we left Hot Zone. Still nothing. I lay on the futon in the back bedroom and fell asleep in the warm sun.

Something woke me. Footsteps crossed the room. I rolled onto my back and opened my eyes. Aidan sat on the edge of the futon, somber-faced, close enough that I breathed in the familiar Aidan scents.

I knew a *We've got to talk* face when I saw one. I didn't want to talk. Seriously did not want to talk, no matter what he was there to say. So I drew his head down, and kissed him.

It wasn't a yank or some kind of whiplash move. He had time to stop me. He didn't. He kissed me back. Now I was awake.

Aidan pulled away, just a little, our faces close. His left hand was by my head, where he'd planted it to support himself, and his right was tangled in my hair. "What if I don't want to kiss you on the same futon where you and Ty made out?"

"It's the same pair of lips," I said.

Aidan laughed so hard that he lost his balance and we ended up face to face on our sides, pressed up next to each other kissing again. I hooked a leg over his and tugged him tight up against me, and it became clear that at least one part of each of us was on the same page.

"Whoa. Let's slow down," he said.

I scooted a little way back and placed my hands on the bed between us. He smoothed a loose tendril of my hair, his face unreadable. And I was pretty good at reading it now.

"Are you sure?" asked Aidan.

What?

He saw I didn't understand. "About this. I mean, are we *us* now or …?"

He turned red. *He's afraid he couldn't be a first choice.* I wanted to kick Brandon's ass right then. *I really don't want to screw this up.*

Horses are easier to read than people. With horses, there's always a path forward, and I can see it. With people … not so much. I'm learning to find the trail. But sometimes it's like studying a foreign language when you don't have anybody to speak it with. Elin would say people can't talk to horses and horses can't talk to people, but they can. You just have to know how to translate.

When you gentle a horse, you make your body language calm, so you show the animal you won't hurt it, but when you reach out a hand, you also have to give it soft words and sounds, or it might shy away. You have to give the horse as much to believe in as you can.

I took a breath. "You're the only person I'd show my hockey card collection to."

Aidan smiled, his face all sharp and smart. "You don't have a hockey card collection."

"If I did … Besides, do you think I let Bonza blow snot on just anyone?"

Aidan's eyebrows shot up. "Is that your idea of romantic?" He wore the exact expression he'd had that first day in our basement when I asked if he wrestled. The difference between that day and today was that now I knew which expressions were his way of putting on armor.

Another true thing about gentling horses is that besides being calm, you have to be confident.

I shifted closer, just a hand's width, but it felt as if I'd traveled miles. "When it comes to being romantic," I said, "I'm kind of a wrestler."

The last rule about gentling horses is that even though you're calm and confident and giving them soft words and sounds, you have to let them come to you.

Aidan gave me another one of those sharp, smart smiles. He twined his fingers into mine. Then we were kissing again, until the back door screeched.

"Hello?" Gary called out.

"Up here," I shouted. Aidan and I sat up, arranging our clothes, smoothing our hair. Gary's steps sounded on the stairs, slow and steady. He appeared in the door. Gary was well on the way to having truth-finding eyes like Dad's. Too bad for his future kids.

"Hey Aidan. I saw your car." No wonder he'd been extra loud. "Congratulations on your show."

"Thanks."

"Gunnar, you don't need to stick around if you guys want to hang out."

I looked at Aidan. "We could go riding."

He smiled, and there was nothing else in it but happy — not hard, not sharp, not blank — just bright, like sun glinting off fresh snow.

The New Us

ON MONDAY, AIDAN met me at the school doors and walked me to my locker. We didn't do anything different, except maybe we looked at each other more, because the school has a strict PDA policy. You can shake hands, but you can't hold hands. You can do a greeting hug, but not a "substantial embrace." Once in an assembly a smart-ass football player asked Mr. Clyde to define substantial embrace. He said, "I know it when I see it." Then he waited a beat and added, all deadpan: "And so do you." Everybody cracked up.

After I got my stuff, we went to Aidan's locker, and then he accompanied me to my first class. I spent most of the class thinking about Aidan and missed everything Ms. Gupta said was on Friday's test. I had to ask a friend to send me notes.

At lunch, Collier was oblivious to the charged looks between Aidan and me as he paged through his social media posts from the show. "Three hundred and thirty likes. Five hundred and twelve likes."

"Nice," said Aidan, his eyes still locked to mine.

"Did you hear from your mum?" asked Collier.

Aidan dragged his gaze away. "Yeah, we Skyped. She YouTubed it."

"Oh, and I posted a warning about those jalapeño poppers," said Collier.

"Did you mention that if you eat them you probably shouldn't drink three rum and Cokes and dance your ass off right after?" asked Aidan.

Collier flipped him off. He still looked pale, and I was pretty sure he'd dropped a few pounds Saturday night. I never knew the human body held that much fluid.

People stopped by to congratulate Collier and Aidan and — to my surprise — Elliot and me. I was laughing at comments Collier was reading aloud (and blushing about some of them) when I happened to glance over at Ryder's table. He stared at me, radiating hate.

Aidan drove me home after school and helped me dismantle everything we'd set up for Fashion Daze practice in the basement. Mum stopped to say hi before heading up to her workroom, and she gave me an extra-long look. She seconded my invitation to Aidan to stay for dinner, but he said he couldn't afford to get any more behind than he already was. He was busy catching up on assignments and studying he'd sidelined before the show.

We texted a few times that night, but Aidan was serious about his work.

Tuesday at school, rinse, repeat. Aidan had to go home after school to study. On the bus, Elin sat by me. "What's up with you and Aidan?"

I shrugged, but I couldn't stop a big grin, and she elbowed me. "Gunnarrrrr."

"It's not a big deal." *Yes it is.* "We're just … you know." But I couldn't stop smiling. "Hanging out." Then I stared for added emphasis. "Don't tell Tor."

In just a day or two, everyone at school figured out that Aidan and I were together. Elliot gave me a few narrow-eyed stares at first, but he finally went back to his normal haughty down-his-nose expression whenever he looked my way. Weirdly enough, Tor didn't seem to notice, maybe because Aidan had been all but living at our place before the show.

Aidan and I couldn't get together as much as I wanted that week because of tests and project backlogs, but we made plans for Sunday. I got nervous when I thought about finally having him all to myself for a while.

FRIDAY NIGHT AND Saturday my family moved me and Gary. Shifting boxes around wouldn't have taken all that long, but Mum's idea of moving turned out to mean scouring the new house and then the apartment after Gary's belongings were out, cleaning everything Mum and Dad gave him (his pick of all the stuff stored in the attic), and then putting everything away.

After Saturday dinner, I retreated to my new place. Mum had been right. Having everything put away made it feel more like home. Weird to sleep somewhere that wasn't where I'd slept my entire life up until now. My old bedroom would become the spare bedroom, because Mum was turning the guest room into additional workspace. She was taking on more commissions now, since only Tor would be living at home in the fall.

Something about that made me sad.

SUNDAY AFTERNOON, GARY and Dad were out in the fields tracking soil temperatures. The sooner we could get seeds in the ground, the better the odds of harvesting without being caught out by an early frost. Mum, Elin, and Tor were at a church meeting. Our congregation was going to sponsor a Syrian refugee family, and they were on the committee organizing everything for their move to Canada. I was waiting for Aidan in the apartment, pacing because I was too nervous to sit.

When his car crunched up the gravel drive, I opened the apartment door and waited. A minute later Aidan stepped inside with the garment bags he'd used for Fashion Daze slung over one shoulder.

"Hey." He kicked off his shoes and then looked around the apartment. "Nice. Can I get a tour?"

We had hardly been alone together all week. Now that we were, with no chance of being interrupted, I was feeling like I had the first time we met. "Um, okay. Kitchenette." I turned a slow circle, pointing. "Door to the basement. Storage closet. Dining nook. We're in the living room. Bedroom through there. Outside door. Coat closet."

Aidan was laughing at me.

"What?"

He glanced at the door to the bedroom and raised his brows, like a question. Then he entered and threw open the closet door. He unzipped the first of the bags, shoved everything in the closet to one side, and hung clothes at the other end.

"What are you doing?"

"Giving you the clothes you wore for the show." He finished unpacking and placed the empty bags on my bed. "Are your doors locked?"

"Always." Otherwise, little brother was likely to barge in unannounced.

"Come here." He held me, and I relaxed into him.

Aidan kissed like Ty, like a guy who knows what he's doing. *He's a lot more experienced than me. What if Brandon was better at this than I am?*

Aidan pulled back. "What's wrong? You went as stiff as a board." He frowned. "Did I do something?"

"No. I just …" *Crap.*

Aidan watched me.

"No wonder people get drunk at parties," I said.

Aidan's face cleared. He'd translated. "Didn't you promise me dinner? I could eat."

"Yeah." I led him through the basement to the kitchen, and we made lentil soup and focaccia again. This time, Aidan leaned into me hard when I passed behind him and steadied him with a hand. And I pressed against him when he peered around my shoulder. We brushed hips and touched when we reached past the other for salt or a wooden spoon, and sometimes, since no one was there to see, we kissed.

We carried our soup and bread to the apartment, leaving the rest for the family's dinner. After we ate, we watched a movie, snuggled in an old afghan, bowl of popcorn between us.

I kept sneaking peeks at Aidan's profile, the way his collarbones and his throat looked so tender, nestled in the open neck of his shirt. How his slim fingers raised popcorn kernels to his mouth. He had those prominent wrist bones that look strong and fragile at the same time.

When the movie was over, I placed the empty bowl on the coffee table and tugged Aidan's arm. He scooted up against me, wrapped his arms around my waist, and rested his head on my shoulder. "So I wanted to ask you something," he said. "You got a trip for your birthday."

"Yeah."

"Where will you go?" Aidan raised up so he could see my face.

"I don't know yet," I said.

He hesitated, looking self-conscious. "Dad said I could have a trip for graduation." He stopped. "You want to go somewhere together?"

He had to ask? "Yeah, of course."

Aidan smiled and then leaned in for a kiss. I met him halfway. Every time I did, it felt more natural. Muscle memory, but more than that. Bigger than that. Holding him felt like holding the world.

Tomorrow was a school day. We disentangled ourselves and said goodbye at the door. And again. And again. And again. Finally, Aidan stepped back and laughed. "No, seriously. I've really got to go."

This time last year, it felt as if nothing would ever change, that we'd all go along living in the same way. I'd see Sam every day, and we'd work out with our friends Sunday afternoons in our basement, and I'd ride the horses. Elin and I would ask for triple-layer dark chocolate cake with inch-thick fudge frosting every year for our birthday. Forever.

When Aidan drove away, me on the apartment steps watching him go, having a life beyond high school felt as if it really was going to happen.

Tethers

AT SCHOOL, THE students who knew what they were doing after graduation walked around looking relieved, and the ones who didn't became more fidgety and anxious as days passed. Jason got accepted to University of Alberta, his first choice since he wanted to study accounting and take over his mum and dad's accounting business someday. Myk got in everywhere he applied, and he accepted his first choice — University of Manitoba to study civil engineering. Katie was headed for McGill to study pre-law. Elliot would study music at University of British Columbia in Vancouver.

Mr. Gilkie helped Rawdon line up a job and apprenticeship with a company so he could study carpentry at SAIT and work at the same time. Becca got accepted to the SAIT culinary program and landed a scholarship and a bursary. I'd been accepted to SAIT too, but I hadn't heard from Agnes Macphail College.

Collier was going to a couture institute in Calgary, and Aidan had been accepted at his second and third choices, but he was still waiting to hear from OCI. One Saturday afternoon I got a text.

Aidan: *I got into the Ontario Couture Institute!*

Gunnar: *Awesome! Tell Mum yet?*

Aidan: *Tonight.*

He was coming after dinner to hang out.

Aidan: *You?*

Gunnar: *Nothing yet. Haven't looked today though.*

Aidan: *You check. I'll wait.*

I logged in and viewed my Agnes Macphail College application status. My pulse shot up when I finally saw something besides *Pending.* STATUS: *Accepted.*

Following was a list of steps I had to take to secure my place and prepare for a move to Toronto, if I wanted to live in residence.

Gunnar: *I'm in.*

Aidan sent a string of party hat and fireworks emojis.

Gunnar: *I have to apply for residence tonight. You help?*

Aidan: *You want to stay in residence?*

I thought I probably did.

Gunnar: *I can't keep the apartment clean and I'm only in high school.*

I went to tell Elin and found her sitting at the dining room table looking at her laptop and frowning.

"What's up?" I asked.

"I've got a full ride at UVic."

Holy crap. She already had full rides at U of A and UBC. "That's awesome." That wasn't what her face said. "Isn't it?"

Elin sagged. "I don't know what to do. If I go away, what happens with me and Jason? Do we try to have a long-distance thing? Does that ever work? But even if I go to U of A, we might still grow apart."

"Can't build your life around what might happen," I said. Elin's brow wrinkled. "You said that to me before school started." That day on the swing — a million years ago.

"What if I didn't know what I was talking about?"

Was this my confident, courageous sister? I hadn't noticed the shadows under her eyes before. "Take a break. I want to show you something. Dress for riding and meet me at the barn."

I KNEW WHEN Elin figured out where we were going because she gave me a sharp glance. When the remains of a soddy came into view, I said, "We'll stop here. We need to be quiet."

We left Deck and Mackie tethered to a rusty old hitching ring. I led the way along the shelterbelt that bordered the soddy, headed for a particular bur oak, and scanned for my prey. There. I pointed to a branch about twice my height off the ground. Elin's eyes followed my finger. A great horned owl perched on a thick platform made of branches. In front of it, two fluffy owlets crowded together on the nest's edge and peered about.

Elin's hand went to her mouth. The parent owl stared down at us, looking furious the way great horned owls always do because they can't help it with that face.

A moment later the other parent owl landed in the nest, a shrew dangling from its beak. The two owlets shrieked, begging for food.

We backed away, giving the owl family some space, and walked to what was left of the old sod house Torvald built when he arrived in Canada.

"I wonder," said Elin. "If they had gone back to Iceland, would they have felt like they were back where they belonged? Or would they have missed this place? Where did they think of as home?"

Now I understood what was bothering her.

Elin turned a face tight with anxiety to me. "What if I change too much? What if I stop wanting to come back?"

"If that happens, you'll do what you have to do. But I don't think it will."

Elin frowned. "You can't know that."

"I know you. Besides …" I threw my arms wide. "Where are you ever going to find anything better than this?" No place is perfect, but our Alberta land was as good a not-perfect location as anyone was likely to find.

Elin laughed, sharp and short. "Says the one who doesn't want to stay."

"I don't want to farm. There's a difference." I might hate big city life, but it would be a mistake to stay on the farm because I was afraid of all the other options. A mistake to stay close by for fear of going further. I would finish my training, get experience, maybe even a Red Seal, but someday I'd end up back here in Alberta.

"You should go to one of the schools in B.C.," I said. "Live by the ocean. In a city. If you come back, it's because you really want to."

Elin kicked at a snow-covered lump jutting from the ground, but I could tell she was listening. "What if it's true that you can't go home again?"

"That just means you can't go back to the home you left." Duh. Things weren't going to stay exactly the same while she was away. "It doesn't mean you'll never feel at home again."

Elin squared her shoulders and lifted her chin. Her expression was so much like Mum that I could imagine how she'd look years from now. She pulled out her phone and took a picture of the soddy.

"I want to take a picture of the owlets." She headed toward the bur oak and spoke over her shoulder. "I'll make a screensaver slide show. To remind me when I'm gone."

I snapped pictures of the horses and the soddy and then followed her. I'd make one too — a tether to home, no matter how far I went.

Getting It

I COULD BARELY drag myself into the school now. I just wanted to be the boss of me. I felt itchy all over — in-my-head itchy — like a snake that needs to shed its skin.

Final class day. Becca and I had just finished our last presentation in Foods and we seriously killed it.

The bell sounded and the room emptied, except for Ms. Freiberg and us. We were still cleaning up. Aidan was going to meet me here.

"You can take that one to Rawdon," said Becca, as I closed up the box I'd filled. "He texted he's in the parking lot." The tiny teacher-overflow and special-needs lot by the nearest exit was usually full and off-limits to regular students, but after school no one enforced the rules. Students in Foods and Building Construction used it all the time. No one wanted to carry a lot of heavy stuff through the whole school to get to student parking.

I popped the exit door bar with my hip and strode out onto the sidewalk and down the gently sloped ramp, looking for a battered, rust-orange and primer-gray truck.

My legs stopped moving like they figured it out before my brain did. Billy and a football player named Mitchell pinned Rawdon against his truck. Ryder stood with two guys who had been in the group I saw in the parking lot the night of the Halloween Festival. Trevis and Boone. Now their attention was focused on me.

"Go back inside," Rawdon yelled.

I set the box down, not taking my eyes off Ryder, my brain whizzing through my options. Leaving was not one of them. No way I'd leave Rawdon out here on his own.

"You're being stupid right now," I said. My head felt tight, like a metal band was squeezing it. Sometimes anger is cold, and sometimes it's hot. Mine simmered just under my skin and threatened to become rolling boil rage. *Stay in control. Do. Not. Fight. Breathe.*

Fighting = expulsion. Expulsion = no Agnes Macphail College. No Toronto. No Aidan.

Trevis moved forward at an angle that would put him between me and the door. Boone walked toward me and pulled something from his jeans back pocket: heavy-duty shears.

WTF? And then it hit me. *My hair.*

Ryder knew when I figured it out, and his smile was ugly.

Five of them and they had a weapon. I was thinking so hard my head felt like it ought to be smoking. I wouldn't be able to prove I didn't start the fight. No security cameras in this lot. *That's why they picked it. No cameras.*

I pulled my phone out, thumbed it on, and framed Ryder. *Record.* I panned from Ryder to Trevis to Boone and over to Billy and Mitchell where they restrained Rawdon.

"This syncs to the cloud."

Boone froze.

"Ryder?" Billy looked over for instructions.

I sidestepped toward the truck, closer to Rawdon, and kept on recording.

"Ryder, what are you doing?" Billy's voice was higher pitched than it had been.

Ryder took a sidestep to match mine. "Kicking his ass."

Dream on.

I focused on Billy — middle-class Billy who wanted to go to university. "It's against the law to restrain someone against his will." I moved closer.

Billy released his grip on Rawdon and stepped back. He might not have known he did it. Putting distance between him and Rawdon. Putting distance between him and Ryder's actions.

Billy took another step back. "Screw this. I'm done." He pivoted and disappeared around the corner of the building.

I panned Ryder and the two older guys again.

"Leave now, and I don't give this to the RCMP." I zoomed in on the shears in Boone's hand.

"This is bullshit." He turned and stalked away.

"Hey, come back here." Ryder's voice held a hint of panic.

Trevis just shook his head and followed Boone.

I panned back to Rawdon. Mitchell was nowhere to be seen.

Ryder backed away, not taking his eyes off us. Like we'd rush him or something. *We're not like your loser friends.* I didn't know how he'd coerced them into doing his bidding, but they'd gone about it all wrong. They should have jumped me the second I was out the door. *How had they known where we'd be and when? Someone in Foods would have known.* That thought led to an ugly place, so I set it aside for the moment.

I wanted to ask Ryder *Why? Why do you hate me?*

Instead I held up my phone. "We'll all have a copy."

Ryder's face twisted. He turned and followed his buddies. I thumbed off my phone and shoved it in a pocket. My heart rate slowed, but I still felt jittery. Adrenaline attack.

"That was smart," said Rawdon. "I thought we were screwed."

Before I could reply, he looked at something over my shoulder and his face went blank.

"This lot is not for students." Coach Mac stood there, hands on his hips. I hadn't even heard the back door open.

"We're leaving," said Rawdon.

"After we've loaded up," I said. I wasn't exactly asking permission. Coach Mac gave me that same *drop the 'tude* look he'd given me in Mr. Clyde's office on the second day of school, but I didn't lower my gaze this time.

It didn't matter that Rawdon wasn't causing trouble. If Coach Mac had come out and found Billy and Mitchell beating on Rawdon, Coach would have figured Rawdon did something to cause it. Because to him, Rawdon didn't count. It took me way too long to understand that, but then before this year, I was always one of the guys Coach thought did count.

Becca and Aidan emerged from the building, Becca carrying a box and Aidan with both our packs. For a moment their steps slowed as they took in the scene, but then Aidan crossed to me without hesitation, dropped the backpacks, and draped an arm around my shoulder, leaning against me. It felt good having him there, like he had my back. I put my arm around his waist.

Coach Mac's lips thinned and the skin around his nostrils bleached white.

"I used to think you were a decent young man."

Aidan went stiff in the circle of my arm.

I used to think you were one of the good guys.

Coach tried to stare me down, but we were the same height. I might even be a little taller. I outweighed him. Only in my head had he been some big, powerful, commanding guy.

Words were building inside me.

I would explode if I tried to keep the words inside.

"I can't believe I ever respected you."

Coach inhaled so hard I heard it, and his right hand fisted. His face went blotchy red. He wanted to hit me. Me, the fag — all he saw when he looked at me now. Me, the queer guy who didn't count. Coach unclenched his fist and stepped back, still trying to stare me down. I didn't look away. Then his expression just crumpled like an aluminum can in your fist, and he spun and walked toward his truck. His spine was stiff. He moved like a guy ten years older. Moments later he peeled out of the lot.

"Hey," said Aidan, and he wrapped me up in a big hug. "I thought he was going to hit you."

He wouldn't have. He would have lost his job and it would have been for nothing, because he still wouldn't have gotten what he wanted. You can't beat respect into people. And he could never make me see myself the way he did.

AFTER RAWDON AND Becca drove away, Aidan and I shouldered our packs and walked around the school to the big student lot. Only two vehicles remained: Aidan's car — and Brody's truck, parked next to it. Brody leaned against the tailgate. No one else was in sight.

He stood up straight as we approached him and shoved his hands in his pockets.

He wants to talk. I stopped, far enough back that I could react in time if he flipped out. Aidan followed my lead.

"I'm sorry about what I did in the mop room."

Aidan and I exchanged an incredulous look.

What about being a dick in general? Are you sorry for that?

When Aidan didn't reply, Brody added, "I don't expect you to say it's okay. It wasn't." He corrected himself. "It isn't."

I thought of a hundred different things to say, but this wasn't about me.

Brody had circles under his eyes. He'd lost weight. I couldn't remember seeing him around school at all the last few months. He hadn't been eating in the cafeteria.

"I can't really say it's okay," said Aidan. "Not yet. But I appreciate your apology. Why now?"

Brody's gaze was fixed on the ground. "You ever think what your life might have been if you had a different dad? Like if my dad was yours and your dad was mine?"

Aidan frowned, the way he did when he concentrated on a design, focused on Brody's words.

Brody still couldn't look at Aidan. "Say you were taught your whole life that some kinds of people were bad and were going to burn in hell like it was a fact. Like the moon doesn't have air and vegetables are good for you — that kind of actual fact. And then you started to think you might be one of those people."

Was he saying what I thought he was? I couldn't be sure: his dad thought all kinds of different people were hell-bound. I remembered Brody sitting in the library watching people going to GSA after I was outed, that first time I went. I'd thought his expression was sad. What if it was more than that?

"Why didn't you go to GSA?" I asked.

"The second somebody told my dad, I'd have been shipped off to conversion therapy."

"Could he do that if you're eighteen?" asked Aidan.

Brody shrugged. "He'd kick me out if I didn't go. That's what he told other people to do to their kids. Tough love."

Doesn't sound much like love to me.

"Couldn't you tell your dad that a lot of churches don't think like that?" I said. Like our church.

Brody laughed, short and harsh. "He doesn't think those people are real Christians."

Those people? *That's not creepy judgy at all.*

"Maybe he'll change his mind," said Aidan.

"No." Brody's eyes were a desert landscape. "No, he'll never do that."

And I got what that meant for him. He could lie his whole life, which would be a really crap one if he did, and stay good with his dad. Or he could tell the truth and get jettisoned from his family like a used-up rocket booster after lift-off. Like dying, only he wouldn't be dead. No birthday greetings from home. No family Christmases. No one who would take his call with good news of a first real job. Or a great new apartment. Or a serious boyfriend or an engagement or maybe even a wedding someday.

I thought of that day in Tall Tall Charlene's Coffeehouse, when I let someone know about me. How good it felt to tell someone who'd get it. But I'd been almost sure that when I did tell my family, I'd still be one of them.

What if Brody's dad had been my dad? *Would I have turned into a self-hating piece of shit who went around taking out his misery on other people?*

"That day in the mop room," said Aidan. "It wasn't me you were trying to drown."

Brody's expression froze for a second, and he blinked really fast. Then he climbed into his truck and drove away.

Détente

ELIN AND I were packing up food to take to Gary's house-warming when Aidan came through the back door.

"Almost done." I slotted the last covered casserole dish into a carrier and then dropped onto a kitchen chair and held out a hand. Aidan sat on my thigh, an eyebrow raised like *are we seriously doing this in front of Elin?* I tugged, and when he relaxed against my chest, I wrapped my arms around him, and he rested his head against my shoulder. Usually we were way more discreet, and I would never have done that in front of Mum and Dad, but they were already at Gary's helping set up.

"You packed?" asked Aidan. He had been for a week. His suitcase looked like a YouTube tutorial on how to pack like a travel professional.

"Yeah." I'd better be. We were driving to Edmonton International Airport early tomorrow morning to start our trip.

"Stacy's coming!" Tor bounded into the kitchen and leaped into the air, spinning. "Stacy's coming to the house-warming!" Spin. "Stacy's coming to the house-warming!" He caught sight of me and Aidan and came to a dead stop just before he would have crashed into the wall.

Tor looked us both up and down, and his eyes narrowed. "Is he your *boyfriend?*"

Aidan braced an arm on my shoulder and turned to look at me, his lips quirking. *He finally figured it out.*

"Yeah," I said. "He's my boyfriend."

Cough. Sam stood in the door. Two spots of color dotted his cheeks.

"Hi Sam," said Elin. "Didn't hear you drive up." No kidding, the way the kid was tra-la-la-ing through the kitchen.

"Hope it's okay I let myself in." He would never have said that before he left. "Gunnar, I was hoping I could talk to you for a minute."

Aidan slid off my lap and offered a hand up. "I'll help Elin load the van." I couldn't read his expression, and I squeezed his hand before I released it.

I led Sam into the living room and waited. He stuck his hands in his pockets. "I don't have a problem with you."

I shut my mouth when I realized it was gaping.

He winced. "I'm sorry. I'm saying this wrong. I just — it's cool that you're gay. I'm sorry about Marky's." Sam's voice was flat, like a hostage reading a scripted statement. He kept glancing away, unable to hold my gaze.

Christmas was half a year ago. Had Gary been waiting all this time to find out if Sam still wanted to be his friend? Did Gary even care now? That was his call, not mine. If Sam wanted to salvage the friendship, I wasn't going to stand in the way.

"No worries," I said.

"So ... we're okay?"

"Yeah." Sam couldn't help who his dad was either. I hoped one day he could step out of that shadow.

"Cool. That's ... cool." Sam ducked his head and took a step back. "Guess I should head over to the house-warming. I want to talk to Gary."

I nodded, and he took another step back. "See you," he said.

"Yeah," I said. "See you there." Not if he saw me first, I suspected.

There would be a lot of people at the party. We could probably avoid each other. All Sam wanted was a truce, not a friendship.

A couple of minutes later I watched his truck rattle up the driveway.

I thought of grade school and sitting by Sam on the bus.

I thought of how he whooped on his snowboard behind Mackie, me laughing aloud for the sheer joy of riding hell for leather through the snow.

I thought of watching the best wrestler on our team, trying to copy his moves — trying to be as good as he was.

I thought of that day in June.

I thought of the last time I saw the Sam-warmth in his eyes — that night he came to see me after I got kicked off the team.

Aidan stood next to me in front of the living room window. I hadn't heard his approach. I could feel him studying my face. "You look like you're thinking deep thoughts," he said.

He slid his hand into mine, and then he waited. I liked that about him. He knew how to be still.

"I'm just thinking," I said, "how sometimes you have to give up the old good life stuff to get to the new."

Real

AIDAN SLID INTO the seat beside me and handed over a latte.

"Thanks."

"You're welcome." He twisted in his seat to see the gate. People were already lining up. We didn't bother. We were in the absolute last boarding group. He turned back to me. "Just think. We'll be doing this again in a couple of months."

"I won't need my passport for that." Not for Toronto. But thinking of my passport made me check the zipped backpack pocket again to make sure mine hadn't disappeared since the last time I'd looked.

Aidan laughed. "Stop being paranoid."

"I'm not." *I was.* Boarding pass. Check. Passport. Check. Extra cash stash. Check. Wallet in pocket. Check. Shiny new credit card in wallet. Check. I hugged my backpack and relaxed against the back of my seat. *Breathe.*

Aidan paged through the guidebook his dad gave him. It was old-school, but Mr. Standish had pointed out you couldn't always get Wi-Fi. "When we get there, we should go straight to the hostel and drop our stuff."

We had discussed all this. Several times. Maybe Aidan wasn't totally the cool, experienced traveler he wanted to appear. The line of boarding passengers was moving fast, and the gate attendant called for our section. We stayed seated and let the line shrink again. Finally, when the last few passengers in the gate area began collecting their things, we took a place at the end.

"Final call for Icelandair flight 692 with service to Reykjavik. All remaining ticketed passengers should now board."

Aidan nudged my shoulder. "You ready for this?"

"Yeah."

I'm ready.

Acknowledgements

Thank you to:

Barry Jowett, whose editing was essential to the process of freeing the book lurking in the manuscript.

Stacey Kondla, my agent (The Rights Factory), who ably shepherded me through the submission process and found a home for *Under the Radar*.

The Writers' Guild of Alberta for its mentorship program, and Kim McCullough, my WGA mentor, for providing the creative space and guidance I needed to finish a first draft.

Kelley Eskridge of Sterling Editing for the right words at the right time and fantastic developmental support.

Luna Ng, for sharing insights from her experience teaching high school in Alberta.

And most of all, thank you to Hendrik Kraay for unwavering belief and support from the beginning.

I acknowledge that I live and write in the traditional territories of the Blackfoot and the people of the Treaty 7 region in Southern Alberta, which includes the Siksika, the Piikuni, the Kainai, the Tsuut'ina and the Stoney Nakoda First Nations, including Chiniki,

Bearspaw, and Wesley First Nation. The City of Calgary is also home to Métis Nation of Alberta, Region III.

We acknowledge the sacred land on which Cormorant Books operates. It has been a site of human activity for 15,000 years. This land is the territory of the Huron-Wendat and Petun First Nations, the Seneca, and most recently, the Mississaugas of the Credit River. The territory was the subject of the Dish With One Spoon Wampum Belt Covenant, an agreement between the Iroquois Confederacy and Confederacy of the Ojibway and allied nations to peaceably share and steward the resources around the Great Lakes. Today, the meeting place of Toronto is still home to many Indigenous people from across Turtle Island. We are grateful to have the opportunity to work in the community, on this territory.

We are also mindful of broken covenants and the need to strive to make right with all our relations.